What the critics are saying

Merinus and Callan seem to be made for each other. Merinus's years with her overprotective family allow her to hold her own with this dominant male. Callan would overwhelm a less independent heroine. There are several laugh-out-loud moments as Callan butts heads with stubborn Merinus. Together they create a sizzling heat that is palpable." – *Denise Powers, Sensual Romance Reviews*

Winner of the WordWeaving Award for Excellence
"Author Lora Leigh pens a lavish, sizzling extravaganza with TEMPTING THE BEAST. Accustomed to her over protective family, Merinus holds her own with this alpha male. Callan is every woman's fantasy lover with his amazing physical prowess. A tale of fierce passion and erotic extremity, TEMPTING THE BEAST blazes a path between sensuality and gripping plotting to present the perfect balance that will keep readers glued to its pages and eagerly seeking its sequel." – *Cynthia Penn, WordWeaving*

"I have never read a more unique story! The characters created here were all devastatingly sensual and I only wish there was more to read. This proved to be a very interesting story woven skillfully from beginning to end. As I've come to expect from the folks at Ellora's Cave, the sex was sizzling, blistering, and intense. This is one story you won't want to miss!" – *Amy Turpin, Timeless Tales*

Discover for yourself why readers can't get enough of the multiple award-winning publisher Ellora's Cave. Whether you prefer e-books or paperbacks, be sure to visit EC on the web at www.ellorascave.com for an erotic reading experience that will leave you breathless.

www.ellorascave.com

TEMPTING THE BEAST
An Ellora's Cave publication, 2003

Ellora's Cave Publishing, Inc.
PO Box 787
Hudson, OH 44236-0787

ISBN # 1843607247

ISBN MS Reader (LIT) ISBN # 1-84360-418-3
Other available formats (no ISBNs are assigned):
Adobe (PDF), Rocketbook (RB), Mobipocket (PRC) &
HTML

TEMPTING THE BEAST edited by Kari Berton.
Cover art by Darrell King.

TEMPTING THE BEAST

Lora Leigh

DEDICATION

Dedicated to: My husband, Tony
Just because he makes life wonderful.

CHAPTER ONE

Washington D.C

"This story is mine." Merinus stared down her family of seven brothers as well as her father, her voice firm, her determination unwavering.

She knew she didn't present an imposing figure. At five feet five inches, it was damned hard to convince the males of her family, all over six feet, that she was serious about anything. But in this one instance, she knew she had no other choice.

"Don't you think this is a little bit much for you to take on, Squirt?" Caleb, editor-in-chief of the National Forum and her second oldest brother, smirked with an edge of superiority.

Merinus refused to give into his baiting. She looked down the long table, directly into her father's thoughtful expression. John Tyler was the one to convince, not his moron upstarts.

"I've worked hard, Dad, I can do this." She fought to put the steely determination in her voice that she often heard her oldest brother use. "I deserve this chance."

She was twenty-four years old, the youngest child in a family of eight and the only daughter. She hated makeup, despised dresses and social functions and she heard often how she was a disappointment to the female race, according to her brothers. She wanted to be a journalist; she wanted to make a difference. She wanted to stand before the man whose picture lay on the table before her and see if his eyes were really that brilliant amber. Perhaps she was more woman than they knew.

She was obsessed. Merinus silently admitted to it, and knew she would play hell trying to hide it. From the moment she had seen the picture of the man in question, she had been nervous, panicky, terrified that his enemies would get to him before she could present her father's offer.

"What makes you think you're the best person for this job, Merinus?" Her father leaned forward, clasping his hands on the table before him, his blue eyes serious, thoughtful as he watched her.

"Because I'm a woman." She allowed herself a small smile. "You put that much testosterone in the same room with just one of the behemoth seven here, and you'll have an automatic refusal. But he would listen to a woman."

"Listen to her, or try to seduce her?" one of her other brothers questioned harshly. "This idea is unacceptable."

Merinus kept her eyes on her father and prayed Kane, the oldest brother would keep his mouth shut. Their father listened to him where she was concerned and if he decided it was too dangerous, then there was no way John Tyler would allow her to go.

"I know how to be careful," she told him softly. "You and Kane trained me well. I want this chance. I deserve it."

And if she didn't get it, then she would take it on her own. She knew her brothers couldn't make contact, but she could. She suppressed a shiver at the thought. Some would say the man wasn't even human. A genetic experiment conceived in a test tube, carried to term by a surrogate and inheriting the genes of the animal his DNA had been altered with. A man with all the instincts and hunting abilities of a lion. A perfectly human looking male. A man bred to be a savage killer.

Merinus had read the notes, experiments and the thirty-year journal of the scientist who carried him within her body. Dr. Maria Morales had been a friend of her father's in college. It was she who had the box ready to be delivered to John in the event of her death. It was his decision who would carry out the woman's last request.

He was to find her surrogate son at the location she had given. Help him defeat the secret Genetics Council by convincing him to come forward, making a way for him to find safety. She had enough proof to get them digging. Kane had done the rest. They had names of the Council, proof of their involvement, everything but the man they created.

"This is too dangerous to trust to her," Caleb argued again. The others were silent, but Merinus knew they would voice their opinions soon enough.

Merinus took a deep breath.

"I get the story, or I follow whichever moron in this room gets it. You won't have a chance."

"This coming from the woman who refuses to wear makeup or a dress?" another brother piped in with a snicker. "Honey, you don't have what it takes."

"It doesn't take being a whore," she replied furiously, turning on the youngest brother. "It's simple logic, dunce. A woman, whether in pants or a dress will draw more attention from a man than any other man will. He's careful, he doesn't trust easily. Maria's notes state that plainly. He won't trust another man. The basic male threat."

"And he could very well be just as dangerous as he was created to be," Caleb argued for Gray as he swiped his fingers through his short brown hair. "Dammit, Merinus, you have no business even wanting to be anywhere near this bastard."

Merinus took a deep breath. She lowered her eyes, staring down at the bleak loneliness reflected through glossy paper. His eyes mesmerized her, even in the picture. There were decades of sadness reflected there. He was thirty years old now, single, alone. A man without a family or even a race to call his own. How terrible it must be, and to be hunted as well was a tragedy.

"I won't stay here," she said loud enough for them all to hear. "I'll follow whoever goes out there and I won't let you hound him."

The silence was heavy now. Merinus could feel eight sets of eyes on her, varying degrees of disapproval reflected in their expressions.

"I'll go with her. I can handle the research part, Merinus can make contact." Kane's voice had Merinus jerking her head up in surprise.

Shock echoed along her body as she realized that the brother who suffocated her the most was actually willing to help her in this. It was hard to believe. Kane was arrogant and ninety percent of the time, the world's worst jerk. He was an ex-Special Forces commander as bossy as any man ever born.

For the first time she looked directly at him. His expression was cool, but his eyes were angry. Deep and hot with fury, the dark blue orbs met hers without their usual light of teasing mockery. The intensity in his look almost frightened her. He wasn't angry with her, she could tell, but Kane was pissed. And a pissed Kane was not a good thing.

Merinus was aware of her father sitting back in his seat, watching the eldest son now with surprise.

"You've put a lot of time in this already, Kane," John remarked. "Six months at least. I thought you would be ready for a rest?"

Kane glanced at his father, shrugging his shoulders with a tight movement.

"I want to see it through. I'll be close enough to help her out if she needs me, but also able to do the research that could be too damned dangerous for her. If she can be ready to leave tonight, then we can do this her way."

"I'll be ready." Her response was instantaneous. "Just tell me what time."

"Be ready at four. We have an eight-hour drive ahead of us and I want to do some recon before morning. Damn good thing you don't care if you chip a few nails, brat, because you'll be doing just that."

He came to his feet abruptly as the men around him erupted into a furious argument. Merinus could only watch him silently, amazed at his decision. What the hell was up with this?

He ignored the heated protests of his other brothers. The arguments of Merinus' safety, the lack of assurance that 'some damned hybrid animal' wouldn't infect her. Merinus rolled her eyes, then bit her lip nervously as Kane's face tightened into a mask of dangerous fury. His eyes went dead. She couldn't describe it any other way. As though no life or light resided inside him. It was a scary look.

The room silenced. No one but no one messed with Kane when he looked like that.

"Be ready, baby sister," he said evenly as he passed by her. "And if you pack one damned dress or a single tube of lipstick, then I'll lock your ass up in your bedroom."

"Ahh, Kane," she whined sarcastically. "There goes my luggage quota. Asshole." He knew better than to think she would pack either one.

"Keep your nose clean, brat." He flicked the ends of her long brown hair as he walked by her. "I'll pick you up this evening."

CHAPTER TWO

Sandy Hook, KY

That was not a sight for virgin eyes. Merinus trained her binoculars on the vision below her, stretched out in the warming rays of the sun, as naked as a man could be and more than a little aroused. That gorgeous, heavily veined shaft of male flesh rose a good eight inches — no less, could be more — from the base below his flat abdomen. It was thick and long and mouth-wateringly tempting. She blew out a hard breath, lying flat on the rock she had found, the only viewpoint into the small sheltered back yard. She couldn't take her eyes off him.

Callan Lyons was tall. At least six feet, four inches, muscular, broad chested and narrow hipped, with powerful thighs and the most gorgeous damned legs she had ever seen. This just wasn't a sight that a nice, prudish little journalist like herself should be seeing. It could give a girl ideas. Ideas like how it would feel to lie next to him, rub over him, kiss that smooth, golden skin. She shivered at the thought.

She and Mr. Lyons had been playing an amusing little game for over a week now. She pretended not to know him, who he was, where he could be found, and he pretended she wasn't snooping around town asking questions about him and his deceased mother and where he lived. It had gone so far as direct conversation several times. Like she hadn't come prepared, she thought mockingly. Papers, notes, memos, pictures, the whole nine yards. She had studied the man for weeks before demanding this story.

She still couldn't believe Kane had stood by her and brought her with him to contact Callan. Not that he wasn't breathing down her neck half the time. He would be now if he hadn't had to run back to D.C. to talk to a scientist they thought might have been involved with the original experiments. And Merinus was supposed to be finding out about Callan's mother and making contact with the elusive object of her fascination.

So here she was, on the story of her life, and instead of the investigative reporting she should be doing on the man below, she was watching him sun himself. But what a sight. Tanned, muscular skin. Long, golden brown hair, the color of the lion that was supposedly infused into his DNA structure. A strong, bold face, gorgeous, almost savage in its planes and angles. And lips, full male lips with just a hint of a merciless curve. She wanted to kiss those lips. She wanted to start with his lips and kiss and lick her way down. Across that broad chest, the hard, flat stomach to the erection rising from between his tanned thighs. She licked her lips at the thought.

She jerked as she felt her cell phone vibrating at her hips. She grimaced impatiently. She knew who it was. It had to be her oldest, most aggravating brother.

"What, Kane?" she hissed as she flipped the phone open and settled it against her ear. She was rather proud that her eyes never once strayed from all that male glory below.

"It could have been Dad," Kane reminded her, his voice flat and hard.

"It could have been the Pope too, but we know the averages on that one," she muttered.

"Bitch," he growled almost affectionately.

"Why Kane, how sweet," she simpered. "I love you too, asshole."

There was a brief chuckle over the line, making her smile in response.

"How's the story going?" His voice turned serious, too serious.

"It's getting there. I have an appointment later today with a woman willing to talk about the mother. She was murdered in her own home. Dad doesn't know that."

Maria Morales, known as Jennifer Lyons in the small eastern Kentucky town had died at the hands of an attacker, not a thief or a random victim, but someone who wanted only blood.

"What do you think you're going to learn researching the mother?" Kane asked her. "You need proof on the son, Merrie, don't forget that."

"I know what I'm after, big shot," she said. "But to get to the son, I need information. Besides, someone's trying to give me the runaround on Morales. You know how I hate that."

There was a puzzle there, just as big a puzzle as the one stretched out on the deck below her. Sweet Heaven. She watched as his hand moved to his scrotum, not to scratch as she assumed, but to caress, stroke. There went her damned blood pressure.

"I'm research, remember?" he reminded her. "You are just contact."

"Well, I can do some of both," she hissed.

There was a weary sigh across the line.

"Have you made contact with Lyons yet? Offered him the deal Dad has set up?" Yeah, the deal of a lifetime, show yourself, tell your story for us, and we'll make you famous. Fuck your life. She hadn't liked that deal to begin with but she knew it was the only one Callan was ever likely to receive that would provide any measure of security.

"Not yet. Getting there." She fought to breathe evenly as his hand clasped the base of that thick cock and he began stroking all that firm, wonderful flesh.

He was going to masturbate. Incredulity flared through her system, especially her vagina, at the realization. Right here before her eyes the man was going to masturbate. She couldn't believe it. His hand barely circled the broad shaft, moving slow and easy, almost lazily from tip to base.

She felt the flesh between her thighs heat. The muscles of her vagina clenched, moistened, her womb contracted as sensual heat speared her body like a bolt of lightning. Her nipples hardened, ached. Her body became so sensitive she could feel the breeze caressing her bare arms now, like the stroke of a ghostly lover.

Gracious, was this how men felt when they watched women masturbate? No wonder they liked it so well. Long, broad fingers stroked over his cock from tip to base, the fingers of his other hand gripped the sac beneath, massaging it in time to the stimulation of the other hand. Where was a damned breeze when she needed it? She was due to overheat any minute.

"Hurry, Merinus, you don't have the rest of your life," Kane grunted. "The bastard has mercenaries stalking him.

I can't keep your ass covered forever, you know. I have three more days here, and Dad's pitching fits over you being there by yourself."

Yeah, mercenaries. She blinked as she watched those hands cover the thick head of his own erection, the tips of his fingers caressing the area just underneath. She licked her lips, wishing she was there helping him. She was a doomed virgin.

"I'll hurry, I promise," she muttered. "Now let me get off here so I can get some damned work done. I don't have time to bullshit with you all day."

She heard him sigh roughly.

"Check in soon. You wait too long to call," he accused her.

"Why should I? You call everyday instead," she told him absently. "I have to go, Kane. Got work to do. Chat with ya later, hon."

She heard him curse as she disconnected and tucked the little phone back into its handy case at her hip. Good Lord, she was going to have a stroke. Cat boy was playing his cock like a finely tuned instrument now. She could have sworn she saw the head pulse, throb. His hips arched, then a thick stream of creamy semen erupted from the tip, splattering on that hard abdomen and coating the rough hand.

"Oh man, let me taste," she whispered, unable to take her eyes from the sight.

Then he stretched, his eyes opening. She breathed in sharply as their gazes connected, a self-satisfied smile stretching across those wonderful lips. Of course, he couldn't know she was there, she assured herself. It just wasn't possible. Was it?

* * * * *

Callan chuckled to himself as he turned his gaze away from where the woman thought she was hiding. Damn her, he could smell her arousal on the breeze, even across the distance of nearly a mile. Didn't she read her own homework? He knew the files she had hidden in her truck clearly stated he had exceptional eyesight, hearing and smell. Though he had never smelled another woman's heat in quite the same manner as he did hers.

He rose from the deck, stretched again, presenting her a glimpse of the tight muscles of his ass as he snickered in enjoyment. Teasing the little journalist was more fun than he ever imagined it would be. Each time she approached him, pretending she had no clue who he was, it was a test in patience, wondering when she would snap. He doubted it would be much longer. Not that he intended to touch her. Callan sobered on that thought. No, it was better he didn't. Hell, it would have been better if he had left when she first arrived, but there was something about her that held him firm, kept him curious. The rumor of a cat's curiosity wasn't folklore, though he could have done without a measure of that specific genetic mark.

"She still up there?" Sherra stepped to the doorway of the house as he pulled shorts over his hips, covering his still hard cock. "Quite a show you gave her, Callan."

She was smiling broadly, though there was a question in her eyes.

"Perhaps I'm enjoying the game too much." He grinned back at her. "She has a unique way of going after a story, you have to admit."

"Or going after you." Sherra moved back from the doorway as he entered the kitchen. "Doc wanted to see you again in the lab. Your latest tests were a little off, he wanted to run them again."

"Off how?" Callan frowned. The monthly tests had never been off.

Sherra shrugged. "The glands along your tongue appear enlarged."

Callan ran the side of his tongue over his teeth, frowning at the slight difference in the feel of them. Nothing to worry about, it had happened before.

"Maybe I'm catching a cold or something." He shrugged.

"Heart rate, adrenaline, semen and blood tests are off too. Could be the equipment, but he wants more samples just to be on the safe side."

"Damn. We need new equipment already?" He sighed. "That shit costs, Sherra."

"Keeps us sane though," Sherra reminded him as he pulled a bottle of water from the refrigerator. "Go keep him happy, you know how cranky he gets if a test gets off. He 'bout went crazy last year when Taber's went haywire, remember?"

Hell yes, he remembered. Taber had been half crazy during that year too. Irritable to the point that he was almost savage. He disappeared for days at a time, no excuses, no apologies.

"Yeah, I remember a cool half million disappearing from the account for the updated machines too." Callan grimaced. "Dammit, he's going to have to take better care of his toys. That was just a year ago."

Sherra grinned, her nose wrinkling, the sharp pout of her lips smoothing out with the smile.

"Better go let him have more samples then, just to be sure," she urged him. "We don't want him purchasing new equipment on a whim."

Callan shook his head, heading quickly to the underground cavern where the lab was located. It wasn't the most perfect place to keep their secrets, but it worked. The cool atmosphere wasn't as damp as most caverns were, it was dry and solid, with a steady underground well and easy access from the house. Doc enjoyed the place and it made it easier to keep their lives secret.

"More tests," he muttered. "I need those like I need this hard cock aggravating the fuck outta me."

He would have taken care of the first problem if it would cooperate with any woman other than the tight-assed journalist stalking him. But no, it wilted like limp lettuce if he even attempted it, then shot up like fire forged steel the second her scent reached him. Inconvenient, to say the least.

The fact that she was the one woman he couldn't have wasn't helping matters. He knew the psychology of it. He wanted her more for the very fact that he couldn't have her. A journalist stalking him was not a good thing. His secrets were many and his survival depended on him keeping them. He kept a low profile, stayed away from town as much as possible and let few people get to know him, which meant there was only one reason why a journalist, especially a Tyler journalist, would be searching for him.

His surrogate mother and her infernal idea that by revealing himself he could attain his freedom was the cause of this. The box she had mailed out to the National Forum and her old college friend, John Tyler, right before her death, hinted at the evidence the man could have.

There were notebooks of memos, test results, lab results, DNA sequencing, the whole nine yards needed to bury him, all missing. They had fought over it the night she had been attacked and killed. Argued for hours while the others steered clear of the kitchen where they screamed and cursed like mortal enemies. In the end, she had won though. He had agreed to go with her to New York the minute he was able to pull yet another team of mercenaries off his ass.

He and the others had left to do just that. When they returned they found Maria in the kitchen where they had left her, lying in her own blood. And now, a year later, Merinus Tyler was searching for him.

Which would be okay, he thought, if he could just fuck her and send her on her way. But he had a feeling the tenacity and determination he glimpsed in her expression didn't leave him much hope for that.

CHAPTER THREE

The Gass Up station, convenience store and diner were all in the same lot. And Callan was there, as well. Merinus pulled into the blacktopped parking area late that afternoon and got out of the SUV slowly as she looked around.

There were half a dozen vehicles parked here and there, several at the gas pumps and one weary looking pickup with its hood raised, waiting to enter the garage section of the station. Taking a deep breath, Merinus moved quickly to the garage section and the lone man standing outside, gazing rather intently at the innards of the old pickup parked there.

The game was fun, but getting old. Still, she was reluctant to be the one to end it. Especially after watching him stroke all that hard, glistening flesh of his hard-on to a serious orgasm. She still hadn't recovered from that one. Neither had the flesh between her thighs. It wouldn't stop throbbing, demanding the hard stroke of that broad-headed penis deep inside it.

She took a deep breath anyway and approached the truck cautiously. Today, Callan was dressed in thin faded jeans and T-shirt, a baseball cap covering his hair. She hoped he wasn't trying for a disguise. If he was, it wasn't working so well. She had seen him the minute the station had come into view.

"Excuse me, could you tell me where I could find Taber Williams?" Merinus asked him cheerfully, careful to stand well clear of him. Oil marked his gray T-shirt and the snug denim that encased long, muscular legs. Besides, if she got too close, she may not be able to keep her hands out of his jeans. She still hadn't forgotten the hours past and the sight of all that hard male flesh. But the game was on again. She didn't know and he wasn't telling. Stupid game.

The broad shoulders stiffened, then the head, covered in a red baseball cap turned just slightly, the eyes hidden by dark sunglasses.

"Not here," he muttered, then turned back to the engine.

So much for small town hospitality, Merinus frowned. He was being rude today. Snarly. Male.

"Do you know where I could find him? Or perhaps leave a message for him?" she asked the wide back. Damn nice form, but hell on manners.

Those broad shoulders shrugged.

"Tell me. I'll tell him." Short and to the point, but he never did raise his head from the object of his attention, namely the motor and not Merinus.

Merinus dug one of her small cards from her jeans pocket and handed it to him.

"This is my cell phone number. Could you ask him to call me as soon as possible? It's important that I get in touch with him." She was becoming irritated with the curt, who-the-hell-cares attitude he was displaying. He could at least bother to pretend to be interested. Maybe she was playing it too cool.

"He'll get it." The card disappeared into oil-splattered jeans.

Merinus narrowed her eyes at the man.

"Could you tell me where he lives? I could just give him the message myself," she finally fought to keep from snarling.

Muscles rippled as he shrugged again.

"Lives here for the most part," she was told.

Merinus waited, but there was no other information forthcoming.

"What about Callan Lyons? Could you tell me where I can reach him?" she asked sweetly, allowing a shade of mockery to infect her tone.

There was a long pause as the man reached into the motor and adjusted wires, then thumped at the metal.

"Did you hear me?" she asked him with false sweetness. "Callan Lyons? Do you know where I could find him?"

Those broad shoulders shrugged again, and Merinus gritted her teeth in anger.

"Who knows where Lyons is," he finally said. "He comes and goes."

Merinus rolled her eyes. Wasn't that the truth? And he looked damned fine coming, too.

"Fine," she muttered. "I'll just check back later."

"You do that, sweet thing," he muttered, glancing back up at her with a tight smile.

Merinus narrowed her eyes. He laid the wrench he was using on the inside frame carefully as he watched her as well. She could feel that gaze, starting at her white sneakers and moving slowly up her bare, tanned legs to the hem of her shorts, then up. He paused at the small streak of bare, tanned abdomen, then over her breasts until he reached her face.

Merinus stared back at him, her eyes narrowed at the insolence she read in his body and expression.

"Anything else?" A single, burnished brow arched above the lenses of his glasses.

"Nothing else," she muttered, turning and walking quickly to the diner instead.

* * * * *

Callan watched her go, hiding his smile as she glanced back at him. Damn, she looked fine, he thought. And she was definitely on the hunt. A flare of regret rose in him as he admitted he would have definitely enjoyed the chase if circumstances were different. If he wasn't who he was, if his own life wasn't hanging by luck alone, then he could have enjoyed a game or two. And he'd be damned if that woman didn't look good enough to play with. It made his mouth water, looking at all the smooth, sexy skin, just faintly tanned and as tempting as sin itself.

But it was, and he was determined that Miss Merinus Tyler would neither become embroiled in his life, nor add to the danger. He could watch her, but he'd be damned if he would let her get any closer. But hell, watching her was damned near as enjoyable as anything he'd ever done in his life. Dangerous woman, he thought. A damned dangerous woman. And her scent. It was all he could do to keep his hands off her, his mouth from tasting her. It was heat and wanting, spice and cream. She could be addicting.

"Damn, she don't give up easy, does she Cal?" Tanner, his younger brother strode slowly from the inside of the garage as Merinus disappeared into the small restaurant.

"No, Tanner, she doesn't give up easy." Callan grinned.

"She's pretty. All that thick brown hair and those big brown eyes." Tanner grinned as he shook his head. "I bet Taber will be real sorry he missed her today."

They both knew better than that. Taber was all for Callan meeting up with the little journalist. Callan wasn't so certain how Taber would feel now that Ms. Tyler was searching for him, though.

"Help me get this truck running, Tanner. I need to head home to sleep so I can patrol tonight. And this motor is refusing to cooperate." Callan twisted at a wire, but still nothing.

"Ahh, you just don't know how to talk to 'em right," Tanner laughed, pushing Callan out of the way as he moved in to look at the motor. "These older motors are like women, man. You have to know how to stroke 'em, and how to speak real soft and sweet to 'em." He ended his words with a slight twist of his wrist.

The motor sang to life with the movement, chugging weakly, but willingly.

"Show off," Callan laughed.

"Bring her in later and I'll tune her up for you." Tanner pulled a stained rag from his back pocket with a grin and wiped his hands.

"Tell Taber to leave the keys to his truck and I'll do that." Callan nodded as he headed for the driver's side door.

"I'll do that." Tanner nodded with a broad grin. "And if you need any help with that pretty thing later, you just let me know."

"I'll be sure to," Callan laughed again, amused by Tanner's less than obvious ploy. "Keep your jeans zipped, Tanner, and we might keep you alive yet." More than one father was ready to take a shotgun to the hot-blooded youth.

Callan didn't wait for an answer. He gunned the motor, then slid the truck into reverse, backing quickly away from the garage before sliding it in gear and heading home.

* * * * *

It was late that afternoon when Merinus left the diner and headed back to her motel room, armed with dinner. She was tired, sweaty and cranky. After spending the better part of the day watching over Callan's house and trying to find the road into it, she was more than a little frustrated.

She had seen his truck leave and return to the large cabin, but she had yet to find a road in. How do you hide a road? And she couldn't get in close enough to follow the graveled track that she could see leading away from the house. To do so meant entering the small clearing in front of it. Not a good idea, as several other people seemed to always inhabit the place.

She had hiked for miles that day in several different directions, and followed more than one wide path through the forest. Still, nothing.

She pulled into the parking lot of her motel and breathed a weary sigh. Dinner, then a shower. Tomorrow, she would try again. There had to be a road up there, she was just missing it. That was all. She was beginning to feel more than a little stupid in doing so.

Her questions around town were getting her nowhere. Those who admitted to knowing Callan only scratched their heads when she asked for directions to his home. The rest just scratched their heads period and played dumb. Small towns weren't her thing evidently, because the people just made no sense at all.

They directed her to the Gass Up station every time she asked about Callan. He was there a lot. She had staked it out first thing. And the very people who swore they didn't know him acted pretty damned familiar with him when they pulled in.

Damn him, he knew she was there. She unlocked the door to her room, flipping the light on as she entered. He knew who she was and he probably had a good idea what she wanted, but he still ignored her. Which was likely a good thing. After that little scene this morning, she didn't know if she could trust herself to keep her hands off him or not.

Merinus ate quickly, staring absently at the television as she considered that damned driveway into Callan's property. It had to be there somewhere. Roads didn't just disappear. Did they?

The problem plagued her through her dinner and her shower. As she stepped out of the bathroom, wrapped in a terry cloth robe, the phone on the nightstand jangled loudly. Frowning, she picked the receiver up cautiously.

"Hello?" She kept her voice pitched low, wondering who could be on the other side.

"Is this Merinus Tyler?" It was a man's voice, rough and cold.

"Who's asking?"

There was a brief silence.

"If you want to find Callan Lyons, get something to write the directions on. You're missing the right turn."

Merinus felt elation fill her. Finally, someone was willing to talk.

"Do you know Callan?" she asked as she slapped a pad of paper on the small bed table and tugged a pencil from the drawer.

"Do you have something to write on? Here's how you get there."

Merinus wrote down the directions hastily, concentrating as she tried to remember the landmarks he was giving her. She admitted she hadn't yet tried that route, but it appeared to go nowhere.

"Do you have it?" The voice asked her.

"Yes, but—" The line disconnected.

Merinus took a deep breath, staring down at the paper. Could she get there in the dark? It wasn't too late. There was still at least a good hour left of light. And it wasn't like she could sneak up on the house anyway.

Throwing off her robe, she dressed quickly in jeans and a sleeveless blouse before slinging her purse over her shoulder and rushing out to the Jeep. The turnoff she was given was only a few miles up the road. Cold Springs, he had said. She remembered seeing the little green sign on her excursions to the neighboring county.

She had him now. She contained her whoop of joy as she jumped into the Jeep and started the ignition. He could run, but if she could find that road to his home, there was no way he could hide from her any longer.

CHAPTER FOUR

Nearly an hour later, she was clenching her teeth in sheer desperation as she made yet another turn along one of the country back roads she had taken in her search for Callan's home. The written directions beside her were giving her few clues to where she actually was as her Jeep bumped and nudged itself along a pitted dirt road that seemed to lead to nowhere.

Applying the brake, Merinus sat and looked around in confusion. How had she done it? She could have sworn she had taken the right road a few turns back.

"Lord, save me from simple minded directions," she groused.

Pushing her hair back from her forehead, she put the Jeep in reverse and turned around in the wide grassy shoulder that bordered the track. Surely it couldn't be this difficult, she thought. Hell, she had never gotten lost in any big city she had ever been in, and now this little hick county was getting the best of her. It couldn't be happening, her brothers would laugh her out of the nation if they found out.

"Dammit." She pulled off the road again several miles later, looked around and admitted defeat. She was lost. Well and truly and irrevocably lost, and she had no one to blame but herself.

Heaving a sigh, she looked around wearily. There had to be a way out of here. Something she had missed somewhere. Getting out of the SUV, she stretched her tired muscles, then paced over to the edge of the road, looking into the valley below for some sign of civilization.

There wasn't a sign to be found. All she could see was the same thing around her, trees and thick brush, and not even the roof of a house or a barn. Not that a barn meant anything around here, she had seen many of them, ransacked and falling down from neglect, nowhere near a house.

After looking around for a moment longer, she walked to the other side of the road and began to climb the forested rise there. Maybe, if she could get further up, she could see something. There had to be a house somewhere. It wasn't like she was in the desert or the rainforest, dammit. People lived here. That farmer had assured her earlier that if there was a road, then it led somewhere. So something or someone had to be out here. And she was going to have to find them soon. It was getting dark, and she sure as hell didn't want to be stuck out here alone after dark.

As she entered the thicker part of the forest, she turned around to make certain she could still see the SUV. As she did, a noise behind her startled her, causing her to turn in fear.

The man stood several feet in front of her, his eyes dark beneath the camouflage brim of his hat as he watched her. Merinus felt her heart begin to race rapidly in fear as his eyes traveled over her body, sparkling with a deadly intent.

"Well, what do we have here?" The man was tall, his camouflage hat pulled low over black smudged eyes, his face hard and menacing in the shadows of the forest.

Merinus felt fear skate through her body. Her heart pumped quickly in her fear, the blood thundering in her ears as she took in the cold, harsh expression of the man's face.

"I'm lost." Merinus backed up as the man loomed over her, a leer spreading across his face. "I was just looking for a way off the mountain."

"Lost are you?" he sneered, his gaze stripping her. "Poor little thing. You need some help, do you?"

He sounded suspiciously like the guy who called with the stupid directions.

"I'm sure I can manage." Merinus backed away slowly, fighting the panic spreading through her body.

As she tried to back away, her arms were grabbed from behind and fear shot through her with the force of a tidal wave. She felt her system clog with hysteria as she felt the hard grip, felt the harder body behind her.

"Maybe we can help you find your way." The voice behind her suggested as the steel hard hands pulled her closer against his tall male body. "Maybe you'd like to party with us a little first, though."

It wasn't a question; it was a statement of intent. Merinus swallowed tightly as she fought to keep her sanity as the fear washed over her. She was in a shitload of trouble and she knew it.

God. What did Kane tell her? What did he say to do?

As the man behind her tightened his grip, she released the muscles of her legs, lifting her feet from the ground. A startled sound from the man behind her was her only warning. As she began to fall, Merinus tucked her body and rolled away from the men then jumped to her feet to run.

Her screams shattered the forest as she heard the first guy give a quick order to catch her. She ran, and she screamed. She didn't try to conserve energy, because she knew she most likely wouldn't make it to the Jeep anyway, so she used it to pierce the lonely countryside with her terrified cries.

She almost made it to the Jeep. She was within feet of the protective shelter when she was tackled, her body slamming into the hard, gravel encrusted ground with enough force to knock the breath from her body and to still her cries.

"Bitch," the man cursed as she cried out. He jerked her arms behind her and she was hauled roughly to her feet.

Fighting to breathe, the metallic taste of her own blood in her mouth, the sickening stench of her own terror wrapped around her as she was once again face to face with one of her attackers.

"I'm a journalist," she gasped. "Merinus Tyler. The National Forum. There will be people looking for me."

"And what's a pretty little journalist like yourself doing around here?" If it were possible, his voice became colder, crueler. "Maybe we should teach you where not to stick your pretty little nose, Ms. Tyler."

Merinus had no warning, she had nothing to prepare her for the hand that shot out and hit her face with enough force to snap her head around and send stars shooting across her vision. As the world seemed to darken around her, she could have sworn she heard deep-throated growls and a vicious feline snarl echo through the forest.

Merinus fell to the ground, dazed she was suddenly released, the sound of her attackers' hard soled boots thudding quickly away from her as several gunshots were fired. Bracing her hand on the rough gravel of the road, she fought desperately to scramble to the SUV. She had to get in the Jeep. The cell phone was there. She would call the sheriff, surely he knew enough about the area to find her.

"Easy." Male hands supported her carefully, even as she shrank from the touch with a ragged cry. "It's okay, come on, let's hurry and get you in the truck and get you the hell out of here."

Merinus felt the soft seat, fought to pull herself onto it despite the hands that lifted her tenderly, if quickly into it.

"Get started now." The rough order was given from whoever jumped in next to her and slammed the door closed.

"What the hell is she doing out here anyway?" a female voice demanded as the motor of the truck fired up and the quick lurch and rough jerking of the vehicle signaled the speed the driver had pulled out with.

Breathing easier now, Merinus raised her head and stared into the most electrifying, golden colored eyes she had ever seen. A gasp escaped her lips, and then to her profound humiliation and distress, she felt darkness closing slowly over her.

"I'm gonna faint..." Darkness closed over her, soft and inviting as she slumped against Callan's chest.

* * * * *

"Shit." Callan cradled her close to his chest with one arm while he braced himself with the other.

He was still fucking shaking. He couldn't help but clutch her against him, his cheek pressed against her head as he thanked God over and over that he had gotten to her in time. What the hell was she doing up there? There was nothing but broken cliffs and wilderness for miles in every direction. He knew she was desperate to find the track into his driveway, but surely she had enough sense to know it wasn't up there.

"Hey, look at this." Sherra extended a piece of paper to him as she fought to move the vehicle quickly down the mountain. "Where are we taking her? Your place or her room?"

"Her room." Callan took the paper from her hand, glancing at the scribbled directions written on it. "Where the hell did she get this?"

He met Sherra's gaze in the rear view mirror.

"Looks like the boys are wanting to play, Callan," she said softly. "They've seen you with her, know she's searching for you."

A tool. That's all she had been to them. A means of taunting him, of taking something they thought he wanted. He hadn't been careful enough. Somehow, he had let the bastards see his interest in her. He lifted her into his lap, holding her closer, absorbing the shock of the Jeep bouncing over the rutted road to protect her from it. She was so light in his arms, her body delicate and small against his taller, broader length.

He inhaled her scent, fighting to ignore the hard throb of his erection beneath his jeans, the desire to caress her skin with his lips. He contented himself with rubbing his cheek against the silk of her hair. A soft, peaches and cream scent lingered in it, as it did on her skin. Tempting him. He always had been partial to peaches in any form.

"Callan, what are you going to do?" Sherra pressed him.

Merinus was in danger now, they both knew it.

"Put Dayan on watch for her," he told her. "She doesn't know him. Tell him to stay as close as possible, just in case. Have him call me if trouble comes around her."

"Trouble doesn't have to find her, she finds it, evidently," Sherra remarked.

Callan smiled, his fingers rubbing over Merinus' arm softly. She didn't back down much, he had to give her that. She was stubborn as hell, but he didn't consider that a good trait in this case.

"She still out of it?" Sherra asked worriedly.

"Yeah. So hurry and get to that damned motel before her nosy ass wakes up. We'll be in for it good if you don't."

He could just imagine her pleasure, which wouldn't be mutual, to find herself in his arms right now. Not to mention the damned questions that would come pouring out of her mouth. She was just waiting on the chance to lay into him, and he wasn't too eager to give it to her. It was coming. He knew the only way to avoid her would be to leave the county again. Something he was going to do soon anyway to lure the damned soldiers away before they learned about the whole Pride. As far as the Council knew, the others had died in that damned explosion more than ten years ago. He wanted to keep it that way.

"Here we are." Sherra pulled up to the motel room door swiftly. She grabbed Merinus' purse, searched around then pulled the key from its depths.

Callan let her open the door before he quickly exited the vehicle, Merinus limp in his arms, and strode inside. He laid her on the bed, noticing the white robe that lay on the mattress, the remains of her dinner on the table. The television was on, the sound turned down, a low light burned beside the bed.

He moved away from her, reluctant, regretting the need to leave before she awoke. He touched her cheek, a fleeting caress, then before he could stop himself, he leaned over, touching his lips to the corner of her mouth, his tongue barely glancing the soft curves. She was as soft and as sweet as he knew she would be.

"Callan, we need to hurry," Sherra whispered from outside the door. "Before someone sees us."

Merinus' lips parted, a low groan vibrating in her throat as her head turned, unconsciously seeking more of the caress. Her tongue touched his, hesitant, unsure. He fought to keep the kiss light, to deny his need to stroke the heated depths of her mouth as he wanted to. He contented himself with a soft tangle with her tongue, then drew back quickly and forced himself to leave the room.

He closed the door softly behind him as Tanner's truck pulled in beside the Jeep. Following Sherra he jumped into the cab quickly, silently, watching the door as Tanner reversed. He stared straight ahead, ignoring Sherra's worried look, ignoring his own needs pulsing hot and demanding through his blood stream. Son of a bitch, he wanted Merinus. He wanted to lay against her, stroke every sweet curve of that slender body before burying his cock so deep inside her that neither one of them would ever be free.

As they pulled out of the parking lot, Callan watched as Dayan pulled into a small, secluded parking area within sight of Merinus' door. She would be watched carefully until he could leave. He should have left sooner, before those damned mercenaries had somehow figured out his attraction for her. Before they decided to use her against him.

"Call Taber in when we get to the station," he told Tanner, his voice cold as he made his decision. "We go after those bastards tonight."

"Sure thing, Callan." Tanner's voice was edged with fury. He may not be personally involved, but Merinus was a female, she was supposed to be protected, no matter the cost. The younger man rarely came to violence until faced with the abuse of a female, young or old.

"Sherra, you go back to the motel, send Dayan back." Callan knew Dayan would be pissed, his answer was to ignore the bastards. "You stick around and watch out for her, take Dawn if you want to."

Sherra was more than capable of protecting herself, but Callan hated sending her alone anyway.

"Get a piece of them for me." Memories and bitterness filled her voice.

"For all of us then." Callan nodded as Tanner pulled into the Gass Up. "Let's get things together and we'll head out."

They knew where the soldiers camped, though the men were unaware of it. Like the others before them, they thought their training and their precautions would hide them from the instincts ingrained in Callan's DNA. They would find out otherwise.

CHAPTER FIVE

Merinus woke up aching the next morning. Not the flu or summer cold kind of ache. The utterly female ache of needing a man. How a virgin was supposed to know what that ache meant, she wasn't certain. But there was no doubt that was the cause of it. Her cunt was slick and creamy, her panties damp, too damned damp to suit her. Her breasts were swollen, her nipples distended and hard, and she could have swore she tasted cinnamon on her lips.

Her lips were sensitive. She ran her tongue over them. They weren't swollen, just sensitive enough for her to be very aware of them. Then she remembered the night before. She frowned, her brows snapping together in instant ire. Damn him. He hadn't even stuck around long enough to wake her up?

She jerked to an upright position, then groaned roughly as her sore muscles protested the effort. Oh hell, now that just hurt. There was no cause for those bastards to act that way. She groaned roughly as she reached for her cell phone. Kane was supposed to take care of this.

She keyed his number in swiftly as she stood to her feet. Waiting on Kane to answer, she shed her clothes and pulled on a big, soft cotton T-shirt until she could get to a hot shower.

"Where the hell were you last night?" His voice came over the line with a stern, cranky tone.

"Watching soldiers," she informed him tensely, knowing better than to tell him the truth. "There are two on the ridge above the Lyons' house. I thought you had that taken care of."

His contacts in the private and government sector put him in a place where he would have, or should have known those men were being sent out there. There was silence across the line.

"Damn," he finally cursed quietly. "Pull out, Merinus. Someone's gone to the trouble to hide these bastards from me. I'll bring Dad and we'll come in—"

"And I'll head for another paper at the first offer," she cut in. "You aren't pulling me off this, Kane."

"Dammit, Merinus, it's not safe anymore."

"So find out who they are and give them a call. Tell them you'll rip their balls off and feed 'em to your favorite dog or something," she suggested. "Make them pull back until I can finish this. Don't start making excuses, either. I know you can do it."

Kane was slick, and he could be mean when he had to. Merinus knew that. No one messed with him, and most people in his little world owed him enough favors that he rarely had to ask for anything twice.

"Geez, Merrie, why don't you just pounce on them yourself if you have all the fucking answers?" Kane growled.

Merinus bit her lip, painfully aware of the bruise across the left side of her face now. Yeah, that one worked really well.

"Okay, I can do that," she mused thoughtfully. "They looked kinda big, but hey, maybe if I throw your name around a little—" She should have thought of that one yesterday.

"Dammit," he cursed. "You would, too. Okay. Okay. Just hang on a few hours and let me see what I can find out here. Stay out of trouble, dammit, until I can find something out."

"I always stay out of trouble," she lied smoothly. If Kane knew the trouble she was getting into he would come down, tie her hand and foot and haul her back to New York so damned fast it would make her head spin.

"Yeah. Right." He grunted absently.

"I'll be waiting on you." Evidently he was already hard at work on his trusty little computer.

"You do that," he mumbled, then disconnected.

Merinus sighed roughly as she flipped the phone off then tossed it on the bed. Dammit. Like she was going to sit around and play dead while he hunted around the Internet for a source of information. Bruise or no bruise, she was hardly finished. And she was growing tired of this game she was playing with Callan.

Glancing at the clock, she winced at the time. Late morning. She had definitely overslept. A shower and lunch first though, then she was tracking Callan Lyons down and that was that. If she had to stake out that damned gas station until hell froze over. Her phone rang, interrupting that furious thought.

"Well, that was fast enough," she said as she brought it to her ear. "Did you threaten their balls or what?"

There was silence over the line. Merinus frowned.

"Kane?"

"Maybe you didn't need as much help as I thought you did yesterday." The male voice was low, rumbling and filled with amusement. "Any woman who could threaten such an important area is tough enough to take on a few mercenaries."

"Or the asshole that left her unconscious all night," she said with thick, exaggerated sweetness. "Callan Lyons, we aren't going to get along if you keep up like this."

That brought a definite chuckle.

"Who said we had to get along, darlin'? I was trying to help out some. That scream you blasted out rocked my mountain."

"Well, big boy, tell me where to find you and I'll come thank you, real personal like." Like her foot up his ass for being so damned difficult.

"Hm, tempting offer," his voice dropped, becoming huskier.

Merinus breathed in long and silent. Oh, what that voice did to her insides. Any minute now her juices would be running from her cunt right down her leg.

"You don't sound tempted enough." She grinned, her own voice lowering, becoming silky, intimate. "Come on, Callan, surely you don't want to have to rescue me again? I'm not going to give up, ya know?"

There was that silence again.

"You sound soft, Merinus, too damned soft for what you're up against," he finally sighed.

"Callan, I can't give up." She sat down on the bed, gripping the phone tightly. "You have to talk to me. I have things to show you, things I have to tell you that can only be done in person."

"I'm not a story, pretty lady, and I know that's what you're after," he told her, his voice so gentle, so soothing she felt stroked, petted.

"Perhaps you are," she answered. "Why would you be hiding from me if you weren't? All I want to do is talk."

"Maybe I wouldn't stop with talk," he suggested. "You don't know me. I could be as mean as those soldiers you tangled with."

"And maybe I wouldn't fight you." She closed her eyes, knowing she wouldn't. Just the sound of his voice had her pulse skyrocketing, her body heating up like a damned furnace.

Dammit, if her vagina clenched any tighter she would strangle his cock when it finally got inside her. What the hell was wrong with her?

She could hear him breathing over the phone, deep and rough. She wondered if he heard her as well.

"Like what you saw the other day?" His shocking question was delivered in a hot, rough voice.

Merinus took a deep breath, her tongue running over her dry lips nervously.

"You knew I was there?"

"Oh, I knew. I could feel your hot little eyes on me, Merinus. Do you think I jack off for the hell of it? I'm a grown man, not a kid. I don't get a hard-on with just any stiff breeze anymore."

Merinus fought the little whimper that edged in her throat. She clenched her thighs together, fighting the ache there.

"Why?" she whispered. "Why did you do that?"

"Because you were watching. Because I know you want me and you don't know what you're asking for."

"I saw—"

"Son of a bitch," he growled. He actually growled the words. "Damn you, woman. This is insanity, you know that, don't you?"

Oh, she knew. She knew it wasn't the story she wanted anymore. It was just saving his life, revealing a major conspiracy, a crime against nature itself. It was more now, and she felt helpless in the grip of what it had become.

"I could return the favor." Where the hell had those words come from? Merinus felt her face flush the minute they came from her mouth.

There was silence again. Long, thick with tension.

"You're tempting me." His voice sounded strangled.

"You know where I'm at," she offered, amazed at the huskiness of her voice.

"Why are you doing this?" He sounded as ensnared by the heated offer as she had been at the sight he had given her.

"I'm not really sure." She swallowed tightly, dragging her hand through her hair as she fought the overriding need pulsing in her body now. "Because I want to be with you. If nothing else, put you through the hell you put me through."

Her breathing was rough, but so was his. She could hear the throb of desire in it, the same as it throbbed through her body.

"I'm too old for this," he said, though his voice lacked conviction.

"Too old for sex?"

"For voyeurism. There's no way in hell I'm actually going to touch you, woman, you'd burn me alive." Once again, there was no real heat in his voice.

"I want you to touch me." She was confused by the intensity of her need. "I don't know what's wrong with me, but I'm sitting here aching for you so desperately I'd agree to damned near anything. This isn't normal for me, Callan."

"So hunt up an old lover."

"I'd have to have one first," she snapped, offended by the desperation in his tone. "Forget it. I'm not going to beg."

"But I might—" His voice was strained, husky. "Tell me you're not a fucking virgin."

"No, I'm not a fucking virgin. Virgins have yet to fuck, remember?"

He cursed. Low, rough, a rumble amplified by the phone connection as heat seemed to sear her across the airwaves.

"I want inside you so bad my cock is about to burst," he snapped. "You're fucking dangerous."

"So jack off again," she snarled. "No, wait an hour first. I want to at least watch."

The phone disconnected. Merinus threw it across the room as a squeal of feminine outrage erupted from her throat. Damn him. She ached. No she didn't, she hurt. And all she could think about was that thick cock sliding into her, thrusting hard and deep, her vagina milking it, caressing it deeper and tighter than his hand had done days before.

Enough was enough. The game was over. She would be damned if she would lie here, virtually in heat, dying for some hick moron's touch that didn't want her. She would take him the message her father sent her and get it over with. Lay the offer on the table then head for home. She didn't need this, and she didn't need him. Now, if she could just convince her body of that.

CHAPTER SIX

"Have you finished hiding from me?"

Callan knew he was in trouble when he saw her approach him moments before. Trouble was always recognizable. It had a scent, a feel, a low vibration of warning that thrummed through his veins. This feeling rioted through his system now. She stood beside him, watching him with a frown as he tinkered with the reluctant engine of his old truck once again and fought to get a handle on his self-control. The scent of her drifted on the breeze, the scent of fresh, clean woman, the beginning heat of arousal. Those scents lay around her now, tempting him, drawing him.

"Are you going to answer me?" she inquired, tilting her head, irritation flashing over her expression.

Long strands of straight, thick brunette hair fell over her shoulder, caressing silken skin and tempting his hands. Dammit, he didn't need this kind of trouble. Not after that phone call earlier, not after the hot surge of lust her offer had hit him with.

"I'm in plain sight. How's that hiding?" He tested a line into the carburetor. "Now what the hell did you want with me? Didn't those soldiers give you a nice little warning, Ms. Tyler? They play for keeps."

She was intent on ignoring the danger of the situation evidently. She leaned her bare arms against the side of the truck, peering into the guts as though she knew what the hell she was doing.

"A friend sent me." She shrugged. That movement caused the gentle curve of her breasts to rise a shade above the scooped neckline of the sleeveless top she wore.

Red. Dammit, it should be a crime for a woman that damned pretty to wear red.

He glanced at her. Her brown eyes, clear and wide, studied the motor intently, rather than looking at him. The sweet spice of her need wrapped around him, making his cock harden demandingly. Big problem, Callan thought. Literally.

"So who sent you?" he questioned her with mild interest. "I don't have a lot of friends."

"Maybe not." She glanced up at him, suspicion riding her expression. "But your mother had a few. My father sent me to extend his condolences and to see if you needed anything."

He glanced at the woman again. Her gaze was knowing now. She had found him and she was more than aware of it. He laid the wrench down on the side of the truck and took a deep breath.

"You should return to your home, Ms. Tyler," he told her quietly, warningly. "This is not the place for you or your father's questions."

Merinus looked around casually, careful to keep her voice low.

"Father can help you, Callan. That's why I'm here."

Frustration filled him now. The naivety of journalists often astounded him. They believed so deeply in their freedoms, the public's right to know and their convictions of justice that they could not see the evil that shrouded them all. The innocence of this journalist fairly took his damned breath away.

"Come with me." He rose to his full height, staring down at her as he took her slender arm in his hand and began pulling her along with him.

"Come where with you?" Suspicion laced her voice. There was no fear though, and he wanted to rail at her for her courage. The ignorance of her belief that she would come to no harm.

"Upstairs. To the office." He pulled her through the garage to the back corner and up the steep stairs that led to Taber's office.

The garage and attached store was owned by the Pride, as were all their holdings. But Taber was listed as sole owner on paper. It was better that way. Less suspicion. Less chance of being found.

Callan jerked the door open and pushed her inside. Closing it carefully behind them, he turned the lock, reasonably confident of privacy now, considering the sound proof room they were standing in. He would have one chance to bluff his way through this, and one chance only. He was considering how to begin when she drew an envelope out of her purse and pulled out the damning evidence.

"Don't bother to lie to me." There was a vein of hurt in her voice, as though she knew what he had intended.

Callan crossed his arms over his chest. He narrowed his eyes on her and let his frustration free in a harsh, rumbling growl that he hadn't intended to give voice to. The low snarl, catlike in sound, dangerous in purpose, filled the air.

He watched the woman blink. The pictures fluttered from her hand, the heat of her body rose, the scent of it thicker, mixed now with fear. The pictures lay on the floor now, incriminating, damning. Callan, as a child, a thick lion's fur covering his body, his eyes, amber gold and bright, shining into the camera. The fur had slowly fallen away, until only a smooth, light scattering of fine, nearly invisible, ultra soft hair remained. The other was a sonogram, and Callan knew pertinent information was recorded on the back of it. Blood type, DNA sequence, anomalies. All recorded. All nails in a coffin that Merinus Tyler could help build.

* * * * *

Merinus watched the tall, powerful man as he bent and scooped the pictures from the floor. His face was expressionless, his eyes hard, brilliant amber in the tan darkened features of his face.

She hadn't intended to show him the proof she carried with her, but she had known he was ready to lie to her. The knowledge had vibrated through her body. Lie. The word had been like a whisper, dark and vibrating. But Merinus had proof. She hadn't come to him with supposition and half-truths. The evidence Maria Morales had sent John Tyler had been conclusive, irrefutable. But to bring truth to the test results and pictures, they needed the man. She hadn't meant to drop the pictures, but the smooth rumble of warning from his throat had been more than a surprise

"Maria was like a little packrat," he sighed, shaking his head as he stared down at the pictures.

Long, thick, coarse, tawny gold hair lay below the nape of his neck, framing a sharply lined face, savage in its angles. Wide, tilted eyes, thick lashes and cheekbones with an odd flattened angle where they should curve high and sharp. His nose was aristocratic, but the ridge seemed smoothed out, much as the cheekbones were.

Merinus ignored the hard beat of her heart as he finally looked at her. Her womb tightened uncomfortably, making her cunt clutch and protest the emptiness there. It was unusual, this sensation. She was well aware it was arousal washing over her. It made her breasts feel swollen, made her nipples harden uncomfortably, and those unusual eyes did not miss the reaction.

"She asked Father to help you," she said, trying to cover her nervousness. "He wants you to come in with me. He has safeguards set up—"

He laughed. His lips twisted into a humorless curve and the bitterness in the sound struck at her heart. He shook his head, his gaze mocking.

"If this is why you have come here, Ms. Tyler, then you have wasted your time." Gone was the good ole boy, in its place a cold, hard creature. She saw it in the tense readiness of his large body, the flash of sharpened incisors at the sides of his mouth.

"You aren't safe," she told him worriedly. "Our research into this has uncovered a plot to kill—"

"And eventually they will succeed." He shrugged as though unconcerned. "When they do, steal the body and write your story and good luck to you in living. Until then, I need no help of yours."

Surprise flared inside her.

"You don't intend to try to stop them? To keep this from happening again?"

"It has already happened again and again and again," he told her coldly. "They used wolves as well. To my knowledge, I am the only known success they have achieved."

Merinus shook her head. She had seen the pictures of those pitiful forms, born so deformed that there was no hope of life. Only Callan, as he said, had been their success.

"You can't hide forever," she pointed out. "You're letting them win, Mr. Lyons."

"I am living. I do not kill; I do not follow their command. They have not caught me, nor captured me again since my teens. I will defeat them until I can no longer, Ms. Tyler. Then, as I said, the rest is history."

"My father is offering you an alternative," she told him.

She fought a shiver that washed over her body as he moved, bringing his body closer to her. Heat suffused her, making the flesh between her thighs moisten. If the feeling wasn't so strange, she would have been amused.

Callan Lyons was watching her with a frown, a question in his eyes as he came closer. She watched him inhale deeply, his eyes narrowing on her. As he brushed against her, the shiver couldn't be controlled. It tightened her scalp, tingled down her neck, then spread out over her body, drawing goose bumps in its wake.

He stopped behind her, his body so warm the heat seemed to wrap around her. She could feel her body wanting to relax against him, wanting to be surrounded by him. Her thighs weakened, and between them she could feel the slow leak of moisture from her inner flesh, preparing her, readying her. Insanity.

She gasped, startled when she felt his chest brush against her back, his head lowering to her ear.

"I am going to unlock that door, Ms. Tyler. When I do, I want you to walk out of here, get in your vehicle and go home. Make no stops between here and there and do not mention my name or what you know to anyone, do you understand me? It just might keep you alive."

Merinus turned her head, a grin edging her lips.

"Are you trying to intimidate me, Mr. Lyons?" Good gracious, where had that husky edge to her voice come from? Maybe the same place that the sharp contraction to her womb originated from.

She felt him tense behind her. His hand moved to her arm, his fingers curling, the backs of them running softly across her flesh.

"Do you know what the Council does to pretty little women like yourself?" he asked her, his voice low, a deep rumble of warning from his chest. "They impregnate you with their latest batch of genetically altered cells. Then they take you out daily, to check the progress. If your body rejects it, then they do it again and again until you either hold the fetus, or you're too weak to be of use to them any longer. Then they give you to the soldiers to use until you die. It's not a pretty way to be taken from this earth."

Merinus bit her lip as she felt pain, overwhelming, intense, striking at her chest. It wasn't fear, it was horror, revulsion, absolute pain for the women who had endured it, the man who had obviously seen it.

"I'm sorry," she whispered, staring back, seeing only the thin line of anger his mouth had settled into.

"You are risking your very sanity being here." His breath caressed her ear, a shiver working over her skin once again as he spoke to her. "Your sanity and your life. You should leave."

His voice throbbed with menace. It pulsed with heated arousal. Thick and husky, it rippled over her nerve endings, seared her cunt.

"So you've said." She stared forward as he moved again, coming back to face her. "I told you, I'm not willing to let them continue to kill and maim, and you shouldn't be either. We can stop them. My uncle, Samuel Tyler, is a Senator and close to the President. He's waiting to do whatever is necessary. I have seven brothers, each one doing their part, and my father is willing to put every resource he has within his paper to back you. We have to make them stop."

"And you think this will stop them?" he asked her incredulously. "Your innocence is to be envied, Ms. Tyler. It's actually quite frightening. You can't take these people down."

She had to. She couldn't stand to live if they managed to kill him. He was proud, determined and too damned remarkable in his very humanity to allow them to murder him. She had to convince him that his only safety lay in revealing the horrors he had escaped.

"You know who they are. You know what they are. You have the rest of the proof that we need to stop them," she argued determinedly. "Your mother died because of this."

"My mother was a victim of a random crime," he growled. "Had the Council struck her, she would have disappeared and her body returned to me in pieces. The Council did not destroy her."

"There was no sign of theft." Merinus had read the police report. "It was a personal crime, Mr. Lyons. Whoever killed her wanted her dead."

Merinus hadn't come to this place unprepared. Her father had made certain she knew everything involving Maria Morales' death and the evidence they had against the Council.

"And they succeeded. But it wasn't the Council." He stared down at her, his eyes hard, furious. "I know their scent, I know the stench of their evil. As cloying and cold as the scent of your arousal is sweet and hot."

Merinus opened her mouth to argue until the last words penetrated her brain. She felt her face flush, her heart rate increase. She stared at him in surprise. How had he known?

"Explain to me why a young, innocent woman is standing here before me, her cunt wet and prepared for an animal? And I am an animal, sugar, unlike any you will ever know."

CHAPTER SEVEN

Merinus trembled beneath Callan's regard. His amber eyes almost glowed, his voice lowered, husky. A quick, very brief glance below his hips showed a bulge that made her more than nervous. Evidently, she wasn't the only one afflicted. And an affliction more than described it. She felt fevered, her skin sensitive, ready for his touch. It was unlike anything she had ever known. It was unlike anything she ever wanted to know.

"I don't know." She heard the nervousness in her voice, the confusion. The longer she stayed in his presence, the worse the temptation to touch him was growing.

She stared at his chest, no longer able to stare into his eyes. Those amber depths drew her in, made her want, made her need things she wasn't certain she should want.

She flinched when his fingers gripped her chin, uncertain, almost frightened now. Had he not been aware of the desires flaring in her body, she could have handled this. Could have handled the direct look from his eyes, the caress of his fingers against her chin. She ran her tongue nervously over her dry lips, aware of the sudden fullness in them, the ache, the throb just beneath the skin.

His eyes narrowed. His thumb reached out, running experimentally over the soft curve, picking up the moisture from her mouth. Her chest tightened as she tried to breathe normally. She couldn't seem to draw in enough air to fill her lungs sufficiently. She felt the need to fight for breath, to release the moan she held there.

"You're dangerous." There was that growl again, rumbling just beneath the surface of his words. "Whatever this is, Merinus, could mean our lives."

"Anomaly." She bit her lip. She had no answers for this.

A mocking curve of his lips showed his disagreement.

"There is no such thing as an anomaly when dealing with one such as I," he assured her. "I'm instinct, Merinus. An animal barely disguised. Any response is one to fear."

"Not an animal." She shook her head, seeing the bitterness in his eyes.

She drew away from his touch quickly. He made her body weak, pliant. She needed all her wits about her now.

"What would you call it then?" There was a thread of anger running through his voice. "If I did as you asked, and by some miracle of God did not end up dead, then I would be known as America's Freak. More experiments, more tests. At least this way, I'm free. As long as I can run faster than their soldiers and hide better than their trackers, then I can survive."

"And is survival enough?" she asked him, angry that he didn't want more. "What about those who will come later? The poor souls that meet their killing criteria? Don't you feel in some way responsible to stop it?"

Cynicism washed over his expression.

"So passionate," he murmured, leaning against the wall, his arms crossing over his chest as he watched her. "I'm one man—"

"With a nation that will back him," she argued desperately.

"Your innocence is to be commended, Merinus," he mocked her softly. Straightening, he stalked closer to her. "As are your motives. But you have no idea of the piece you've bitten off here. It's bound to choke you."

He gripped her arm, jerking her against his body, allowing his erection to cushion against her stomach. Merinus breathed in harshly, her hands bracing against his chest as he locked her to him.

"You spout off with your morality and your ideas of justice, and all the while your juices froth from your cunt, tempting me, driving me insane with the scent. It's not the story you want and it's not justice. You want to be fucked by the Cat Man. Admit it."

He gripped her hips, ground himself against her. Merinus gasped out, fighting against the slow relaxation of her body against his, the needs suddenly swamping her. Where had they come from?

"I don't know why," she cried out hoarsely, shaking her head. "It wasn't like this before I came here. I only wanted to help you."

"Doesn't this frighten you, Merinus?" His hand gripped her hair, pulling her head back. "Aren't you scared of this sudden lust? Because if you aren't, you should be. It has me damned near shaking in my boots with my need to lay you over that desk and fuck you until you scream with your pleasure."

Merinus shuddered, then cried out when his head lowered. His lips went to her neck, his teeth scraping over it in a slow, dangerous gesture. Merinus shook. Her hands gripped his powerful arms, she stared at the ceiling in dazed rapture as his tongue swiped over her skin. The moist roughness, the sandpapery rasp had her going to her tiptoes, silently demanding more. Her head tilted further, exposing the vulnerable curve of her neck. Her skin tingled, screamed out for more.

"Damn, you taste good, Merinus. Damn good." He licked across her skin again, and she cried out.

She couldn't believe the sensation. Like rough velvet, only better. A sharp spasm of need rippled through her womb, the clenching muscles of her vagina had her whimpering in arousal. What was this? Why did it feel so good when her neck had never been an erogenous zone before?

Then his lips covered hers. Merinus had been kissed before, many times, but nothing like this. His tongue swept into her mouth and the taste of him was intoxicating. Her tongue met his, drawing him deeper, caressing over him, luxuriating in the taste of him. Hot, spicy. The taste was all male, dark and elusive, conquering. She groaned against his lips, needing more, needing to examine and discover the origin of his taste. But he moved, drawing back, his lips going to her neck once again.

His teeth nipped at her skin briefly, a growl emanating from his chest as one hand moved from her hip to below her breast. He was close, so close to the torturously swollen mound, the throbbing nipple. She whimpered, pressing against him, uncaring who or what he was, caring only about the primeval response of her body to his.

"Get out of here," he rasped, though he refused to release her. "Get out of here before I do something neither of us will survive."

His mouth moved from her neck, along her collarbone, sipping, licking as he weaved a path back to the scooped collar of her shirt and the rise of her throbbing breasts. Merinus was burning alive for his touch. Her nipples hardened further, jutting against the soft material of her shirt, hard, desperate for the warmth of his mouth. If he didn't touch them, if he didn't suck them deep into his mouth she was going to explode. Oh God, if he did, she would explode anyway. She was close, so very close to orgasm it terrified her. Her blood pumped, rushed through her body. She trembled in his grip, her body arched against the arm at her back as a desperate moan whispered from her throat.

She felt the bottom of her shirt jerked from the waistband of her shorts and pulled quickly above the swollen mounds. Her nails bit into his shoulders, confusion, desire, fire tearing through her.

"What the hell have we done to each other?" His voice whispered the confusion churning in her body. His hand moved, cupping her breast. The dry heat of his flesh against hers had her hips arching in desperation. His thigh slid smoothly between her legs as he turned her, bracing her against the wall, allowing her the minute release of riding the hard muscled thigh pressing between hers.

Oh, that felt good. Her clit throbbed, ached, swelled painfully at the friction she created as she rode him.

"Callan," her cry was a shocking mixture of fear, overwhelming need, and questioning desperation as his mouth covered the hard nipple that rose pleadingly from her breast.

He drew on her, the sensation spearing into her womb, her cunt. His tongue rasped over the hard flesh, the texture of his tongue was rough but incredibly gentle, deeply erotic. He suckled her, laved her, then nibbled at the flesh as she writhed on his thigh, moaning, begging for release.

"Son of a bitch." He pulled back from her, staring down at her with eyes glittering with lust and confusion. "This isn't normal, Merinus. This need should not be here."

He jerked her shirt back over her breasts, restoring order to her clothes, if not her senses.

"Sit." He pushed her onto the couch that sat against the wall and began to pace the floor.

Merinus shook her head. It wouldn't stop. The pulsing, throbbing need was only intensifying.

"What did you do to me?" she gasped, shaking her head. "It won't stop."

He paused, turning to her.

"What?" He frowned, staring into her eyes, confusion crossing his face.

"It won't stop," she gasped, fighting for control. "You did something to me. Now make it stop."

Callan came to his knees before her, staring into her eyes, frowning at whatever he saw there. A tremulous laugh escaped her throat.

"Damn, Callan, you really need to watch those kisses. They're dangerous."

"They have never been a problem before," he growled, his fingers lifting to her forehead as though checking for a fever.

"Share them around do you?" she asked, gritting her teeth against his touch. "I don't like this. I think I'm going to call my brothers to come out and kick your ass now."

She wouldn't. Not really. They would welcome the chance to take her seriously, especially Kane, her hot shot Special Forces brother who held a grudge against the world.

"What are you feeling?" he asked her quietly. "Besides the obvious?"

"The obvious multiplied as high as you can go," she breathed out, clenching her thighs together. "Do you know I'm a virgin? Seriously, virgins shouldn't be this turned on. It has to be bad for their health or something. We're an endangered species, ya know?"

She ignored the shock in his expression.

He tilted her head, his gaze going over her neck, then he jerked her shirt up again, examining her breast. Merinus looked down, almost grinning at the site of the love bite that marred her nipple.

"Callan, that tongue of yours is dangerous." She moaned as his thumb raked the hard flesh.

She heard his low moan an instant before he covered the other peak with his mouth. Her hands went to his hair, holding him close, feeling his tongue stroke her gently, his mouth drawing on her tightly. She squirmed against him, moving her body lower, wanting to press herself tight and hard against the bulge that threatened to burst the seams of his jeans.

"God, I smell you. So hot and sweet," he gasped as he pulled back, his head lowering as he rested it in the valley of her breasts. "I want to taste you so desperately Merinus, that it rages through me."

"What?" Shocked pleasure electrified her body.

"I want to bury my mouth in that hot little cunt of yours," he groaned. "I want to lap every bit of your cream and stroke you with my tongue until you give me more."

The cream in question wept slowly from her vagina in mute plea for just that. Her swollen clit throbbed, her womb spasmed. His mouth nibbled at the curve of her breast, his tongue stroking the swollen flesh, the rough texture of it making her shiver with need.

"Please, do something," she groaned, her thighs tightening on his as he pushed his cock deep into the vee of her thighs. "I swear, Callan, your touch is like a drug."

He stopped. She felt his muscles tense, then an oath sizzled from his mouth as he jerked away from her.

"I'm going to regret asking. But what's wrong now?" She laid her head back against the couch, breathing heavily as she dragged her shirt back down.

She could hear him fighting for breath as well. She opened her eyes, watching as he stood several feet from her, watching her.

"If you don't get out of here, I'm going to fuck you," he rasped out savagely. "Think about it, Merinus. You don't know me. I'm a stranger to you. A genetic animal that's getting ready to tear your clothes from your body and fuck you on a grease stained couch. Is that how you want your first time?"

Merinus frowned. "Well, it didn't top my list of things to do today. But I've always been good at improvising."

She could think of no reason not to lie back on the couch and let him have his way with her. She didn't understand his problem and her body was in such a riot that she really didn't care.

"Merinus, think," he snapped furiously, moving to sit on the opposite end of the couch as he raked his fingers through his hair. "You've never been assaulted by lust in such a way. This cannot be normal."

"How would I know?" she frowned. "I told you, I've never done this before. Have you?"

"Have I what?" he questioned her suspiciously.

"Have you ever had sex before?" she asked him impatiently. "You seem so reluctant, I was just curious."

"Of course I have had sex before." He frowned. "It was a required subject before my escape from the labs. I had sex every day for over two years."

Shock tore through her system.

"You were sixteen when you escaped," she said, horrified. "That was too young."

He shot her a glare. "I was recaptured at seventeen and held until I was twenty before I destroyed the labs. You need to be certain of your sources, Merinus."

"They taught you how to have sex?" She couldn't imagine anything so barbaric.

"Of course, killing a person can be done in many ways. They taught me how to bring pleasure and how to inflict pain." He sneered. "I know every way imagined to fuck a man or a woman, with any degree of each sensation."

Merinus swallowed tightly, blinking over at him.

"That's horrible," she whispered. "Why would they do that to you?"

Overriding her lust was her terrible pain for this man. He looked disgusted, both with himself and with her.

"They did that to train me," he reminded her coldly. "I was to be a killer, Merinus. There are many ways to kill, to maim, to force the information you want from your victim. I was taught all those things. But that does not answer the question of our present problem. I don't remember a time when my kiss has ever drugged a woman."

"Maybe it's just me," she breathed roughly. "You kiss really good, Callan."

His lips kicked up at the corner and his eyes filled with a weary sort of humor.

"You are a dangerous woman. How are you feeling now?"

"Horny," she sighed. "Very horny, Callan."

The hot throb between her thighs was threatening to soak through her shorts. She was so ready, so needy she felt ready to explode.

"This could be a problem," he sighed.

"Why, because you are too?" she mocked him. "Yeah, really complicates your little survival idea doesn't it."

Merinus rose to her feet. She was tired of this. If she didn't get away from him she was going to beg him to fuck her brains out. Just what she needed to start her week off.

"Where are you going?" He frowned as she picked up her purse from the middle of the floor and took a deep breath.

"Back to camp."

"Camp?" He sounded incredulous.

"Yeah, camp," she stated. "I set a tent up on the lower piece of your property a few hours ago. You can find me there if you want to talk, or whatever."

Incredulity crossed his expression

"You are camping on my creek?" he asked her incredulously. "You're trespassing. When did you do that? Do you think those damned soldiers won't find you there?"

"I set it up this morning. I told you, I'm tired of waiting. I'll find my way to you sooner or later if it kills me."

"Those soldiers just might," he reminded her. "And you can't stay there, Merinus. It's trespassing," he repeated.

"So sue me, since you don't seem to be willing to fuck me." She shrugged. "I'll be waiting, Callan. But I'm a pretty impatient person, I'd hurry if I were you."

"Or you'll do what?" he asked her suspiciously.

"Or I'll call my brothers and let them have the job after all," she told him, unlocking the door. "And trust me, they would put your Council soldiers to shame for sheer tenacity. I'm the welcome wagon, the Tyler Seven are hell."

She swept out of the office, leaving only her scent. Clean, fresh, so fucking hot it made his cock throb. He collapsed against the back of the couch, staring at the nearly empty room, breathing harshly. Dammit, this wasn't a good thing. She hadn't even made it out of the building yet, and it was all he could do to keep from dragging her back and making a damned lust filled meal out of her on the couch.

He groaned, the thought of pushing his head between those silky thighs, his tongue lapping the sweet moisture that produced that intriguing scent was nearly more than he could bear. He licked his lips and bit back an oath. Something was wrong. It shouldn't be this strong.

Pulling himself to his feet, he strode to the desk and jerked the receiver from the phone base. Dialing quickly, he waited for a voice to answer.

"Doc Martin's." Sherra's voice was carefully cultured, smooth and cool.

"Get Doc out to the house as soon as possible. I have a problem."

There was silence on the line.

"What kind?" she asked him worriedly.

"Physical. I need some tests. Just get out there."

He hung the phone up before she could answer. He was throbbing, his flesh sensitive, his body demanding relief from the little journalist that tempted him so desperately.

Lust wasn't like that. He knew he was intensely sexual, more than a little driven in that area, and he knew it wasn't like this. It didn't drug, it didn't intoxicate. It didn't dig its claws into your loins, demanding satisfaction. Which meant it could be a problem. An instinctive, genetic problem only now showing itself. Shaking his head, he could only pray he was wrong as he headed for his truck and the peace of his home.

CHAPTER EIGHT

"It may take a few days." Doc Martin, the only scientist left alive from the original five that had worked with the creation of Callan and the others, set the dozen or so vials in a small box and began to pack his instruments.

He had blood samples, saliva samples, hell, even more than one semen sample. Despite the manual releases, though, Callan's cock still throbbed. His blood rushed through his veins and he couldn't get the scent of that damned woman from his body.

"Any guesses?" Callan asked him.

Doc shrugged. "It could be anything, Callan, though I say we can safely narrow it down to a sexual problem. I won't know anything conclusive until the tests are finished. And I need samples from the woman as well. You need to bring her here tonight, let me get those samples to test alongside yours."

"No." He couldn't trust himself anywhere around her.

"From what you say, she's affected as well, Callan," Sherra stated from behind the doctor. "We need to know what's going on. This isn't just about you. It could affect all of us."

The full Pride was assembled, the other three watched him somberly, more than a little concerned at the news of this new problem they were facing.

"Let's wait and see what mine say. If she's still experiencing this problem, then we'll see," Callan suggested a bit desperately. "Until then, there's no sense in alarming her." No sense in tempting the lust raging between them.

"It's dangerous enough that he's had any reaction with a normal person," Dayan said darkly. The cougar breed was brooding, his brown eyes unsettled, angry, his expression more savage than usual.

"We aren't monsters, Dayan." Beside him, Dawn, the youngest of the pride, also a cougar breed, protested softly.

"What do you call it, Dawn? Do you want to fuck a normal male and take the chance that your nature will destroy him?" Dayan sneered.

Callan watched Dawn flinch, her face paling, fear flashing across her expression.

"Enough," Callan growled. "What's happened to you, Dayan, that you would turn on the women now? There is nothing to indicate we would hurt anyone."

"She's not normal. She has no business—"

A savage snarl erupted from Tanner's throat. Bengal, unpredictable, and fiercely protective of the women, as a young male his temper often ran hot and impatient.

"Enough, dammit." Callan came to his feet, staring at them all. Taber and Tanner had placed Dawn behind them and now faced Dayan, incisors showing, their expressions masks of anger.

"They're at it again," Sherra sighed. "It won't go any further."

"It should not be going on this far." Callan turned to her angrily. "Is this what you do while I'm drawing the Council soldiers from our home? Fight amongst yourselves?"

"Only when Dayan attempts to take over," Tanner burst out. "You left Taber in charge, he has no right to order us, or Dawn and Sherra."

"He is getting out of hand, Callan," Taber's voice was less violent, but the potential of it throbbed just beneath the surface. The jaguar breed his DNA was mixed with could be calm and patient, or savagely aggressive.

"Dayan?" Callan questioned him, his voice hard.

Dayan shook his head. "We are not normal." He seemed more subdued now, backing down from the others. "It's insanity to pretend we are."

"None of us attempt to pretend that we are normal." Callan raked his fingers through his hair in frustration. "Go home. See if you can find your patience before tomorrow night. I want you and Taber patrolling the ridge for soldiers. We can't let down our guard, especially now."

Other than a brief nod, Dayan did little to respond before he turned and stomped from the room.

"Dawn?" The young woman still seemed to cower behind Tanner and Taber. "Come out of there, little sister. Why would you still be frightened?" Because shadows and memories tore at her, tormented her. He knew well why she feared.

She moved from the safety of the other two men, glancing back at Taber as though for reassurance.

"Dayan is trying to force her to move in with him," Sherra said as she began to help Doc pack their supplies. "His desire for her frightens her."

Dawn paled. Callan breathed a weary sigh. There were days he wondered if they would survive with their sanity in tact.

"Take her home with you, Sherra," Callan ordered. "I don't want her left alone."

He ignored Dawn's look of surprised thankfulness.

"Keep her there," he continued. "I'll have my hands full running Ms. Tyler off. I need no other worries."

"Good luck," Doc said as he studied a page from the thick notebook he had stolen from the lab years ago.

"What have you found?" Callan frowned, easing closer.

Jacob Martin shook his head worriedly, his lined face creasing into a scowl as he read the information he had found.

"There was a case of this, with the first Leo created, about ten years before you. He was kept in another location. This occurred with a female scientist, actually." He turned worried eyes to Callan. "It affects not just you, Callan, but the woman as well. The two of you are in a 'mating frenzy'."

"Mating frenzy?" Callan asked carefully.

"I must have missed this, because you've never displayed these symptoms before." The scientist shook his head in confusion. "It's just a small notation, really. The Leo and the female were destroyed, so there were no tests done regarding the phenomena. But extreme sexual distress, fevered conditions, heightened senses, the ability to scent the female's arousal, were all notated. The scientist labeled it as 'mating frenzy'. A condition similar to that of feline animals."

Callan sat down as he breathed out wearily.

"No tests mean no way of knowing what will happen," he said wearily.

Doctor Martin shook his head. "There was mention that several scientists wanted to study it, see if the Leo could breed with the woman, but those over the project wouldn't allow it. They destroyed the pair."

Callan braced his elbows on his legs, his hands hanging between his knees as he lowered his head, shaking it in horror. The decisions of life and death were made so easily within the hell they had been created in.

"Someone has to keep an eye on the woman. I need those tests from her, Callan," the doctor warned him. "We need to track this, for the others if for no other reason. If it happens with you, then it will happen with them. And we don't know if the woman is in any danger from this."

Callan wondered if the night could possibly get any worse.

"You need to check on her, Cal," Sherra warned him. "Or let one of us."

"I'll do it," he growled, he wanted none of the other males around her. "I'm taking the cell. Doc, you and Sherra hang around here for now. I'll contact you if she's still — " He shrugged.

"Horny?" Sherra grinned mischievously.

"Aroused," he snarled. "I'll let you know when you can leave."

* * * * *

Merinus was aroused. She lay on the sleeping bag within her tent, naked, her body sheened in sweat, pulsating, throbbing with a fever of lust. Her hands cupped her breasts, her fingers pressing against the hard nipples and she couldn't contain her moan. It felt so good.

Almost as good as when Callan had touched her there. She rolled the hard little points between her fingers, her head tossing. Her breasts were so swollen, so sensitive, they were nearly painful.

Her skin tingled. One hand ran over the damp contours of her flat stomach to the smooth flesh between her thighs. Slick, wet heat greeted her fingers. Her clit throbbed, pulsed. She shivered at the feel of her own fingers glancing over the hard little button. Need arched like electricity over her body. Hungry, consuming. She wanted, needed Callan.

She admitted she was in a hell of a mess now. Somehow, someway he had made her crazed for his touch, his kiss. That kiss had been so hot, spicy. The taste of his mouth lingered in hers, making her crave more of it.

Her fingers slid down the thickly coated slit of her cunt. Her thighs tightened, her legs trembled. Oh, she ached. Her fingers tweaked at her nipples, pulling at them, tightening around them until she was moaning heatedly. Her hips bucked against her fingers as they circled her clit. Oh, that felt good. But not as good as Callan could make it feel. She wanted to feel his mouth on her clit, sucking, his tongue stroking it as he had her nipples.

She panted for air now. Remembering the moist, heated warmth of his mouth. Her fingers moved more firmly on her clit, a moan working from her throat as heat swelled in her, around her. She was on fire. Dying. What had he done to her?

"Callan," she whispered his name tremulously.

She would laugh, if she weren't so hot. If the need pulsing through her body wasn't so intense, so searing.

She wondered where Callan was. Surely he had some idea what was happening to her? Was this his punishment for her daring to come out here and try to drag him into public awareness?

This wasn't working. Breathing hard, her fingers stilled on her flesh. She wasn't going to climax, not the way she was doing it. Dammit, she knew she should have bought that damned book on masturbation. But no, she was convinced she could find some buff, muscled god to take care of the job for her. Here she was, stuck in bum fucked nowhere, so horny she was burning alive, and no muscle god to put out the fire.

"Dammit," she slapped at her sleeping bag, frustrated tears coming to her eyes. "I'll kill him when I find him. I'll let Kane neuter him. I'll blow his balls off with my gun."

She groaned, turning over on her side, breathing roughly. She could get through this. She blew out hard, attempting to find some measure of control. She could do this, she thought. She really could make it until tomorrow, then she was stalking into that damned garage and Mr. Callan Lyons, Catboy Extraordinaire, was going to take care of this damned problem, one way or another.

CHAPTER NINE

"Sherra, get up here if you want those blood samples." Callan's voice was low, he could feel and hear the growl emanating from his chest. The 'mating frenzy' was building in him, but he knew Merinus was being tortured by it. He could hear her breathy moans, smell her heat.

"Dammit, Cal, bring her to the cabin," Sherra argued fiercely. "A tent is not the most romantic place. And it's sure as hell not a good place to retrieve samples."

"If I touch her, I'll lose control, Sherra," Callan whispered.

Admitting it took all his strength. He couldn't touch her, couldn't get close to her. He heard the silence from Sherra's end, thick, tense.

"Okay, pull back. We'll come out there and get her. You stay out of range of her, Callan. We need her blood and saliva samples before you touch her again."

"Then you better get up here fast. If she threatens to neuter me again, all bets are off."

Callan disconnected the cell phone and moved further away from her camp. He couldn't bear her moans. And the scent of her was making him crazy. His hands clenched into fists, his body tightened with his need. He could feel the small, minute protrusion beneath the head of his cock flaring. The barb. He knew it was there. He had seen the X-rays of it countless times, but never, in all the years he had been having sex had it flared to life. Now it throbbed.

It pulsed with a life of its own; the nearly unbearable swelling of it was a demand in and of itself.

How long he waited, Callan wasn't sure. Time was measured in the throb of his cock, the beat of his blood through his veins, the lust that seemed to build steadily.

"Hey bro," Taber bent next to him as Dawn and Sherra moved quickly for the tent. "Tell me what to do."

Callan shook his head, sighing deeply.

"Find a cure." He grimaced with a harsh laugh. "Talk about a major complication here, Taber. Until then, you and Tanner scout the area, make sure we don't have any watchers. I'll follow Dawn and Sherra as soon as they get Merinus from that tent and headed to the house."

Taber nodded. He clapped Callan on the shoulder, a gesture of affection they all practiced, then moved quickly away. Callan leaned back against the boulder behind him and breathed a hard sigh. Dammit. Way too complicated.

* * * * *

"Merinus. I'm a friend of Callan's. Can I come in?" The female voice was soft, incredibly gentle.

Merinus jerked into a sitting position, pulling the sleeping bag to her breasts as she stared at the zippered door.

"Where is that dirty bastard?" she cursed angrily, reaching out and pulling the tab down furiously. "I'm going to kill him."

The two women framed in the opening moved in purposely. The door was re-zipped and they regarded her curiously.

"Merinus, we need to get you dressed and to Callan's home. Our doctor is waiting there."

"There's a cure?" She narrowed her eyes on them.

"Sort of." The blonde grimaced. "If you'll get dressed we'll explain everything on the way out of here."

"I don't know if I can walk out of here," Merinus moaned, anger unfolding in her again. "I don't know what he did to me, but it's not pleasant."

"Callan is in little better shape at this time. Now, my name is Sherra and this is my sister, Dawn. We'll help you get dressed. My Jeep got pretty close, so you shouldn't have to walk far."

As Sherra spoke, Dawn jerked a pair of light sweat shorts from a backpack and a loose, sleeveless top.

"Good, loose clothing should be better." Sherra took the items and held them out to Merinus. "Do you need help dressing?"

"No." Merinus clenched the material in her hand. She had removed her clothes for a reason...didn't they know that?

Heaving an irritated sigh, she clenched her teeth together and dressed herself quickly. Moving wasn't comfortable. But then again, breathing wasn't comfortable. It didn't hurt, exactly. The pleasure was just so intense that it was damned impossible to contain her moan when the light cotton material fell over her breasts, stroking her nipples.

"Oh God, I'm going to kill him," she mumbled, flushing with embarrassment.

"You have my permission." Sherra unzipped the door and moved out of the tent. "Can you make it? We brought a friend in case you couldn't walk."

Merinus shook her head, embarrassment flaming her body now.

"I can walk. Let's just hurry up and get there."

Thankfully, Sherra was right. The Jeep was much closer to the tent than Merinus had been able to bring her Blazer. It was still running and the air conditioner was blasting.

"Hang on and we'll hurry," Sherra promised her as she bounced out of the parking spot.

Oh, now that wasn't fair. Merinus felt ecstasy shimmer up her spine as they bounced over rocks and ruts. She closed her eyes, holding tight to the steel bar beside her and the edge of the seat. Each jarring of her body only incited the fever raging through her.

"Definitely need to write a story on this. What does he call it anyway?" Merinus asked. "I feel like I'm in damned heat."

"Close." Sherra shot her a concerned look. "It's called a 'mating frenzy'. We didn't even know it existed until tonight. We don't have much research into it. It's only happened once, before we were born."

The statement didn't take long to hit Merinus' brain.

"We?" She turned to her in shock. "There are more like Callan?"

Sherra nodded, watching the rough track she was driving over carefully. "There are five of us. Three males, Dawn and myself. The evidence on us was destroyed in the lab. Only the files on Callan remained. Thankfully, the scientists were trying to double-cross their masters and didn't tell them about their little side experiments with the rest of us."

There was bitterness and rage in the woman's voice, not that Merinus blamed her. She could only imagine the horrors two young women would have endured there.

"So, you have your own doctor then?" Merinus panted as they bounced over a succession of ruts. Oh, glory. She closed her eyes. If she didn't climax soon, she was going to burn alive.

"The only scientist left. He helped us in the labs, then helped us escape. He watches over us, makes sure everything is okay physically. Sometimes mentally." Sherra shrugged. "He's a good man. Kinda old now, but a good man."

"Oh hell, Sherra, please watch those bumps," Merinus sighed dismally as the woman accelerated over a washboard road. "Oh, God. I'm dying here."

"I'm sorry, Merinus, we really need to hurry." The Jeep shot forward.

Despite the narrowness of the dirt track, the sheer drop from the side of the cliff, the woman pushed the Jeep at an incredible speed, steadily climbing up the nearly impassable road.

"We're not far now," Sherra promised her as they hit the top, then curved around and headed down another cliff. "Just a few more minutes."

A sharp turn again and they were running straight up the middle of the wide creek that ran through two mountains. Several miles up the creek, they turned again to a graveled road that led to a rustic, large log cabin. No damned wonder she couldn't find the road, she thought. There was no road.

"Just pull into the garage," Dawn said from the back. "We need to take her downstairs."

"Doc has a little lab below the cabin, in a cavern we found when we first came here. The dry, cool conditions there are perfect for his work."

The vehicle bounced into a wide garage off the side, then came to a jarring stop.

"Come on. Callan will be here in a minute, and I want you safely out of sight when he shows up." Sherra led her to a door that opened to a cool stairwell.

"I thought the point would be to get very close to Callan," Merinus sighed. "I don't like this, Sherra."

"Well, give Callan time and you'll like it even less," Sherra chuckled. "He's bossy and arrogant. We love him, but he's hell on the nerves."

"What about the bed?" Merinus followed the dimly lit stairs, close on Sherra's heels as they curved and led into a large open cavern.

The stone room was brightly lit, with assorted tables, computers, bright lights and complicated machines.

"Where's Frankenstein?" she jeered, coming to a halt and staring around in amazement.

"I told you, he's on his way." Laughter echoed in Sherra's voice. "Come on, meet Doc and we'll get those samples we need."

Samples. Blood samples, saliva, even a swab of her vagina. Merinus lay back on the flat bed, a sheet covering her, her body damp with sweat. Sherra, Dawn and the grandfatherly doctor moved around her constantly. Even her sweat was being tested. It wasn't comfortable, but compared to the raging lust zinging through her, it wasn't bothersome.

"Okay, I'm ready for the antidote now," Merinus stated when she began to feel the deep, hard contractions of her womb, coinciding with the hard, throbbing pulse that attacked her vagina. "Time to do something here, guys."

Doctor Martin was bent over a complicated microscope, computers and gadgets whirring as he pressed in several commands to the keyboard, raised his head and checked his readout. He sighed, shaking his head.

"Doc?" Sherra stood at his side, reading the display on the computer screen herself.

"A mating," the doctor muttered, running his hand through his thinning gray hair as he glanced up at Sherra. "Look at the results of combining his sperm with her vaginal secretions."

"Okay, it's now time to explain to Merinus." She heard the waver in her own voice and admitted to the fear that was becoming impossible to hold at bay.

What did she really know about these people? They could be dangerous. This could be some elaborate show for their own experiments. She felt her body tremble, not just with lust, but with trepidation.

"It's okay, Merinus," Dawn assured her, her voice soft, hesitant. "No one's going to hurt you. I'm certain Doc and Sherra are almost finished."

Merinus looked up at the other woman, seeing sympathy, shadows of nightmares and pain in her dark, whisky brown eyes.

"I think its time to call in the Amazing Seven," she whispered, thinking of her brothers. They could fix anything. "My brothers," she explained to Dawn's confused look. "They'll be really pissed over this. I've really stepped into it this time."

Kane, hard-nosed asshole that he was, would scream and yell at her, then he would likely kill Callan. Maybe that wouldn't be the smartest route, at least not until this problem with her hormones was fixed.

"Do any other sperm samples react to the excretions?" She heard Sherra ask the doctor.

Oh Lord, this was bad. They were combining the samples taken from her body with other men's cum. Merinus gritted her teeth.

"Enough." She didn't wait for the doctor's response. "Get me a phone. Time to call home."

"Merinus, it really is okay." Dawn glided forward, her heart shaped face concerned as Sherra and Doctor Martin turned to her. "Just a bit longer and we'll be finished."

Merinus sat up on the bed, intending to move to her feet. To dress. To leave. A hard shudder worked over her body then, her vagina spasmed and a fierce jolt of incredible need shook her body, forcing a moan past her throat.

"This is bad," she whimpered, bending over clutching her stomach. "Oh God, this is bad. Time to go home."

"Merinus." Sherra rushed to her side as beeps and pings began to echo through the cavern as the machines, attached to Merinus' body by electrodes, began to go off. "Just a minute—"

"Time's up." Callan stood in the entrance of the makeshift lab, his hair flowing to his bare shoulders, his golden eyes glittering with lust.

Merinus gasped as he came toward her. She had to touch him, had to have him against her. He looked big and hard and so warm. There was no hesitation in her when he reached for her, lifting her from the lab bed.

She groaned aloud when his fiery skin touched her, his arms lifting her against his chest as he turned and stalked from the room. The sheet trailed to the floor, rasping against her skin as it slowly fell away.

"Is it going to hurt?" She couldn't keep her lips from his chest. She had to taste him. She bit at hard muscles, licked the small wound as his body shuddered.

"Hell if I know," he growled. It rumbled through his chest, a deep, predatory sound that had her shivering in pleasure. "And it's too damned late to worry about it."

CHAPTER TEN

Callan carried her through the darkened house, his steps quick, stalking as he moved through a large kitchen, a rustic living room, then into a long hall. Then he was turning into a doorway, kicking the door closed as he passed it and moving to the wide bed on the far wall.

Merinus didn't have time to think and Callan didn't make her beg. The moment her back touched the mattress he was moving over her, his lips taking hers, his tongue plunging forcefully into her mouth.

He tasted so good. Eagerly, her tongue mated with his, the spicy taste of his mouth easing the incredible pain of lust that gripped her body. Like a drug addict in the first seconds of her 'fix', her body began to ease, the harsh contractions in her stomach to lessen. But she wasn't taking chances. Her hands gripped his hair, holding him to her as his mouth devoured her. Lips and tongue mated with hers, hard, hungry, her response urging him closer, urging the kiss deeper.

His arms went around her, blunt nails scraping along her back as she arched to him, her nude body twisting closer, desperate to mate every cell in their bodies together. His hard chest, with its fine sprinkling of golden brown hair rasped her nipples, engorging them to the point of pain. Powerful thighs parted hers, a hand at her back moved to cup her breast, and still he kissed her.

He licked at her lips, nibbled at them, drew her tongue into his mouth and sucked at it before teaching her to do the same. More of the incredible taste of him. She arched closer, the bare flesh of her cunt jerking against the long, hot thickness of his erection as it lay against the soft flesh.

"So good," he whispered against her lips, the rumble of pleasure that echoed through his chest making her shiver. "Your kiss, Merinus, the taste of you, is exquisite."

"So taste more," she gasped, her head arching back as that rough, rasping tongue stroked over her neck.

Oh, that was good. Real good. Hot, with a gentle abrasion that had her panting as he moved slowly to her breasts.

"Don't tease me," she begged, twisting in the grip of an erotic heat that was burning her alive. "Take me, Callan. I can't stand it much longer."

"I want to taste you first," he growled, his tongue licking her breasts, his lips nibbling sporadically. "I want to bury my mouth in your cunt, Merinus. The smell of your heat is making me starve for the taste of you."

His hand moved to her abdomen, stroking its way to her parted thighs. She almost screamed when his fingers, thick and hot entered the narrow, soaked slit of her pussy. She opened her eyes, seeing his grimace of pleasure, the raw lust that transformed his face. Then in amazement she saw his arm lift, his hand moving to his mouth.

Two fingers glistened with the frothy cream of her body. She whimpered as he took them into his mouth, his eyes darkening on a sigh of ecstasy as he tasted her. His lashes lowered, becoming heavy with sexuality, his lips were fuller, his face tense, tight with the needs that surged through his body as well.

"You taste as delicate as spring, as hot as summer," his rough whisper sounded tortured. "I have never tasted anything so good, Merinus."

"Oh, hell. You like to talk," she moaned. "Oh God, I never could stand that in movies. It's too sexy, Callan."

He smiled, the curve of his lips tight.

"I want you to know how hot and sweet your body is, Merinus," he told her darkly, moving, edging lower along her body. "I want to tell you how I'm about to lick that sweet cunt of yours, eat that delicate cream from your body."

Her hips jerked involuntarily to the rough growl in his words, as well as the words themselves.

"Ask me to eat you," he demanded roughly. "Say the words for me, Merinus."

"Oh, God." Her eyes widened as his face poised over the desperate, aching part of her body.

He was watching her heatedly, his eyes glittering, savage, hot.

"Say the words for me," he repeated. "Give me permission to devour you."

Merinus licked her lips, panting hard as he spread her legs further, his fingers barely glancing over the moisture glazed flesh.

"Yes," she moaned, shaking, desperate for the touch. "Eat me, Callan. Please lick me. Lick me now—" Her head fell back, a hard shudder wracking her body.

His tongue rasped through the slit of her lips from bottom to top. Slow, sliding, erotically rough and so hot she felt her flesh melting. His hard hands gripped her thighs, holding them apart when she would have clenched them around his head.

"Mmm," his low moan of pleasure vibrated against her clit. She felt the small bud throb, beg.

Merinus gasped for breath as he licked her, his tongue dipping into the tight entrance of her vagina, swirling around, gathering more and more of her taste as his heated growls of pleasure echoed against her body.

She was mindless now. She could feel the sensations building, her skin tingling, the pressure increasing in her clit as he stroked around it, over it, sucked it lightly into his mouth.

"Oh yes, suck it." The shocking words erupting from her mouth did little to dim the haze of need sucking her in, as his mouth sipped at her flesh. "Oh yes, Callan. Yes. Just like that," she was almost screaming now as he suckled her clit deeper, harder. "Please. Oh please—"

It was building in her. Her body tightened involuntarily, every bone and muscle in her reaching for his mouth, the hot draw of his lips, the moist wash of his tongue. It was killing her, killing her with pleasure, building, increasing. She could feel her heart struggling to keep up with the demands her arousal was placing on it. It beat hard and fast, bursting through her veins, a pleasure in and of itself. Then one hard male finger slid past the soft folds of skin. His mouth suckled her clit faster, his finger pushing inside her, filling her, burning her.

She heard her scream as the pleasure burst inside her. Desperate, hard, her hips bucked and she felt herself dying. Her climax was like a tidal wave, tearing through her, heaving her body, shaking it, shuddering through it, destroying her as she held tight to his hair, praying for some anchor to hold her to earth. It was never ending. Hot pulsing relief spasmed through her cunt, causing it to grip tighter about his plunging finger, soak his hand, her thighs with a rush of liquid that would have terrified her at any other time.

Then his mouth was there, devouring the release, his tongue plunging into her vagina, building the pleasure again as the sandpapery texture of that organ rasped her tender flesh.

"I'm going to fuck you first," he growled, his body moving powerfully, his hands lifting her as the thick head of his cock lodged against the entrance to her vagina. "I'm going to fuck you until you scream again, Merinus. Over and over. Scream for me, baby."

She screamed. One hard thrust buried the thick, steel-hard erection into her body to the hilt. She felt his scrotum slap against her buttocks, watched his hard face twist into a grimace of sublime pleasure, his eyes closed, his body arched, tight, tense.

* * * * *

Callan fought for breath, for control. She was so tight and hot around his cock, her muscles gripping him like a slick, velvety fist. Control. He had to fight for control. He could control the raging lust beating at him, demanding a hard, fierce ride. She was tossing beneath him, her hips bucking, driving him harder into the soft flesh of her cunt, grinding against him.

Gritting his teeth, he eased back, wanting to scream himself at the incredible pleasure from the friction of her flesh against his. His cock was so sensitive it was nearly unbearable. He could feel the small barb-like protrusion emerging from beneath the head of his cock, slowly, unfolding from its former hiding place. He prayed. He prayed to a God he had once doubted that it would bring her no harm. That the once inactive portion of his cock, the small, curved, hard protrusion would not bring her harm. Because there was no way he could stop.

She squirmed beneath him, fighting for breath, her body damp with perspiration, her female honey coating her inner thighs, as well as his. He thrust inside the tight depths of her body, groaning on every stroke at the tight heat clasping him, the sensitive swell of the barb raking her tender flesh, driving him insane with the pleasure it washed over his body.

He gritted his teeth against the sensations as he braced his body over Merinus'. She was bucking against him, her head twisting against the sheets of the bed, arching desperately, begging now for release.

"Callan—" Her plea was a hard gasp, a breathless moan as her hands went to his shoulders, her nails biting into his skin.

His sharp growl at the added sensation surprised him. He felt his cock swell, pulse. He drove against her harder, deeper, one hard hand spanning her hip as he held her still, the other under her shoulders, arching her breasts to his devouring mouth. He couldn't get enough of her. Her nipple was hard, succulent, the grip on his cock tightened each time he drew on it.

She was getting close. So damned close. And so was he. He could feel the white hot fingers of fire moving down his spine now, the swelling of the barb, the lengthening of the tiny hard membrane. Then all hell broke loose. He slammed inside her, deep, hard, as he felt the membrane extend fully, felt it rake across the silken flesh of her vaginal walls, the area of the elusive g-spot. It lodged there, causing his thrusts to become hard jerks in fear of tearing her, hurting her. But the pleasure. The pleasure was unlike anything he had ever known. It wrapped over the head of his erection like tiny fingers of paradise, at the same time he heard Merinus scream. Her body arched, her eyes widened, she stared at him in dazed, wild hunger for a second before her orgasm hit. She clenched around him, the action making her so tight and hot he could do nothing but follow her. His guttural growl as he felt the harsh ejaculations into her body shocked him.

The barb, so feared for so many years, destroyed his sense of balance. He could feel it moving, stroking the sensitive spot it had lodged in, each movement had Merinus crying out, jerking, tightening, her orgasms lengthening as he came inside her. She was breathing hard, crying now, her head tossing with the extremity of her pleasure before his own began to ease, and he felt the little protrusion recede, allowing him to pull weakly from her body.

Merinus still trembled. Her cheeks were wet with sweat and tears as she gasped for breath. Her breasts were swollen, her nipples hard little peaks that had not eased with her climax.

"Merinus," he whispered her name gently as he eased her into his arms, lying beside her, his hand smoothing down her damp back. "Don't cry anymore, baby. I don't think I can handle it."

Her breath hitched, one hand clutched at his back, the other around his neck.

"Did I hurt you?" He was terrified that perhaps he had, and was unaware of it.

She shook her head against his chest. A weak movement as her tongue stroked over his skin. Callan took a deep, careful breath after that small caress. He was still hard, he could easily take her again, but he feared for her. She was virgin, and there had been little gentleness in him when he had slammed inside her tender body.

She whispered against his chest.

"What?" He moved back, staring into her dazed, distressed eyes. "What did you say?"

"I need you again." A tear fell down her cheek. "I need more, Callan."

She was exhausted. He could see it in her expression, in her eyes and hear it in her voice. She was shy and confused and frightened by the overwhelming sensations that were controlling her body.

"Shh, don't cry, baby. You need only ask." He smiled softly, his thumbs wiping the tears from her eyes.

She was so tired it worried him, but he couldn't ignore her need, not when it was his own as well. He turned her to her side, bringing her leg over his as he tucked her buttocks against him.

"We will do this easy," he promised her. "I know you're tired, Merinus."

She shook her head, gasping, moaning as the thick length of his cock re-entered her, stretching her, sliding in deep. The tight clasp had him gritting his teeth at the renewed pleasure.

"You feel so good," he murmured at her ear as his fingers went to the swollen bud of her clit and massaged it gently. "So tight and hot around me, Merinus. Unlike anything I have known."

"We're drugged. That's why," she gasped. "You drugged us, Callan."

"Then I would stay drugged forever, Merinus." He nibbled at her earlobe, loving the sharp intake of her breath, the way she thrust back at him. "There is no pleasure on this earth as good as the feel of your pretty cunt wrapped around me."

"Oh God, why did that just sound so sexy?" she groaned, tightening around him, shivering at the feel of his lips against her neck.

"Because it is sexy," he assured her, smiling. He licked the soft flesh just beneath her ear, loving the little gasps she made. "It's sexy and erotic and hot as hell." He pushed harder into the tight sheath, gritting his teeth now at the pleasure.

"We'll kill each other before the need goes away," she panted. "Callan—" A plea stole from her as he felt the shivers working through her vagina.

He felt it as well, the barb's re-emergence, the added stroke over her tight muscles.

"Does it hurt you, Merinus?" He was tortured, terrified he had been wrong, and she was in pain, despite her need. "Tell me if it hurts you. I'll try to stop."

He buried his head in her damp hair. God help him if he was hurting her. God help them both.

"What is it?" she gasped as his strokes became deeper, harder.

Callan couldn't control it. His hips began to thrust his cock harder inside her, the ultra sensitivity of the barb making the pleasure so damned good he wanted to howl with it.

"Does it hurt you?" he demanded again, gritting his teeth, fighting for control.

"No," she cried out, her hand moving to grip his slamming hips. "Ah, more. I need more."

He pushed her to her stomach, moving behind her, instinct guiding him now, the pulse of pleasure overtaking his mind. Spreading her thighs wide he slammed his hips into her buttocks, feeling his scrotum tighten against the base of his cock as he drove deep and hard inside her. His head lowered, his teeth gripping the sensitive area between shoulder and neck as she screamed out in pleasure. And it was pleasure. She was begging for more, held still by his hard body, his plunging hips, the sharp teeth that held her still for his invasion.

He was the animal he had always feared. In the back of his mind, Callan was appalled at his own actions, but helpless in the face of the frenzy overtaking him. The barb was only half erect, sensitive, sliding, gliding over tight vaginal walls and smooth flesh. It was more than he could bear. He could control himself no longer.

Primitive, throaty, his growl demanded her surrender, her submission to him as he powered inside her, over and over. She was crying out now, her body tight, reaching, desperate. The barb extended full length, scraped, she screamed out in desperation, her muscles locking on his erection as her orgasm swept over her once again. Callan plunged deep and hard, his own climax rocking his soul, the growls constant now, rumbling from his chest as he felt the hard spurt of his semen inside her, the burning grip of her muscles, the wash of her own release.

Then she was still. Slowly, the inner muscles unlocked and Callan felt his own erection begin to subside minutely. Her body became pliant, relaxed and he knew that either sleep or unconsciousness claimed her. Either, he knew, would be a welcome relief for her.

Panting, he lay down beside her. Jerking sheet and comforter from the foot of the bed, he covered them both, weariness lying heavy on his shoulders. He tucked her body close to his, breathing in her scent, her warmth. He was exhausted. Never had he climaxed so hard, so deep. As though his seed were being jerked from his soul, rather than the tight sac beneath his cock.

"Mine," he whispered the word as his grip tightened on her, exhaustion draining him. He was aware he made the claim, and he admitted it terrified him clear to his soul.

CHAPTER ELEVEN

Merinus awoke, tender and groggy. She shifted in the bed, seeking the warmth that had held her through the night, but Callan was gone. Opening her eyes she blinked, stared up at the ceiling and tried to ignore the pressing need that still throbbed in her vagina. Damn, talk about a potent kiss. She licked her swollen lips experimentally. Callan had nibbled on them more than once, licked them. His tongue, the rough texture of it, the stimulating feel of abrasive velvet running over her skin, the memory of it caused her to shiver.

She needed a shower. Dried perspiration itched on her skin, made her feel grungy. The smell of sex, hot and wild, lingered on the air and on her body. She grimaced. Rising from the bed, she stepped gingerly over the cool hardwood floor, moving to the opened door on the far right of the room. A bathroom, complete with a large sunken tub and a brief written message on the counter greeted her.

Bathe. Relax. Stay in the house. I'll return soon with your things. So much for her camp, she sighed. After the hours it took to set it up so neatly, it might have been nice to actually use it for longer than a few hours. She wondered how long he had been gone, then decided it didn't really matter. He would return soon enough, and she desperately needed that bath.

She ran the tub nearly full, adding a liberal portion of bubbling bath salts she found at the edge of the tub, then eased herself into the hot water. She washed her hair quickly, wrapped it in a towel then lay back against the rim to allow her body to soak. She glanced down her body, seeing the red abrasions on her skin, small sensitive points where his tongue had stroked her a bit roughly. Her breasts were still swollen with need, her nipples still hard.

She couldn't understand it. The events of the day before seemed more like a dream than reality. But reality was the tenderness between her thighs, the flush on the smooth mound of her cunt, the sensitivity of her body. The need for Callan wasn't as intense, as harsh as it had been the day before, but it still throbbed in her. She still ached for him. It made no sense.

"Merinus." Sherra's voice called through the closed door, her knock light. "Can I come in?"

Merinus checked the bubbles covering her, then sighed deeply.

"Yeah. Come on in."

The other woman entered the room, concern marking her pretty features, lingering in her light blue eyes.

"If Callan's DNA is lion, then what's yours?" She didn't bother to beat around the bush. There were more than just Callan and she knew it.

Sherra sighed. She sat gracefully in a padded chair at the end of the tub.

"Snow cat," she said quietly. "Dawn and Dayan's mix is cougar.

Tanner is Bengal. Taber is jaguar, Callan is lion." She watched Merinus carefully, her expression composed, calm, but her eyes were shadowed.

"What's happening to my body?" She would ask the questions of their DNA later. Right now, there were more pressing problems.

"It's a mating, Merinus," Sherra said gently. "Our tests aren't conclusive yet. Doc's still working on it. But it seems to be pheromones. Chemistry is the culprit. Yours matched with Callan's and his body reacted to it. There's still so much we don't know about our bodies. Aren't certain of. Unfortunately, we'll need more samples. I had hoped to catch you before your bath to begin them. Your body will give us more answers than Callan's can, as the mix of his semen and your body's secretions are contained within you."

Fear raced through her now.

"I'm not on birth control," she whispered, her voice trembling. She couldn't believe she hadn't thought of that before.

"Don't worry," Sherra rushed to reassure her. "The semen of our males has never been compatible with a female before. But just to be on the safe side, the injection doc gave you last night would prevent conception, should the reaction have changed that."

"And this 'thing' going on with my body?" she asked her hesitantly. "Will it stop?"

Sherra sighed roughly. "We think so. Callan's semen seems to have a counteracting agent in it, but it appears very slow acting. In time, I believe it will go away."

"Man, I really stepped into it this time," Merinus breathed wearily, closing her eyes at the problem she now found herself steeped in. "This is not good."

"Perhaps for Callan it is," Sherra said softly. "He was growing very angry, very hopeless, Merinus. He leads us. Protects us. Maybe this was what he needed. I can't say he was relaxed when I saw him this morning, but he now plans for more than just his death."

"And what are those plans?" Merinus asked her, watching her through the steam of the bath.

"Providing for you. Protecting you," Sherra informed hesitantly.

"No." Merinus shook her head fiercely. "This is just a story. This chemical thing will go away, and so will I. I can't stay here. And if he goes back, then I go to the next story. This is not permanent."

"That's what you think." Callan stood in the doorway, his face dark, the savage lines pulled into a mask of male arousal and hard purpose. "You cannot leave me now, Merinus. No matter what either of us would wish." He glanced at Sherra, the look hard, commanding.

"I need those samples, Callan. Quickly," she told him as she came to her feet. "And Merinus is sore—"

"I do not need you to tell me my responsibilities, Sherra." He flashed her a sharp look. "I have always seen them through."

"Of course you have," Sherra said worriedly. "When she's finished, please, we need her in the lab."

"I'm not a guinea pig," Merinus burst out. "I won't be poked and prodded at incessantly."

She flushed as Callan arched a brow sarcastically. Then her body heated as her gaze skipped to his thighs, then back up. He was aroused. Ready for her. Again. Her body heated up further, her blood pumping harshly through her veins.

"Leave, Sherra. I will have her there soon for your tests." Callan moved aside, allowing the woman to escape, then closing the door behind him.

Merinus stared at him from the depths of the tub, breathing heavily, her body reacting to the fiery glitter in his slumberous eyes.

"I won't take you again, yet," he promised her softly. "But soon. Do you need help now getting out of the bath? I can fix you lunch before you are forced to endure Doc's testing."

Merinus' eyes narrowed on him. He was commanding, forceful. She hated that in a man.

"I'm a grown woman, I think I'm capable of bathing myself," she told him sweetly, patiently. She felt everything but patient inside.

"Merinus, while your body is demanding my touch, it is not a good idea to push me with your female stubbornness," he warned her, male aggression stamped on his features. "I am not fully in control of myself right now. I could not promise you I would be gentle if you pushed me."

Merinus' lips thinned. How typically male. She opened her mouth to speak, but stayed silent as his hand rose, demanding.

"Hear me well," he gritted out. "Finish your bath. Then come eat. Your clothes are on the bed. I have tried to tell you, I am not whatever fairy tale you have worked up in your head. At this moment I am more instinct than I am control. I am more the animal I was created with right now, Merinus. Do not push the animal, because even I cannot predict its response."

The heavy grief in his voice silenced her anger. His eyes were filled with bleak memories, emotions she couldn't define. But she saw the pain there. Pain and a terrible loneliness.

"I'm very independent," she whispered. "I can't change that. Orders don't sit well with me."

He shook his head. "I don't have the patience to tamp down the beast that demands submission. For now, perhaps it would be best to control your independence in the face of something neither of us can predict. Now, once again. Do you need my help?"

"No. I think I can manage." She couldn't help her anger. She saw no reason for him to lose control over something as simple as allowing her choices. And she wouldn't tolerate it for very long. Only as long as it took her to get the hell out of there.

"You're angry." He tilted his head, watching her with narrowed eyes. "I can smell it, Merinus. It mixes well with your lust." He breathed in deeply as though savoring the scent.

"Why don't you go away and let me finish my bath," she snapped. "I didn't ask you to come in here."

She watched him grit his teeth.

"I would suggest wearing loose clothing, perhaps one of my shirts that I laid on the bed for you. Your skin is still sensitive, and clothing will irritate it —"

"I know how sensitive my skin is, Callan," she informed him, fighting to keep her voice calm. "I know what my body is doing, and why. I don't need any other explanations, all I need is privacy."

His golden brows snapped to a frown. A rumbling growl emanated from his throat.

"And don't do that growling thing at me." She was tired, horny and irritated. She didn't need any more male aggression. "Go away and leave me alone. When I'm done, I'll find you."

"You, Merinus Tyler, are an irksome woman," he accused her.

"Just go ahead and say 'bitch', my brothers do it all the time," she snapped back. "Now, go play Lion-O someplace else. I don't have time for it."

"Lion-O?" he questioned her, clearly offended at her reference to the cartoon character.

"Lion King?" she asked sweetly. "I'm not here to pamper your ego. Now leave me alone."

She watched his fists clench. His eyes narrowed further, giving him a predatory, dangerous appearance. He opened his mouth to speak, then seemed to change his mind. He turned and stalked from the room, jerking the door open then slamming it with a bang. Merinus flinched, then clenched her thighs together. Damn it.

* * * * *

"I heard you were in town asking questions about Maria the other day," Callan said as he set a cup of coffee beside her sandwich plate when she sat down at the table. "Why?"

He seemed less than pleased by the information. He sat across from her, cradling a steaming cup of coffee himself, his amber eyes watching her unblinkingly.

"She was murdered." Merinus refused to apologize or back down. "She was special to my father, Callan. I could tell by the way he talked about her. I want to know who killed her and why."

He was silent for long moments. Long enough for Merinus to pick up a half of the roast beef and tomato sandwich and bite into it.

"It's none of your father's business, nor yours," he berated her softly as she ate. "You are once again involving yourself in a place where you shouldn't."

Merinus watched him carefully, gauging the tension in his body, the growl of warning in his voice.

"Did you kill the person responsible, Callan?" Merinus forced the words from her mouth, needing to know the truth. She wouldn't blame him if he had, but she had to know.

The realization of how little she knew him weighed upon her. She had spent the night in his bed, his body connected to hers, driving her to heights of pleasure she never imagined existed. She knew he had been bred to kill, but had no idea if he had crossed that line between his humanity and animal instinct.

"I don't know who killed her, Merinus." He shook his head wearily. "I wish I did, then I wouldn't have to wonder anymore. And I could repay him then, in kind."

The implication that he would kill was heavy in his voice. Merinus finished her sandwich, but her enjoyment for it had dulled somewhat.

But you suspect someone?" she asked him.

"Hell, I suspect everyone," he growled. "It could have been anyone. The Council is good at getting nice, ordinary folks to do their dirty work. I know, I've seen it done before. My list of suspects is as long as four different counties and just as wide."

"Do you know what they were looking for? Surely Maria said something before she died?" Merinus probed cautiously, aware of the tension in his body, and the buried anger in his heart.

"What she said didn't matter," he finally sighed. "She didn't name her killer, she asked for your father. I begged her to tell me who did it and she refused. She protected them, and I swear I haven't been able to figure out yet who she was protecting."

"Who would she have protected? Who was that close to the two of you, Callan?" she asked, fighting to keep her voice even, the suspicions concerning the killer's identity to herself.

"We trusted no one, and those close to us couldn't have done it. They wouldn't have done it." He shrugged. "Whoever it was will show themselves eventually, and when they do, I'll be waiting."

The finality of his voice sent a shiver down Merinus' back. It was cold and hard and filled with menace.

"Callan…"

"Enough questions about Maria. I'll solve that when the times comes. How are you feeling now?

Merinus sighed roughly.

"Callan, you have to do something soon," she whispered. "You can't keep hiding."

The bright, golden brown depths were filled with sadness, arousal, and regret as he watched her. His lean, tanned face was striking in its sheer maleness. His eyes, despite the dark emotions, were so beautiful they made her heart clench.

"When I can hide no more, then I'll leave here, Merinus. It's all I can do." He shook his head at the futility of her argument.

"We could help you, Callan." She tried to stem the tears, but they only fell harder as she felt her heart breaking not just for him, but for Sherra and for herself as well.

"No, Beauty." He grinned at her, though there was no humor in his smile. "No one can save me and we both have to accept that. I'll ensure your safety, and that of the others, but they know about me. There is no safety for me."

"But Callan—" He stood from the table, halting her words.

"If you're finished eating, then I promised Sherra I would bring you to her. They need those samples and I need you soon before I die."

He pulled her from her chair, his lips going to hers, his tongue swirling into her mouth. Merinus groaned. The kiss was hot, so tempting, his taste alone enough to nearly make her peak.

"I wanted you for lunch," he whispered as he nibbled her lips. "Right across the table, Merinus, with my head buried between your thighs. Your taste is enough to make me drunk." His teeth scraped her neck, his hand roaming beneath the dark blue, soft shirt he had loaned her.

His hands clenched on her buttocks, parting the flesh, his fingers tucking into the crevice as he pulled her closer. Merinus gripped his shoulders, moaning low and deep as his mouth whispered over her skin, moist and hot. Then he was kissing her again, drawing her tongue into his mouth, possessing her, making the heat in her body rise, the need between her thighs pulsate.

"Callan." Sherra spoke behind him, her voice firm. "We're waiting on her."

He raised his head, staring down at Merinus while she shivered in his arms.

"Hurry, Sherra," he warned the other woman as he let Merinus go slowly, reluctantly. "I'll wait up here for her."

"Come on, Merinus. It shouldn't take us long," Sherra promised, casting Callan an impatient look.

Merinus sighed. "Damn it. Sex wasn't supposed to be this complicated." But she followed the other woman anyway, determined to hurry and get it over with, and get back to Callan's arms.

CHAPTER TWELVE

By the time the tests were completed, Merinus was nearly in pain, the arousal was hitting her so hard again. She could feel the moisture glazing her inner thighs, the heat and need building in her cunt like a volcano preparing to erupt. The pressure was tremendous. But on top of that was another problem. As hours ticked by, Sherra and the doctor both began to wear steadily on her nerves. Or more to the point, the touch of their hands, even protected by the latex gloves, did. It made her literally sick to her stomach, made her skin crawl, made her want to shrink from them as they came near her.

She couldn't fully explain the sensation, even to herself. She knew though, if she had to tolerate one more minute of it, she was going to be sick. And she needed Callan. She was desperate to touch him, to feel the incredible warmth of his skin, his hands stroking over her. She was cold, aching, frightened.

"No more tests," she informed them as she dressed, buttoning Callan's shirt with shaking fingers over the throbbing mounds of her breasts. "I can't stand it anymore."

"The tests are necessary, Merinus," Sherra told her with a sigh.

"Look, I cannot fucking tolerate being touched anymore," she snapped, almost in tears, her skin still crawling from the sensation of someone's hands, other than Callan's on her. "Do you understand me?"

Shock crossed Sherra's expression; bemusement filled the doctor's.

"How do you mean, Merinus?" Sherra's voice stayed soothing, but Merinus heard the confusion in her voice.

"Just what I said." Merinus fought her tears. "Where's Callan? He was supposed to come for me."

She had to find him. Her body was going crazy, rioting. Tiny fingers of sensation were washing over her skin, leaving her shuddering, shaking.

"Callan's upstairs, just as he promised he would be." Sherra reached out to touch her, but Merinus jumped back, flinching away from the contact. "Merinus, something else is evidently happening. You have to let us help you."

"Get away from me." Merinus shook her head.

"Sherra, get Callan down here," Doctor Martin had watched the byplay silently, but his voice now became commanding. "Get him down here quickly."

Merinus gripped the side of the bed. Her legs shook as she fought to stay upright.

"I want to go home," she panted, suddenly terrified by a thousand different feelings and sensations assaulting her. "Make them take me home, Doctor."

"I will discuss it with Callan, Merinus," he promised her softly, but she heard the indulgent tone of his voice. He was merely placating her. Lying to her.

She shook her head, fighting to stay upright.

"Where the fuck is Callan," she cried out, disoriented now. She was sweating heavily; she could feel the moisture running down her face, between her breasts. Her heart was beating hard, laboring, her lungs fighting for breath. "What did he do to me?"

Her fists clenched as she felt herself collapsing against the bed.

"Let me help you, Merinus." The doctor reached for her.

She felt his hands on her arm and jerked back, fire seemed to lance her skin, searing her flesh as she fought to get away. She stumbled over the bed, going to her knees, feeling the scrape of the hard floor as she fought to right herself.

"Don't touch me!" she screamed out.

She was crying now, her stomach cramping. She clasped her abdomen, bending over, rocking against a pain she had never felt before. She was terrified. So scared that her entire body was shuddering now. She was cold, shivering, filled with dread and on the edge of hysteria.

"Merinus." Callan's shocked voice echoed around the room.

Seconds later his hands gripped her arms, pulling her against him.

"What the hell is going on?" His voice was raised, furious, the dangerous growl rumbling in his touch.

"Withdrawal," the doctor sighed. "I believe, Callan, your woman is in withdrawal."

Callan felt fear course through his body. Merinus was clawing at him, fighting to get closer to him, crying. She was hysterical with fear or pain—he couldn't say which.

"From what?" He lifted her head, staring down into her face.

She was pale, her eyes dark, nearly black with shock.

"From you," Doctor Martin stated roughly. "I don't know what to do for her now."

Callan cursed.

"Help me," she whispered desperately, her tears hot on his flesh, her body shaking, her skin cold and clammy. "Please, Callan. Please help me."

He lifted her quickly into his arms, his lips going to hers, his kiss swallowing her cry as he turned from the others. His tongue went to her mouth, tempting hers, mating with it. He knew when the need had been at its height the night before, his kiss had soothed her, eased the clawing need. God help him and her if it didn't now.

He kissed her desperately, aching, hurting for her as she twisted in his arms, fighting to kiss him deeper, her lips and tongue mating with his, a hot moan of need whispering into his mouth, making it nearly impossible for him to control his own lusts now. But she eased. Slowly. The hard shivers that coursed over her body lessened, her whimpering cries became moans of desire.

"We need the saliva sample now." He heard the doctor at his side. "We cannot touch her, Callan. I need your help."

Moving his lips from hers, Callan laid Merinus back on the cot. She was watching with dazed need, like an addict needing a fix. Dear God, what had they done to her. He gripped her jaw gently.

"Easy," he whispered as she flinched back, seeing the doctor. "It's okay, baby."

The swab went around her mouth quickly.

"Your turn." A clean swab poised at his mouth. Callan allowed the swab, watching Merinus carefully.

"No more tests," she whispered. "I can't stand their touch."

"Then let me," he asked her, his voice soft, cajoling. "We must find a way to stop this, Merinus."

"I need another vaginal swab and Sherra needs blood. Now, Callan." The doctor's voice was imperative.

Merinus was shaking her head.

"Shh," Callan moved to her side. "Concentrate on me, Merinus, and it will go quickly. Hold onto me, baby."

He wrapped one of her arms around his neck, the other he stretched out on the bed for Sherra, clasping their hands, holding her still. Then he lowered his mouth to her. She had the softest, sweetest lips, her tongue branded his when he touched it, her kiss made him weak, made his cock throb.

He felt her jerk when Sherra inserted the needle into her arm, but she didn't fight it. The same when the vaginal sample was taken again, she endured it, focusing on his kiss, his touch, rather than the degrading tests that were required.

"I'm so sorry," he whispered against her lips when they were finished.

He picked her up in his arms, striding quickly now from the lab. Damn them. Him, Sherra, the doctor. What had they done to Merinus? Withdrawal, somehow she had become dependent on whatever primal drug his kiss released into her system. Dammit, they didn't even know what it was, didn't know how to control it.

His arms tightened around her. He couldn't stand this unbearable knowledge of what he was doing to her, the futility of trying to find a way to ease it.

"Now," she whispered desperately as he entered the main part of the house with her. "I need you now, Callan."

Her fingers were digging into his shoulders, her voice weak, pleading.

He couldn't make it to the bedroom with her. Her body wasn't the only one affected, she wasn't the only one steadily losing control. He laid her on the couch, ripping the damp shirt from her body then quickly shedding his jeans, before going to his knees between her spread thighs.

His erection was steel hard, hurting from the need. Her scent was like a brand to his senses, hot and seductive, just as addicting as their kisses, as the need for orgasm. He knew she was still sensitive, still sore. He fought for control. How he found it, he would never be certain.

He slid into her, moving back to watch narrowly as the smooth folds of flesh parted around the width of his cock. Her vagina hugged him, sucked him in. His fingers smoothed over the silken flesh of her cunt, his eyes going to hers slowly.

"You wax?" he whispered, drawing his finger over the glazed skin until he could circle her swollen clit.

The pearl pulsed beneath his finger, begging for his attention.

"Yes." Her head tossed as he touched the sensitive flesh, as his cock slid in to the hilt, throbbing at the entrance to her womb.

"Why do you do this?" he asked her, gritting his teeth against the tightening of her inner muscles over his flesh.

Her eyes opened, dark, seductively, her lips parting as she moistened them with her tongue. His hips bucked against her.

"A friend convinced me to try it," she panted, grinding against him, her breasts arching to his hands, her breathing harsh as he caressed her swollen nipples. "I like it."

"Why?" he gritted out. "Tell me why you keep it like this."

He slid nearly free of her body, his teeth clenching, perspiration dampening his entire body as he slid into the tight depths once again. Her muscles clenched, hot, milking his flesh. He had to keep his sanity. His control.

"It feels better," she gasped. "Freer."

"I feel nothing but hot satin against me, Merinus," he gritted out. "You destroy my control like this. Hot velvet inside, silk and satin out. You make me mindless."

He leaned over her, the fingers of one hand sinking into her hair, his lips nibbling at hers as he drew back, then inched in slowly.

"Oh, Callan." She shivered against him, her hands clutching at his back, her nails biting into his flesh. "I need you harder. Please, do it harder."

He resisted temptation. He wanted her slow and easy first. He wanted to take her to the edge of madness where he seemed to teeter each time he touched her.

"Feel how tight you are, Merinus," he groaned against her neck, his tongue lapping at the perspiration there. "Feel how my flesh stretches you, fills you. You were created for me alone."

Her cunt tightened on him, her muscles spasmed as he whispered the words against her neck. He pulled back, his hand tightening in her hair, the other holding her hip, keeping her still as she fought to buck against his body.

His lips tracked to her breast, swollen, curved so sweetly, her nipple poised like a ripe little berry atop it. He licked it, allowing his tongue to rasp it, his teeth to grip it as she jerked against him, trying to force a deeper contact. And all the while his cock moved slowly inside her, pushing past tight, slick muscles, pulling back, dragging the emerging barb across her tender tissue.

"You'll kill me," she panted. "What in the hell is that, Callan?"

"What does it feel like?" he murmured against her breast. He was terrified to tell her, afraid disgust would ride the heels of her desire if he did so.

"I don't know. Intense." She gripped him hard, making him grimace as he dragged his flesh nearly free of her, then pushed forward again. "Firm," she panted. "It feels like a little finger raking over—me." Her cry of pleasure electrified him as he felt the barb emerge further.

He wouldn't last much longer. Control. He stilled, deep inside her, fighting for breath until he felt the small protrusion relax marginally. Damn, this was killing him. The sheer pleasure of the elongated growth scraping over her flesh was almost soul destroying. There had never been anything like it.

"Why did you stop?" she whimpered, pressing against him as he drew her nipple into his mouth for a quick taste.

"Slow and easy, Merinus," he growled.

"No." She shook her head. "Fast and hard. Oh God, Callan. If I don't come soon I'm going to die."

She was dazed, beseeching, clenching around him, her soft cream sliding over him. He wouldn't last much longer. The barb was pulsing, a demand of its own, his cock was throbbing, demanding action, demanding the fierce hard friction that sent him spiraling into climax.

"I don't want to hurt you." He kissed her breast again. "I know you're tender."

"No. I'm dying." He felt her legs lift, encircle his hips and his control disintegrated.

Merinus cried out as the thrusts began. Hard, hot, driving into her. The thick expanse of his cock stretched her, biting at her flesh, whatever the hell that little thumb of silken torment located on his erection was doing to her, would kill her. It scraped over the walls of her cunt, caressing nerves she never would have known existed, swelling against her, pulsing, separating from the driving flesh of his erection.

Her legs tightened around his hips, driving him deeper within her as she fought for breath. It was so good. His scrotum slapped at her buttocks, the flesh of his lower abdomen raked her swollen clit. She felt fire in her vagina, in her womb, burning her, searing her. Her muscles clenched around him, loving the feel of the rough rasp of whatever it was that stroked the inner walls of her. It was hot. Oh God, it was killing her with pleasure, like a hard tickle. That's what it was. A strength destroying tickle that locked her muscles, stole her strength.

"Merinus, baby," he groaned against her breast. "I can't control—"

The little thumb lengthened, raked, locked his cock deep inside her, then impaled the ultra sensitive tissue in the very depths of her cunt. It moved, pulsed, tickled and stroked until she exploded. She screamed, feeling the hard jets of his semen as she climaxed around his flesh, her hips arching, her clit erupting in pleasure, lava thundered through her veins, bubbling with the fierce ecstasy as she pulsed around him, milking his cock, soaking his flesh.

His hips jerked against her, his rumbling growls vibrating against her breasts as he breathed harshly at her shoulder, groaning in the throes of his own frenzied release. Then slowly, she felt the pressure ease. Once again it was only his cock, thick, softening only marginally as he pulled free of her.

"Once I rest," she said drowsily. "You're gonna tell me what that was, Callan."

She snuggled against his chest as he collapsed beside her, dragging an afghan from the back of the couch and wrapping it around her, her breasts cushioned against the incredible heat of his chest, her body languid, sated for the moment.

"If I have to," he whispered at her ear, somber.

"Hm, you have to." She yawned. But first, a nap. Her eyes closed, her body relaxed against his heat and she drifted quickly into rest.

CHAPTER THIRTEEN

"I have work to do." Merinus kept her voice carefully controlled, calm, as she sat at the kitchen table the next morning, staring down at her untouched cup of coffee.

Breakfast had been completed in silence, despite the amount of people who had ranged around the table. There were six of the Breeds as they called themselves, Merinus and the doctor. The sheer scope of the story she was now looking at terrified her. Not because of the implications of it, but due to the part she now played in it.

The others had left after eating. The other three males disappearing outside, Sherra, Dawn and the scientist returning to the lab while Callan stayed and watched Merinus in concern.

"What work do you have that doesn't require you to be right where you are?" His broad, bare shoulders lifted in a shrug, as though her forced confinement here was not a problem.

"Where's my cell phone?" She ignored his question. "And I want you to take me back to camp. I have interviews to do—"

"If I am your story, then why would you need to do other interviews?" he asked her curiously.

"Your mother's death—" she began.

"Is not part of this story, Merinus," he finished for her. "Her death was not at the hands of Council members, I have told you this already. And it is a mystery you cannot solve. So let it go."

His voice was quiet, smooth. He watched her with those golden eyes, still hot with lust, but shadowed with demand.

"I have a life, Callan, a job," she told him firmly. "I have to get back to it. And I need my cell phone back. I have to talk to my family, let them know I'm okay."

"What will you tell them?" he asked her, his eyes showing an amazing degree of genuine confusion. "You cannot tell them the truth, Merinus. Not until we have this figured out."

"They'll worry. And if they worry, all seven of my brothers will head out here and start kicking ass until they find me," she warned him. "It would be easier if you would just let me call them and let them know I'm okay."

"I have no problem with you calling them." He shrugged. "I have problems with what you might say. I will not have a team of scientists or Council killers following on their trail. I've had the two who attacked you taken care of, do not bring more down on our heads right now."

Shock scattered through her system.

"Taken care of?" she whispered. "How did you take care of them?"

Irritation flashed over his features. "I slapped their hands and sent them home to their mommas," he snarled. "How did you think I was forced to do this, Merinus? They are killers. They would have raped and tortured you and given no thought to your pain or your life. Why does it matter how I took care of them?"

He stood to his feet, stalking to the sink with his empty cup.

Merinus pushed her fingers through her hair, breathing out roughly. Anger rose in her as the situation began to overwhelm her.

"Did you kill them?" she asked him furiously.

He had his back to her, staring out of the kitchen window, his shoulders tense.

"I had no choice." Heavy, cold, his voice whispered through the room.

"Then you are no better than they are," she cried out.

"There is where you are wrong." He turned on her, his eyes blazing, his mouth pulled into a snarl that revealed deadly incisors. "I did not ask them to create me, Merinus. I did not ask for the DNA they coded into my body, nor did I ask them to train me to kill. I did not ask them for any of their 'gifts'. I most certainly did not ask them to stalk me, torture friends and make my life hell because I would not slaughter innocents for them. And I will not tolerate them sending their soldiers out to destroy me, nor what I hold as mine, Merinus. It is the law of nature. Only the strongest will survive."

Rage trembled along his body, in his voice.

"This isn't the jungle," she yelled back at him, standing to her feet as she placed her palms flat on the table. "You wouldn't have to kill if you would let the world know what is going on."

"God, such innocence," he growled, throwing his hands up in exasperation. "Fickle public that America possesses. We would likely be burned at the stake as monsters."

"Get real, Callan, it's not the Middle Ages anymore," she burst out. "Don't you think the public has a right to know? To be aware of the atrocities going on? Show them for the monsters they are and it will ensure your safety."

"It will not do this," he snapped, shaking his head roughly. "You have no idea of the men you go against, Merinus. Men whose social, financial and political resources span not just America, but also other nations, other pocketbooks. You will not take these men down. You cannot stop the killing."

"You won't even try," Merinus argued fiercely. "Look at you, Callan. Hiding, never knowing what the hell is going on with your own bodies, unable to get the help you need, when you need it. This isn't living."

"This is the best I can do." His eyes were blazing. "Let me tell you an alternative, Merinus." Her name was a curse on his lips. "An alternative is living in a structured lab, taken out only for tests and training, or breeding purposes. It's cold and sterile and a worse hell than you could ever know. At least here we are free."

"As long as you kill?" Her fists clenched as she fought to understand the life he lived. The war raging against him, through him.

"If they would cease to try to kill me, then I would no longer kill them," he informed her coldly, arrogance settling over him like an aura of danger.

"You can stop it," she pointed out furiously.

"As can they," he told her as she watched him fight for control. "I would not kill their damned mercenaries if they would cease in sending them out."

"Go in. Father can help you." She couldn't understand his need to hide when help was being offered.

"I am not a freak for your tabloids to ponder my humanity over." He shook his head sharply. "I have as much right to live as you or your brothers. I will not have that questioned, nor will I leave it up to a fickle public to decide my fate."

"This isn't how it happens." Merinus clenched her fists angrily. "The public will help you."

"Only if your 'spin' on the story is better than that of my enemies," he said loudly, bitterly. "And trust me, Merinus, you are good, as are your brothers. But they will bribe your scientists, your doctors. They will jerk every weapon you have out of your hands until I am branded as no more than a monster. And then, there will be no place where I can hide."

"That won't happen," Merinus assured him.

Merinus knew her father, uncle and brothers had been very careful. They wouldn't take a chance with his life.

Mockery washed over his face.

"Will it not?" he asked her. "Jacob thought he could aid us and refuse their offers. He returned home to the brutal deaths of his wife and children. A lesson. How many of your scientists would risk that?"

Shock sped through Merinus' body. She knew the Council killed indiscriminately, she had the proof of it. But hearing Callan voice it, so coldly furious, made it somehow more real.

"I promise you, my family has made a way for you," she whispered. "Look at us, Callan. Look at me. I can't be away from you for more than an hour without my body going into some kind of crazy withdrawal. I can't live this way."

"It will only be temporary," he promised her. "Doc will fix it."

"How do you know?" she cried out. "What if it can't be fixed, Callan? What if we can never be free of each other? What if we don't want to be?"

"I didn't want to be born an animal, or an experiment. Wants don't count." His voice held a ring of finality.

"And if Doc doesn't fix it?" His attitude only spurred her anger further. "What about me, Callan? Will you just run away and leave me to deal with it as best I can?"

He grimaced, turning away from her. She watched his muscular back heave with a harsh breath, his head lower.

"If I must," he told her softly, refusing to look at her now. "I will if I have to make the choice of revealing my secrets, or being with you, Merinus. My family must come first."

"I know about your family," she told him, unreasonably furious at the stand he was taking. "What's to keep me from telling?"

He turned to look at her and the blood chilled in her veins. His eyes were cold, stone hard and as emotionless as his expression. Gasping, she backed away from him, fighting an instinctive fear that rose inside her.

"Callan." Sherra's voice stopped him from answering.

The tall blonde stood in the kitchen doorway, a syringe in one hand as she faced them.

"What do you need, Sherra?" he asked her sharply. "I have no time for more of your tests."

Merinus watched Sherra's eyes narrow.

"Good, because I would more likely try to kill you rather than test you," she said sweetly. "I've brought Merinus' contraception injection. Perhaps you need to go outside and get your control back while she takes it."

Callan gave her a hard look.

"You don't intimidate me, brother," she informed him, moving into the room in determination. "And you shouldn't try to intimidate Merinus. This is hard enough on her."

"I do not try to intimidate, Sherra," he reminded her darkly.

"No, you usually succeed," she admitted. "But now is the wrong time to practice that tough attitude. Go stalk something non-human for a change, while I explain to Merinus why you were forced to kill to save the young girl those soldiers found a few hours after we rescued her, rather than letting her think you did it in cold blood."

Callan's eyes narrowed, while Merinus' widened.

"What?" she whispered in disbelief.

"Yes." Sherra nodded, stopping beside her and indicating Merinus should lift her arm for the injection. "When he went back to track them, disable them, then send them home in shame, they were in the process of attempting to brutalize a young girl they had kidnapped earlier. When he interrupted them, they elected to fight rather than surrender, and when Callan would have still shown mercy, one of them attempted to kill the girl anyway."

Merinus took a deep, hard breath as she looked at Callan.

"They are still dead." He sneered. "And they would have died for touching you alone."

* * * * *

Callan watched Merinus blink at his statement. He hadn't meant to reveal that, but the words had come out anyway. He had no intentions of leaving those bastards alive, as he would have normally done. He had been in a killing rage after rescuing Merinus from their hands, intent on destruction. The soldiers had just made it easier for his conscience to bear the weight.

They had touched what was his. He recognized the emotion, the origin of the fury now. They had laid their hands on his woman, put their scent on her. They had crossed a line Callan had never known existed. One that assured their deaths.

It worried him, this attachment he had for her, the violent emotions that swirled in his brain and in his body. He wanted to deny them, not just to her, but to himself. How could he walk away from her if he couldn't go more than a few hours without touching her?

He watched, fighting to keep his face expressionless as Sherra gave Merinus the injection. He knew Doc wasn't giving her a normal contraceptive. The injection wasn't as powerful as the Depo-Provera shots given in a gynecologist's office. They lasted only days and didn't affect the system as severely.

"I hate these shots, Sherra." He could still hear the throb of anger in Merinus' voice.

"I know," Sherra soothed her as she pulled the needle free. "We have all the samples we should need for a while. Until there's a change."

"There better be a change soon," Merinus said firmly. "I'm getting sick of this. There are things I need to do."

She needed to leave. Callan tamped down the instinctive fury he felt at that thought. She wanted to leave here, to put distance between them if he continued to refuse to give in to her demands to return with her, to reveal himself. His teeth clenched. She was so innocent, too damned innocent. There was no way he could be free of the Council as easily as she believed. If it could have been done, then Maria and Doc would have found a way to do so before her death.

"Callan, Doc still needs samples from you," Sherra informed him, disrupting his thoughts. "Daily. When will you be in the lab?"

Callan shrugged. "Whenever you are ready. Send Dawn up to stay with Merinus."

"I don't need a babysitter," Merinus retorted, her earlier anger still evident in her voice.

"Too bad," he told her, unconcerned. "I am not comfortable leaving you alone, so I will ensure you are not alone. Your wishes in this don't matter."

He ignored Sherra's look of surprise, Merinus' narrowed eyes and flash of stubbornness.

"Geez, Callan, I think all this excess testosterone flooding your system is putting you in overload." Sherra frowned.

"Testosterone overload?" Merinus gave an unladylike grunt. "More like asshole overload if you ask me."

Callan growled low and deep at the defiance in her voice.

"And don't you go doing that growling thing at me." She pointed her finger at him commandingly. "I've had it with you this morning, Callan. Don't bother leaving that lair in the basement if you can't act decent."

His cock was throbbing. He could smell her arousal already and he could feel his blood pumping hard and demandingly into his cock. He should throw her across the table and fuck her into a screaming orgasm before leaving her. That would teach her to defy him in such a way.

The thought of her, stretched out across the dark wood of the table as he drove inside her was nearly an irresistible vision of lust. She would throw her head back, beg him to ride her harder, deeper. He breathed in deeply.

"Let's go." He stalked across the room as he ordered Sherra to follow him. "Another minute in this woman's company and I will become violent."

"Or I will," Merinus muttered, though her voice sounded weaker, more petulant than furious as it had before.

Strange, she had not pouted since he had first set eyes on her, he didn't expect to hear it coming from her now. Let her pout, when he returned to her, he would show her who the dominant one was between them. He would make her scream for her release, beg him to throw her into orgasm. And he knew how to do it. The Council had been amazingly thorough in his lessons. Sex could be a weapon as well as a pleasure. A tool to kill, or to cajole, whichever the situation warranted. He would show her that foreplay could be a torture, a lesson in pleasure so incredible it bordered on pain. His cock jerked at the thought. Damn it, tests first, then he would show his woman who was boss.

CHAPTER FOURTEEN

She wasn't about to wait on him. She was fed up with tests and orders, and the throbbing, heated need that pulsed through her body. All she had to do was get away from him. That was all. The enforced confinement only bred the dependency her body was harboring for him. If she could just get away from him, then she could control it.

Merinus hurriedly dressed in jersey shorts, a light tank top and her running shoes. She tucked some cash in the zippered pocket of the shorts, then slipped from the house. She knew the other three males were patrolling the hills around the cabin for mercenaries, but she hoped they were overlooking the main road in. A vehicle could be heard easily coming in, she knew. That area wouldn't be a weak point.

Taking a deep breath, she sprinted across the yard and worked her way into the forest that bordered the road. Staying close to the graveled track, she kept just inside the tree line, jogging quickly toward the main road.

It wouldn't take Callan long to find out she was missing, and tracking her sure as hell wouldn't be a problem for him. She had to get to camp. Callan may have stolen the cell phone she carried with her, but there was a spare hidden in the Jeep. And the Jeep was still there. She had heard him discussing it with the others that morning. He wanted them to get the Jeep and begin taking her camp down, removing all traces of her from the area.

Despite Sherra's attempts to ease her fears, Merinus feared Callan's intentions. He spoke so easily of killing those soldiers. What was to keep him from killing her when their passion had ended? When his body no longer craved her, when his lusts dimmed for her. She would become an inconvenience, one that knew his secrets.

Fear rushed through her veins, giving her the added adrenaline needed to push herself, almost at a run, over the two miles of rough terrain to the main road. There, luck was with her. She had no more begun a hurried jog down the pavement when a car passed, then slowed.

Relief washed over her when she saw the young girls watching her expectantly.

"Hey, ain't you the journalist that's been running around town?" the blonde, gum snapping driver asked her with a smile.

The girl waitressed evenings at the small restaurant she ate in, Merinus remembered.

"I need a ride back to camp," Merinus told her urgently. "Could you drive me there?"

She was sweating, her blood thundering through her veins. She needed Callan. She swallowed at the bile rising in her throat as she fought the weakening symptoms.

"Sure. Get in. You look kinda sick, though. Sure you don't want to go to the doctor?"

Merinus pulled the back door open and slid in thankfully.

"No doctors." She barely halted the shudder of her body at the thought of someone touching her. "Just take me to the access road to my camp. I'll be fine from there."

She wondered if her Jeep was still there. Another cell phone was hidden there, a spare, just in case, Kane had told her. She had to get to that phone.

"Sure. No problem." A heavy foot hit the gas and the car shot forward.

Merinus bit her lip, fighting the need to scream out at her to stop, to take her back to Callan. Addictions could be cured, she told herself. Detox. Kane had gone through it a long time ago, and he told her once, any addiction could be cured. All you had to do was fight it. Just fight it.

She could fight it, Merinus assured herself.

Her fists clenched in the pockets of her shorts, her body throbbed and the air became stifling. She tasted blood from her teeth biting into her lips and she was forced to clench her teeth instead. Control, she chanted to herself. Control. Kane said all it took was control.

* * * * *

The roar that erupted from Callan's throat when they realized Merinus was missing almost shocked him. He knew it shocked the others. Dawn whimpered. Sherra flinched. The three men whose sole job it was to protect the house paled.

"You didn't even know she was out there?" The primal growl in his voice had the three men taking a step back.

"We were above her, Callan. There was no reason for us to believe she would try to slip away from you," Taber defended them all.

"And why would you not patrol the road? Do you think no one would think to use it?" he growled harshly. "What the hell is it there for?"

"We would have heard—"

"Nothing if they were on foot as Merinus was," Callan rasped furiously.

The rage pulsing through his body was hot and violent. Damn her to hell, she had run from him. Taken money and the keys to her vehicle and ran, despite the needs raging through her body. And she needed. He knew, because the hot throb of lust was making him demented.

"We miscalculated," Taber admitted.

"You fucked up, there's a difference," Callan accused him. "She's headed for camp." He pushed his fingers through his hair, fighting to think. "She'll want her vehicle so she can run. Let's go."

He turned on his heel, unwilling to wait any longer.

"Sherra, you and Tanner head for town, make certain she's not there. The rest of us will head to camp. My damned luck she's fucking called in the Marines by the time I get there."

The Marines or those damned brothers she kept threatening him with. That woman thought her brothers could move the damned world if they wanted to. He bit back an oath of disgust as he jumped into the Bronco and turned the key. Taber and Dayan followed quickly, settling into their seats as Callan tore out of the driveway.

"She's becoming a liability, Callan," Dayan charged as they sped onto the main road minutes later. "A danger to us."

"Shut up, Dayan." Callan flicked a glance at the other man through the rear view mirror.

He watched fury wash over Dayan's face, his brown eyes narrowing in offense. Callan was passed caring. Respect came with a price. He and Taber had fucked up, and Callan would be damned before he would accept the responsibility for that himself. They each had a job to do and he had done his part. The other males had failed in theirs and the price could end up being their lives if they didn't find Merinus.

"She shouldn't have much of a head start on us." Callan fought to restrain the animalistic growl rumbling in his throat. "No more than an hour, and she would have taken much of that jogging to the main road."

"Could be less if she didn't get a ride right off," Taber offered.

Callan flicked him a sarcastic glance. Of course, she would have got a ride right off. No one around here left anyone walking.

"If she's called her family, you'll have to let her go, Callan," Dayan pointed out. "We'll all go into hiding again. There's no other choice."

Callan refused to answer him. He turned sharply onto another graveled path, a short cut that would take him right to the area Merinus had parked her Jeep. The drive was mere minutes compared to the half hour it would take by going around. He prayed he got to Merinus before she got to that damned Jeep. If she managed to get out of the county before he caught up with her, then they were both in more trouble than he even wanted to consider.

Callan would not even consider letting Merinus go. He couldn't. Not yet. Not now. Not while his body was inflamed, his natural instincts to subjugate his mate rioting within his body. He couldn't believe she had made such a damned foolish move. That the strong, determined woman he was getting to know would run in such a way. That she was brave enough to tempt the beast lying just below the surface.

* * * * *

She was sweating, her breathing laboring in her lungs by the time she reached the small clearing where her Jeep was parked. It was still there. She was almost crying in relief as she stumbled against the vehicle, fighting the zipper to her shorts pocket and struggling to pull her keys out. She nearly dropped them twice before she managed to fit the key into the lock and twist it.

She scrambled into the interior, shuddering, her body weak, unsteady as she groped at the glove box to open it. The door finally fell open, revealing the spare cell phone that Kane insisted she keep up.

Flipping it open, she keyed the rapid dial and listened for the call to go through.

"Merinus!" His voice was a desperate yell across the line.

"Kane," she gasped, lying across the seat now, clutching her stomach. "Oh, God. I'm in trouble, Kane."

She could hear him cursing, raging. There was fear in his voice though, and worry.

"Dammit, Merinus, I told you this was fucking stupid," he screamed again.

"Just shut up," she tried to yell back, but her voice was weak. "Come get me, Kane. He'll find me and I can't drive. You have to come get me. This is big. God, bigger than we knew—" The soft growl at her back had her freezing in terror.

"Merinus?" Kane questioned into the sudden silence.

Merinus whimpered. She felt him behind her, big, hard, aroused. She knew he was aroused, knew he was furious.

"Hurry, Kane—" The phone was jerked out of her hand as she was lifted from the Jeep seat.

She heard Kane screaming at her, watched as Callan closed the line, slowly, deliberately.

"That was a mistake," she snarled in his face, her fist striking out at him, catching him off guard.

He released her long enough for her to scramble away from him then dash through the trees as she ran for the main road. If she could get close enough, maybe someone would hear her screams for help. Someone would know she was in trouble.

* * * * *

"Leave her," he ordered Dayan and Taber as they started after her. "Pack this shit up and hide it. Jeep and all. I'll meet you at the house in a few hours."

Callan tossed the ringing cell phone into the Jeep with a snarl.

"You just going to let her run?" Taber asked him curiously.

"She's headed away from the road, not to it." He shrugged, knowing how often greenhorns got lost in the area due to the paths that pretty much looked the same. "Do as I said. I'll catch her."

"Uhh, Callan, maybe you should let me go after her," Taber suggested. "You're not exactly calm right now."

"She's safe. For now," Callan assured him. "Just do as I said, and I'll meet you back at the house later."

Callan was furious. He couldn't believe he hadn't managed to get to her before she made that damned phone call. The last thing he needed was the Tyler newspaper clan descending on the little town, looking for him. He should have taken care of the camp and her Jeep sooner. That was a miscalculation on his part. And he would have never suspected she was carrying two cell phones. All he could seem to consider right now was the fact that she had run from him. Deliberately, had left the house and tried to escape him. She belonged to him, at least until whatever the hell it was that made his cock throb decided to stop. Until then, she was a necessity to him. Just as he knew he was to her.

He could smell her heat beckoning him. Fear and confusion and arousal. It was a heady scent that sent his own pulse pounding, his erection jerking in response. He didn't run after her, he stalked her. Moving around her, behind her, choreographing his moves as he pushed her towards the area he wanted.

A clearing in the heavy growth of the forest, a secluded, private area sheltered on three sides by cliffs, with only a narrow entrance in or out. He wanted her there, in the privacy of the place he had chosen as his own.

It didn't take him long before he was following her through the entrance, his steps light, silent. He could hear her breathing heavily, cursing. He smiled, her brothers must have taught her those curses, because no lady could have thought of them on her own.

She was sitting beside the stream, sweat dampened, her head lowered as she muttered weakly about "damned animals and superior men."

"Oh, you've had it now." She stared up at him, her eyes dark, glittering wildly with lust and defiance. "He'll hunt you down like a dog."

"Wrong species, darling." He smiled slow and sure.

She narrowed her eyes on him as he stripped the shirt from his back.

"Asshole," she muttered, her breathing becoming harsh, heavy as he kicked the leather moccasins from his feet.

"Mine." He growled.

Her eyes widened as he stripped his pants from his body, his cock springing free, hard, jutting. He watched her nipples harden further beneath her shirt.

"I'm not yours," she gasped, her protest weak.

"Take your clothes off, Merinus," he told her softly. "If I attempt it, I'll tear them from your body. You should have never run from me."

"Should I just wait around—"

"Take the fucking clothes off before I rip them from you," he threatened her again, his fists clenched as he fought the urge to do just that.

"I don't want you." But she did. He could smell her want, feel it in the heat radiating from her body.

"Now." He made a move toward her, satisfaction filling every pore in his body as her shirt came off quickly, then her shorts.

She was naked. Gloriously, beautifully naked. She stared up at him, flushed and furious, her breathing harsh in the sudden silence of the glade.

"Kane will come for me," she warned him darkly. "Him and the rest. He won't let you keep me like this."

"He'll have to find you first," he told her softly, smiling with his victory as he came toward her. "And I promise you, he won't find—"

Stars exploded in front of his eyes as her foot connected with his balls. He blinked, fought the onrush of bile rising in his throat, and fought for breath as he fell to the ground.

Fuck. That hurt. He wheezed, fighting for breath, aware of the jerkiness of her movements as she pulled her clothes back on. She was weak, her body trembling, the need pouring through her making her clumsy. Son of a bitch, she was going to want for a while. Then she was off and running again.

Callan pulled himself weakly to his feet, fighting for breath and mentally cursing the little bitch for everything she was worth. Or wasn't at that moment. Damn her. He was going to tan her hide.

He jerked his jeans from the ground, intent on stepping into them when he heard her scream. Terror filled the sound. He dropped his pants and with more than a little pain, sprinted after her, fury rising inside him once again. He'd kill whoever scared her. Then by God, she would pay for this little stunt.

CHAPTER FIFTEEN

Dayan had her. He wasn't touching her, but he didn't have to. His face was a mask of fury, his lips pulled back in a snarl, his incisors showing as he growled out another warning at her. His eyes seemed to glow, his body tense and ready for attack. Merinus was on the ground again, scooting back desperately as he advanced on her.

"Callan," her scream ricocheted around the clearing as Dayan reached for her.

Callan acted on instinct. He saw the intent in Dayan's face, the twisted fury and hunger that raged in the other man. He launched himself at him, a savage snarl erupting from his throat as he tackled the other man.

Callan had known killing rage only one time before. The haze of blood before his eyes, the need for death in his tense muscles as he threw Dayan away from Merinus, the savage snarl of fury should have been enough to warn the other man. Instead, Dayan rolled to his feet, facing the proclaimed head of the pride, snarling in defiance.

Callan narrowed his eyes, seeing the blood in Dayan's eyes, and knew the time had come to reassert his supremacy within the Pride they had established.

* * * * *

Merinus watched in growing horror as the other man challenged Callan. He was younger, both men were in superb condition and ready to fight.

"Oh, shit," she whispered, coming to her feet, backing away slowly.

"Taber," Callan called out, never taking his eyes from Dayan. "Don't you fucking touch her."

Merinus looked around desperately. The quiet, black haired Taber emerged from the trees, his jade green eyes concerned as he watched the other two men.

"Don't make me touch you, Merinus," he warned her as she turned to run in the opposite direction. "It wouldn't be pleasant for either of us."

A scream of fury echoed through the clearing. Merinus swung around just in time to see Dayan go flying over Callan's shoulder to hit the ground hard. He came up quickly though, launching himself at Callan once again. Callan stepped aside at the last second, a smooth, gliding motion that put him out of touch, and he smiled when Dayan hit the ground once again.

Dayan shook his head this time, appearing rattled by the fall.

"If you had touched my woman, Dayan, I would have had to kill you," Callan warned him as the other man came to his feet. "I will have no one's scent upon her other than my own."

Merinus rolled her eyes. What was it with him and scents?

"You are his mate, Merinus." Taber must have caught the reaction. He stood close to her, but not touching as he watched the fight progress.

They were throwing punches now, though few of Dayan's wild swings actually connected. The man was working himself into a froth of fury. Growling, spittle flying as Callan faced him calmly.

"I'm not a fucking mate," she sneered.

"Watch your mouth. Even Sherra and Dawn do not handle such language," he told her with a frown, then winced as Callan threw Dayan to the dirt once again.

"Oh, God," Merinus muttered as both men were suddenly on the ground, teeth bared, fists flying.

Callan's blows were harsh, hard. Merinus heard his fists connecting with Dayan's flesh, heard the other man's grunts of pain, his snarls of rage. She had never seen anything so vicious as the blood and blows that rained between them. Until finally Dayan fell back, nearly unconscious, as Callan jumped to his feet.

Savage, glittering amber eyes shot to Merinus. She watched, her throat dry, eyes widening as his cock slowly hardened as he advanced on her.

"Get him out of here," his voice was a harsh rasp as he grabbed Merinus' arm. "Get back to the house. I'll deal with him there."

"You already dealt with him," Merinus protested as he began to drag her back to the stream.

His hand was hard on her arm, almost bruising as he forced her behind him.

"I'll deal with him further," he said, male fury crackling in the air. "But you I will deal with here."

He pushed her to the grass, moving quickly between her thighs before she could strike out with her feet. He gripped her fists in one hand, stretching her back, anchoring her along his body as his cock pressed the jersey material of her shorts against the soaked entrance to her vagina.

"Callan." She hated the fear that tinged her voice.

He was too angry, too intense. She didn't know how to handle the animalistic, savage side of his nature.

He ripped her shorts from her body, tearing them from her and leaving them in shreds.

"I warned you I would rip them from your body." The shirt went next.

Her furious struggles didn't deter him in the least. He held her still, watching her body as she writhed against him. Merinus was breathing hard, her skin sensitive, the rasp of the fine hairs on his body caressing her was nearly driving her mad. They were downy soft, stroking against her. The hair on his legs rasped her inner thighs, the tip of his cock nudged at her tender entrance.

Merinus felt the blood thundering through her veins. She wanted him. Oh, she wanted him so bad it was about to kill her. Inside her, deep and hard, making her scream in her need.

"You ran from me," he growled, sinking a bare inch of his erection into her.

Merinus felt the tiny thrust, her muscles clenching around it, weeping for more. Her clit throbbed, her breasts ached, the sensitive nipples so hard and hot she wondered if they would burst.

"I won't let you—" She shook her head, her back arching as another inch sank into her.

"Mine," his vow was low and rough.

"No—" She was crying from need now. Her drenched cunt begging for more of him. "I won't let you do this to me. I can't."

He pushed in a bit more. Merinus held her breath, feeling the tight stretch of her muscles as they conformed to his width. She pulsed around him, feeling more of her juices easing around his flesh. She was slick, frothing with lust.

"Tell me," he ordered her, his voice dark, rough. "Tell me you are mine, Merinus."

He stared down at her, his eyes bright, intense as he held her securely while pushing inside her by slow, torturous degrees. She was shamefully aware of the pulse of her inner flesh as it milked him, caressed him. She was drowning in her own lusts, her own needs.

"Touch me," she begged shamelessly, her breasts pressing against his chest. "Please, Callan, touch me."

His tongue licked over her breasts. Rough, rasping her flesh, she arched against him, needing more.

"Tell me, and I will give you what you need," he told her tautly. "Say the words, Merinus."

"No." She shook her head, her hips twisting as she fought to get closer to him, to drive that steel hard flesh deep inside her.

"You will tell me," he groaned, his hand gripping her hip while the other held her hands anchored to the ground.

She looked up at him, seeing the savage lines of his face, the determination in his eyes. His body was hard, so hot against hers it nearly scorched her. She had to fight to keep the words he wanted from pouring from her mouth. He wanted surrender. He wanted to dominate and possess and she refused to allow it. She couldn't let him. If he did it now, there would be no stopping him from doing it later.

"Are you mine?" she asked him instead, her muscles clenching on the few scant inches of hard flesh flexing inside her. "Who do you belong to, Callan?"

His eyes narrowed.

"My brothers will be here soon," she told him, panting, fighting to keep her sanity. "They'll take me home. Whose will I be then?"

"No," he snarled, his hips pulling back, then easing his erection inside her again, no further though, than it had been before.

"No, you aren't mine?" she whispered, gasping as his teeth nipped at her breast, his tongue stroking over her nipple.

Oh, how she wanted to give in.

"You will not leave," he growled, nipping her again, then licking the wound.

His teeth were hard, sharp, the little flashes of heated sensation speared to her womb, causing it to clench hard, deep.

"How will you stop me?" she whispered, staring up at him, straining to get closer, to get him deeper inside her.

He breathed in hard. Rough.

"You are mine. Mine, Merinus." His hips plunged hard, driving his cock deep inside her, causing her body to scream with pleasure, with an overload of sensation that made her cry out as her teeth sank into his shoulder.

There was no stopping him then. He moaned, harsh and wild into her neck as he began to pound into her. He filled her cunt, stretching the sensitive tissue deliciously, stroking it as a million bolts of erotic electricity sizzled along her channel. Deep, driving thrusts that had her screaming, begging for release. She felt his cock throb, then along the soft tissue of the roof of her vagina it began. At first, just a soft nuance of change. A stroke, like a whisper of sensation. A separate pulse, a heated prong of pleasure she couldn't stand. It raked against nerve endings she never knew existed, made her twist, fight for more.

"Merinus," he groaned her name as it began happening, his voice fraught with unbearable pleasure.

"What is it?" Her head twisted as it became firmer, stroking her harder, driving her higher. "Oh God, Callan. I can't stand—"

She screamed with what little breath she had left. She felt it extend, pulsing as it lodged in the ultra sensitive muscles in the depths of her flesh as Callan's release began bursting inside her. She couldn't stop her own climax. It tore through her body to the pulse of that nubbin stroking the exact center of her sensations. Her legs tightened around his hips, grinding her clit against him, feeling the hard beat of release there, as well as deep inside her womb. She was pulsing, erupting, begging for breath as the pleasure seemed never ending, until she collapsed against him.

His arms were tight around her. She never knew when he released her hands. His head was buried in her neck, his own breath heaving from his chest as he fought for air. His body was tense and hard, dominating.

"Mine," he whispered again into her neck.

Merinus felt tears come to her eyes. She was naked, stretched out on the grass in the middle of a damned forest with a man she didn't even really know still lodged inside her body. Her flesh still shuddered from her orgasm, her vagina clasped around his erection, unwilling to let him go, and she was suddenly terrified.

"Let me up," she whispered, pushing at his shoulders, fighting the weariness and the fear rising inside her.

She felt his lips at her neck once again. Warm, the caress sent tingles of sensation over her body. Her nipples beaded once again and she felt the fluttering need in her womb as her body responded to it. Her breath hitched, she felt her tears as they fell from her eyes and rolled down the sides of her face.

"Merinus?" His voice was soft, low, a husky purr of satiation as he levered himself above her.

She turned her face from him, shifting her back, suddenly aware of the rough ground on her flesh. He moved from her, and she could barely control her sobs as she felt the firm length of his cock slowly draw from her inner flesh.

"Did I hurt you?" He eased her up, his hands gentle as they ran over her body, his expression somber, remorseful.

Merinus shook her head, fighting her tears. She was damp with sweat, his semen and her juices leaked from between her thighs, a warm reminder of the fiery orgasm that had gripped her moments before.

She heard him sigh wearily as he moved away from her, then he was drawing his shirt over her head, tucking her arms into it, covering her body. He moved away from her then, jerking his jeans from the forest floor and pulling them on. His moccasins came next, his movements graceful, fluid, despite the anger she could feel pulsing from him.

"Stay here. I'll get your shoes," he ordered her.

Merinus nodded, staring at her bare feet, the red polish that needed replacing on her toenails, the dirt on her feet and legs.

A broad, male hand moved to her chin, turning her face to him. She jerked away, hiding her face, her tears. His hand gripped her chin, pulling her face up as he stared down at her, his expression brooding.

"I told you not to push me," he reminded her, his tone harsh. "Now will you stay here, or must I drag you with me to find your damned shoes?"

She nearly choked on her sobs as she fought to contain them. She nodded jerkily. She couldn't speak, if she did, she was terrified she would lose the control she was fighting so desperately for.

He released her, demanding nothing more, then turned and stalked away. Merinus wrapped her arms around her waist, biting her lip as she tried to stem the tears that fell from her eyes. She was suddenly so frightened she could only shudder with it. What in God's name had she gotten herself into?

"Here." Callan knelt at her feet. With gentle hands he put her shoes on, then tied them quickly.

Rather than moving when he finished, he continued to kneel there, his head lowered, his fingers caressing her ankle.

"I'm sorry." His voice was edged with frustration. "I didn't mean to hurt you."

His head raised, his eyes dark with concern and bemusement. As though he too were treading in waters so unfamiliar the threat of drowning was imminent.

"Kane will come for me," she whispered. "You have to let me go, Callan."

His lips twisted bitterly. "I know," he agreed, his hand lifting, his thumb wiping her tears from beneath one eye. "But to take you, Merinus, he'll have to kill me."

The finality in his voice terrified her. The resounding echo in her heart shattered her last hope that she would ever be free of him.

"You said you could walk away," she sobbed. "That even if it hurt you could walk away."

"And an hour later I found you gone and lost my sanity," he told her bleakly.

She shook her head. This couldn't be happening. Not like this. It wasn't supposed to be like this.

"Kane won't let you keep me," she said, desperate for him to understand, to let her go. Desperate to make herself believe, despite the agony throbbing inside her. She didn't want to be free of him, and that frightened her more than anything.

"As I would refuse to let any man hold Sherra or Dawn against their will," he answered her, his expression drawn into lines of acceptance. "This will be up to you to solve, Merinus. One of us will die if you try to leave with him. I won't let him take you."

"You said the doctor would find a cure." Her fists clenched as she rejected his brutal statement. "You said he would make it better."

"And while you were running, I learned he cannot." Callan reached up, pulling her hair back from her face as he watched her. "It will have to ease on its own, and he believes it will. But he believes it will never go away completely. This need, Merinus, whatever it is, could be something neither of us will be free of. Something I'm not certain I want to be free of."

She heard the curious note of vulnerability in his voice. A bemusement that he felt that way.

"I have to call my brothers. They have to know I'm safe." She knew Kane was going crazy with worry. He wasn't safe to be around when he did that.

Callan sighed wearily, rising to his feet.

"Come on. Let's go back to the cabin. We'll discuss it there." He held his hand out to her.

Merinus stared up at him, anger and pain shattering her.

"You won't let me call them, will you? You won't let them help me."

"I won't let them take you," he corrected her. "And if they can find you, they will try to take you, Merinus. They will convince themselves you can be cured. That the need can be taken away. I don't believe it can. I believe nature is having its last laugh on those crazy bastards who created me."

"What do you mean?" She shook her head, even more confused than before.

"The hormone releasing from my body to yours counteracts the contraception injection the doctor's been giving you," he told her softly. "We were created to be unable to breed, our semen incompatible with normal humans. But that hormone is changing that, slowly. Reversing the DNA coded into us. We're mated. Nature will allow us no other choice."

Merinus felt her world tilt. Her hands pressed to her stomach, she had to fight for air.

"Am I—?" She swallowed tightly.

"Not yet," he assured her. "But eventually you will be. There's nothing we can do but see how this anomaly intends to work itself out."

"No." Desperate, pleading, she came to her feet, her hands gripping his arms. "No, Callan, you have to do something to stop this. Wear a condom. That would protect me."

Mockery slashed across his face. "What, Merinus, unwilling to breed with an animal after all?"

Shock held her immobile for only a moment.

"Damn you," she lashed out at him. "I'm unwilling to be an experiment for you. You don't love me, Callan. I'm nothing to you but a bodily function. I refuse to have a child under those circumstances."

"A condom will not work anyway," he told her bitterly. "That part of me that gives you such pleasure, that swells and throbs within your flesh would not allow it."

"What are you saying?" She shook his arm, her nails biting into his flesh. "A condom would work, Callan."

"A condom would split when the barb swells from my cock, Merinus. At full erection, it fills the back of your tight little cunt, locking it into your flesh. It doesn't hurt you, because it's blunt-tipped, but it's too large for a condom to sustain."

Merinus felt the blood drain from her face. Her knees weakened, her heart beating sluggishly within her breast.

"Barb?" Her voice was strangled now as she fought the rising nausea erupting in her stomach.

"I told you I was an animal, Merinus," he growled. "Do you not remember me warning you, that day at the station?" His gaze was hard, cold as he watched her now. Merinus felt the chill of it running over her body. "You should have believed me."

Merinus let go of his arm, fighting to breathe past the panic filling her.

"Then we just fight it," she said, her lungs fighting to draw air past the constriction in her throat. "We don't— don't—" She waved her hand at the erection showing beneath his jeans.

"Fuck?" he questioned her sarcastically, arching a golden brow in inquiry.

Merinus shook her head, her temples throbbing, her pulse rocketing through her body.

"Withdrawal is just that." She fought to breathe evenly. "We'll get over it. We just abstain."

"Fine," he growled. "You can abstain all you want. I'm not so willing—"

"No." She shook her head, moving away from him. "You have to, Callan. You have to. We can't bring a baby into this. Please. Babies are innocent. They don't deserve this."

She was crying again. Her stomach was rioting with nerves, her chest tight with pain. She could feel panic overwhelming her, hysteria rising inside her. She couldn't have a baby. She wasn't ready for a baby.

"Come on, we need to get home." His arm went around her waist.

Merinus jumped back from him. Terror was freezing the blood in her veins. She shook her head, holding her hands up, backing away from him.

"You can't touch me," she whispered. "We can't let this happen, Callan. We can't. I won't let you do this to me."

"Merinus, let's go home. We'll settle it there," he told her, his voice pitched to a soothing level.

"Damn right we'll settle it," she gasped, determination hardening her voice. "We'll settle it in different rooms, Callan. On different sides of the house. This is over. I refuse to have a child, now or in the near future. Especially with a man determined to risk everything he is for pride. I'll be damned if I'll trust you to protect our child, when you don't even take measures to protect yourself."

She watched the anger settle in his face, in his eyes.

"I will allow no child of mine to be tested or taken from me, Merinus," he informed her coldly. "You can count on that."

"And just how the hell do you think you can ensure that?" Incredulity sped through her.

"I will ensure it," he raged, gripping her arm and moving her steadily along the path back to the vehicle. "The conversion hasn't been completed yet. When it has been, we'll deal with it. Until then, I will not let you go. Brother or no."

"You can't keep me forever." She stumbled against him, shivering as the soft, ultra soft hairs of his chest caressed her arms. Damn him. He didn't have to feel so good. He didn't have to do this to her.

"We'll just see about that."

CHAPTER SIXTEEN

Callan half dragged Merinus into the house, his expression stony, his eyes glittering with renewed anger. That was just fine, Merinus thought, because she was none too calm herself. Anger pulsed through her body as hot and pure as the desire did.

"I need a shower," she snapped, jerking away from him as he slammed the door behind them.

The whole gang was assembled now, she thought sarcastically as she watched the interested expressions of the six other people in the room. Even Dr. Martin was there, calmly sipping his coffee as he eyed them.

"Good idea," Callan agreed. "When you're done, you get your ass to the bedroom where you can't get into any trouble."

She cast him a mocking glance.

"I remember Kane saying that one. He learned better, too."

Several snickers and varied coughs sounded through the room. Merinus didn't wait around to see who did what, or Callan's reaction to it. Checking to be certain his large T-shirt covered her rear sufficiently, she swept through the house, heading for the bedroom and a hot bath.

"She called her brother." Callan watched Merinus disappear into the hallway. "I expect the full brood to descend on us. It's time to make plans."

"I told you she was trouble," Dayan growled, his eyes glittering with hot anger beneath the bruises that marred it.

Callan stared at the man, seeing a fury that worried him.

"I would refrain from such comments until I forget the fact that you were ready to attack her," Callan ordered him tightly. He would never forget the sight of Dayan ready to spring and attack.

Dayan's lips curled, and Callan nearly lost his control again.

"Get outside and patrol the house if you can't contribute something to this conversation." Callan stalked to the coffee pot, pouring a large mug and fighting for composure.

He heard a chair scrape eerily over the wood floor. Seconds later, the back door slammed with window rattling force.

"Anyone else?" he asked without turning around. Silence greeted the question.

He turned back to them, seeing the concern on their faces.

"Kane's Special Forces," Taber informed him quietly. "A higher quality than those buffoons the Council keeps sending out. His brothers aren't slouches either. He's trained them. They'll find the house. They'll come in loaded to hell and back to take her."

"I figured that already," Callan snarled.

He knew everything there was to find out about the family. Seven brothers and her father, each man confident, strong. They were arrogant and commanding forces to be reckoned with alone. Together, they would be a small army.

"If he takes her, or if he kills you, she'll suffer," Dr. Martin spoke up. "The withdrawal won't go away according to my tests, Callan."

"What about your theory on conception?" Callan quizzed him sharply.

Dr. Martin shrugged. "The hormone produced only during pregnancy slows it down, but little else. What worries me is the effect your hormones are having on her contraceptives. It counteracts them. And somehow, someway, a minute amount of your sperm has become perfectly normal. There's a chance, albeit slim, that she could conceive at any time."

Callan rubbed at his neck wearily. More complications, more test results that did little to help them.

"We need to meet with her brothers before this goes any further," Taber said worriedly. "We can't take a chance with you, Callan. Or with her."

"Let her call them, Cal," Sherra advised on the end of Taber's statement. "They have to be terrified for her. She's their baby sister. John's child. Maria would have hated this."

The reminder of his surrogate mother and her devotion to John Tyler pierced at him.

"It wouldn't hurt to let her call," Taber agreed. "Let her arrange for them to meet with Doc before they come in like the damned Marines. Merinus won't thank you if you hurt one of them."

She would likely try to kill him herself, he grimaced.

"Maybe you're right," he sighed. "Maybe it would calm her down some. She's like a damned volcano ready to erupt."

"And when she does, it's your ass that's gonna get burned," Sherra told him with little sympathy. "Your attitude with her sucks."

Callan frowned.

"It's normal." Doc grinned. "The mating ritual of all animals. The males fight for dominance over their females. Human males have lost the fight in the past generations with feminism and equal rights and getting in touch with their sensitive sides," he snickered. "Callan's DNA refuses to allow him the choice in dominating her. It's part of his genetic code."

Callan snarled. Just what he needed, a fucking scientific explanation of the problem.

"Great," Taber muttered. "Just what we needed to know."

And the need to dominate was growing worse. Callan's fight with his needs, his sexual desires, was a constant battle now.

"I'll need more samples from Merinus after your next, um, association." The doctor cleared his throat, ignoring Callan's look of amazement at his choice of words. "As her body reacts so violently to any touch but yours, I suggest you come with her."

"I guess I'm here for the night again then," Sherra yawned, stretching tiredly. "So I'm heading on to bed."

"Me too." Dawn, the most silent of the group, rose from her seat.

She carried her cup to the sink, rinsed it, then set it in the basin.

"Let's go, Tanner." Taber was on his feet, slapping Tanner on the back as he rose. "Time to go to work."

"Yeah, work," Tanner grumbled, but there was no hesitation in his movements. "Man, remind me when I get all dominant to find a woman that doesn't argue. You could hear Merinus cursing Callan all through that forest."

"Watch your mouth," Callan ordered darkly.

Tanner grinned, lifted his hand in a friendly salute and followed Taber out the kitchen door. The house was silent now, emptied of the Pride and their worries, concerns and affections. It left Callan feeling tense, almost alone. The feeling left him longing for Merinus. Not just sexually, but for her companionship, the measure of understanding he had found in her, despite her anger.

He rose to his feet and paced into the living room. He turned the television on low, hoping to fill the silence that had never bothered him before. As he lowered himself wearily to the chair, a small vibration in his jeans had him frowning in surprise. Merinus' cell phone. He pulled the device from his pocket, stared at it a moment, then flipped it open.

"Yeah?"

There was silence over the line.

"I want you to give this phone to Merinus." The command in the male voice had Callan's brows lowering, his possessive instincts towards Merinus flaring.

"And may I ask who's calling?" Callan smirked. As though he didn't know.

The silence again. The echo of quiet rage.

"Is she alive?" Had he been a lesser man, a shiver would have worked down his spine, Callan thought.

"Of course she's alive," he said arrogantly. "Killing innocent young women is next year's job. This year I'm just stalking asshole soldiers."

"You have enough of them following after your ass," the voice snapped. "I sent my sister there with an offer of help, not so you could abuse her."

Callan came to his feet.

"I have not abused her," he growled furiously. "If anything, that woman has, at every opportunity done her best to foil my best attempts to keep her from my problems. I blame you, Mr. Tyler, as her older brother, for her willfulness and her total disregard for authority. Your sister is a menace."

Frustration edged a deeper growl from his throat as he allowed his frustrations rein on the man who had most likely caused Merinus to develop such traits.

"Then you will have no problem giving her this phone so I can make arrangements to collect my willful sister," Kane remarked smoothly, suspiciously. "I'll be landing at the airport in a matter of hours. I expect her to be waiting for me."

Callan stilled. "I don't think that's possible, Tyler." He kept his voice smooth, calm. "Regrettably, your influence on her has been detrimental. She is a stubborn, determined woman, but she is now my woman."

Silence again. Callan imagined the man was fighting for control himself, a way to ease his sister from whatever danger he believed she was in.

"Don't make me come in and take her," Kane warned silkily. "You wouldn't like it, Lyons."

"And your sister would not survive it," Callan answered him quietly. "Do not make that mistake."

"Harm her—"

"I could no more harm her than I could harm myself," Callan grunted. "Your sister is not in any danger from me. But she can't leave me now, for her own safety, it's out of the question."

"She's in more danger with you." Kane said dangerously.

"She is tied to me now, Tyler, in ways you do not understand," Callan sighed. "You may see your sister. You may speak with her, but at a time that is of my choosing."

"And you expect me to calmly accept your decision?"

"No, knowing Merinus must have learned her willfulness from somewhere, I would suspect I had better be watching over my shoulder for a while now." Callan grimaced. "But never fear, Mr. Tyler, I have grown quite used to that habit anyway, so it will be no hardship."

Callan happened to glance up at that moment, Merinus' scent drawing him, heating his blood. She stood in the doorway, her arms folded across her breasts, a frown marring her expression

"You're wasting your time," she told him patiently. "If that's Kane on the phone, then you won't convince him of anything."

"Who says I wish to convince him at all?" he asked her, allowing a smug smile to tip his lips. "I merely grew bored with my own company."

"Let me talk to her, Lyons." Tyler's voice was suddenly imperative, coldly furious at his ear.

Merinus stood patiently in front of him, her hazel eyes suspicious, hopeful. He sighed roughly. He should have never answered the damned phone.

He covered the mouthpiece carefully, watching her.

"I won't mention the others," she said softly. "But if you don't let him talk to me, he'll become dangerous, Callan. I don't want you or my brothers hurt. And you can bet Kane's not alone."

Callan snarled softly. A complication they of course did not need.

"Talk to him, but Merinus, remember. My Pride would give their life for yours. Don't betray them." He didn't think she would, but they hadn't survived this long on faith alone.

She came to him slowly, her slender arm reaching out for the small phone. Callan handed it to her, watching her, assessing her soft expression as she brought it to her ear.

He listened to her talk to her brother. He heard the tremble in her voice, her unwavering faith in Kane as she talked to him. Argued with him. Assured him.

"It's not that simple, Kane. I can't leave him," she finally said softly. "I know you don't understand, but I'll explain it all when I understand it myself."

Callan reached out, his fingers gripping her other arm lightly.

"Tell him we will meet with him. You and I and Dr. Martin. Alone, Merinus. I will not have your whole tribe breathing down my neck."

She looked at him in surprise.

"As though I don't know he has your whole family in that plane with him." He grunted.

He listened to her relay the message. She was silent for long moments, sadness filling her eyes.

"You and Dad only, Kane," she finally said firmly. "Or I can't do it. You know I wouldn't ask if there were any other way." She was silent for long moments, then came back with a sharp edge to her voice. "Listen, asshole, this isn't your decision. Stop playing He-Man on me, you know it doesn't work."

Callan winced. At least the brother didn't have to deal with the Lion-O crack. Then she started arguing with Kane. Furiously, her tone steel hard, her smartass cracks causing him to wince in sympathy. Long moments later, it appeared she had won, though.

"You can set the details with Callan. If you two can manage to talk civilly?" She arched a dark brow at Callan.

"I am always civil," he informed her archly.

She rolled her eyes, extending the phone to him. "Try to be a little more civil then. Because your version of it definitely leaves something to be desired."

He accepted the phone from her, watching as she then turned her back on him and stalked into the kitchen.

"I see you are as successful in getting your way with her as I have been," he said snidely into the receiver. "I hope you train your lovers better than you have trained your sister."

"I'm going to kill you, Cat Boy," Kane hissed, furious, no longer able to hide his ire. "Slowly. Painfully."

"You may wish to," Callan agreed, his tone pure sarcastic implication. "But I doubt she will give you her permission."

He could hear teeth gnashing over the line. He knew his assumption that Merinus controlled the strong men of her family was correct. She was like a tiny general, directing their movements where she was concerned at all times.

"When you land, there will be a woman awaiting you. She has natural, pure white blond hair and light gray eyes. Her name is Sherra. She will know who you are, and approach you herself. She will give you the details of the meeting. Will you abide by this?"

A strange, tense silence filled the line. As though Kane were holding his breath, or his surprise.

* * * * *

"Sherra," he whispered the name on a sigh that had Callan frowning in confusion. "I'll watch for her."

Callan sighed. The brother was no easier to deal with than was the sister.

"Be certain you do," Callan sighed. "For the sake of your sister's sanity, Tyler, hold your rage at a simmer long enough to hear the problems surrounding her. Perhaps you will draw a bit more sympathy for my position by then."

The phone disconnected. Callan grinned mirthlessly. He well understood Kane's problem. Just as Callan felt sympathy for his plight as Merinus' brother, unwillingly of course, so too did Kane feel sympathy for Callan. Though Kane was furious at the suspicions he had regarding the relationship between Merinus and Callan.

"You two finish consoling yourselves?" The scent of her hit him like a fist to his loins.

She stood in the entrance way once again, a sandwich in one hand, a glass of milk in the other. She walked over to the couch, her movements graceful, her body tempting in the soft jersey shorts and light sleeveless T-shirt she wore. Her nipples were hard little points beneath the material; her eyes were dark with the lust building in her body. And she seemed determined to ignore it, and him as well.

She lifted the remote from the coffee table, scanned the channels quickly, then settled on a blood thirsty action adventure that set his teeth on edge. He sighed restlessly, dragged his fingers though his hair then stalked from the room. He would be damned if he would sit there, her scent making him crazy for her, while she watched television. If she wanted to ignore it, and him, then by God let her have her way. He would see which of them came crawling first.

CHAPTER SEVENTEEN

Merinus watched Callan stalk the house as she ate. When she lay down on the couch, her thighs clenched tightly together to try to finish watching the movie, he growled and stalked back to the bedrooms. She sighed wearily. Her cunt was so hot it felt on fire. She could feel the dampness on her panties, the slick juices coating her bare cunt flesh.

She was miserable. Empty. So empty she wanted to scream at him to take her, to fill her, to ride her hard and deep like he had in the forest. That dominance, the rougher sex, the utter loss of control he displayed only spurred her lust higher. She shivered, remembering his teeth locking onto the sensitive skin between neck and shoulder, the sharp incisors barely piercing the skin, the sensual pain edging her pleasure higher. She hated that. Hated knowing that she was so depraved she would enjoy it; that she needed it again, only hours later.

She shifted her position on the couch, her head cushioned on the pillowed armrest, her thighs pulled up to her abdomen. Oh God, she hurt. The muscles of her vagina clenched, spasmed. It wept slowly in hot, pulsing arousal. She bit her lip, her eyes going to where Callan stomped into the kitchen. The refrigerator opened, a lid popped. He stalked back to the doorway, his gaze heavy lidded, dangerous as he watched her. He lifted the bottle to his lips and took a long drink.

"I can smell your scent all through this house," he growled as he lowered the bottle, now only half full. "What are you trying to prove by denying us both?"

Merinus felt drowsy, sensual as his eyes went over her. She wanted to roll to her back, spread her legs and plead. She fought the desire, her muscles tightening as she stared at him, denying herself and him.

He looked so damned sexy standing there. Tall and broad and aroused. His face was tense, his body taut. The muscles in his abdomen were tight, drawing her gaze to his thighs. Oh man, he was like a perfect sculpture of some sex god.

"I can't take the chance," she whispered, turning her gaze back to a show she had little interest in. "I won't conceive—"

"There is little chance of that as of yet." Callan shook his head. "You are grasping at excuses, Merinus."

She was, she knew. She was terrified, not of Callan, but of herself. She was terrified of the building needs, the utter lack of mercy her lust had on her emotions. She couldn't separate emotional need from sexual need anymore. Not since this morning. Not since he had taken her, hard and dominating, controlling her body, her responses. Not since he had held her those minutes afterwards, his tongue rasping gently over the small wound on her neck.

The mark was still there. She could feel it throbbing, pulsing in time to her heartbeat, begging for his kiss, his caress. The sharp little pain of his teeth clenching it.

"I have to control it," she whispered.

Her brothers would be here soon. They would have an answer. She knew them, but she would have to be careful. They would take her from Callan and she couldn't allow that. She barely controlled her whimper of emotional pain, not just sexual. Her body ached for him, but her heart hurt. She didn't want to leave. Not yet. She just wanted this 'thing' tormenting them to ease. She wanted to lie in his arms, without the sexual heat building. She wanted to be held by him, touched, cared for. And she was terribly afraid it was nothing but the chemical lust for him. He seemed to have none of these needs.

His cock was hard. It strained against the soft material of his sweat pants, tenting the cloth, drawing her gaze and holding it. She swallowed tightly, licking her dry lips as she wondered how he would taste. In the heat of the frenzy of lust in the last days, it was an experience she had not been given time for. She realized now that she wanted it. She wanted to run her tongue over the bulging head of his cock, feel it jerk against her lips, discover the difference in it that occurred as his orgasm neared.

She closed her eyes, fighting the need. Fighting not just his desire, but also her own.

"Merinus, this will not work," he warned her, his voice hardening. The latent male dominance that lurked just beneath the soft growl had her trembling.

His voice was rough when he took her, too. When he climaxed, his chest rumbled with an animalistic grumble that made her shiver to think about it. He was the ultimate male animal, sexual, arrogant in his prowess and his abilities. Muscular, strong, every bone and muscle in his body in perfect shape. She wanted to taste the skin stretched over those hard planes and angles. She wanted to lick him, nibble at his flesh and hear him groan her name. She wanted to stretch over him, rub against him, find some relief for her aching nipples against his hot flesh.

She opened her eyes, focusing on the flames and explosions playing out on the television. It was safer than staring at the hard cock threatening to burst through Callan's pants, but it provided little distraction from the flesh between her thighs pulsing and screaming out its demand.

"I can make it work. I'm incredibly stubborn, ask my brothers," she told him, her voice sounding much more determined than she felt.

"I need to ask your brothers nothing," he growled forcefully, his voice beginning to rumble. Oh, she loved that sound. Even though it did feel as though the vibrations of it echoed in her womb. "You are the most aggravating female I've ever met in my life."

Merinus shrugged. The movement caused her T-shirt to shift against her hard nipples. She almost groaned at the pleasure. Damn. She wished he would just go away. Go away or take the decision out of her hands and pound into her until she was screaming out her orgasm. That was what she wanted. She wanted what she had earlier, Callan's hands rough on her body, in her hair, driving her to heights she had never known existed. And yet she didn't want it. It equally drew her and terrified her.

"I could ease you in other ways, Merinus," he whispered. He still hadn't moved from the doorway.

She glanced up at him. He watched her intently, waiting for any sign of weakness. She steeled her resolve. She could do this. She could make her body do as she wanted it to. Not the other way around.

Merinus swallowed tightly. "No. I'd beg you to complete it, Callan. It doesn't ease until you come inside me."

The fiery wash of his seed, blasting hard and hot inside her cunt was the only relief from the building pressure. No matter how many times she climaxed, how many different ways, it was only that final action that allowed her body to cool down from a boil to a simmer.

"You risk my self control this way," he told her softly. "As your need builds, so does mine. Just as it happened this morning. You tempt the beast taking you, rather than the man, Merinus."

She looked into his face. The beer bottle was empty, though he still gripped it tightly. His face was drawn in a mask of concern, of desire. His amber eyes almost glowed, hot and demanding. Her pussy heated further. Oh, she wanted him. She could fuck him for hours and never get enough.

"You aren't a beast," she told him, her voice soft as she glimpsed the regret in his eyes.

It bothered him, she knew, these needs, the domination he fought to keep from exerting over her, the control he fought to hang onto. He didn't like the instincts raging at him, any more than she liked those raging at her.

"But I am, Merinus," he sighed, looking down at the bottle he held for long moments. When he looked at her again, there was remorse, and acceptance. "I don't deny what I am. To do so would risk my sanity. And you can't either. You can never forget that the animal is there, lurking beneath the surface. It's dangerous to do otherwise."

The problem was, the beast within him didn't frighten her nearly as much as it seemed to bother him. She felt her inner muscles tighten, her womb clench with the heated memory of his loss of control. How much more dominant could he become, she wondered, then shivered at the thought.

"Merinus, don't do this," he told her, his voice tormented now. "You are denying yourself and me. I don't want to hurt you."

She heard the plea in his voice. She wanted to give in, she wanted to turn to him, to ease the fire ripping through her body, but she couldn't. Not now. Not yet. It wasn't a need to tempt him, or even her curiosity in the face of the lack of control he warned her about. She no longer controlled her own body, and she knew this was the root of her problem. She needed that control. She needed to dictate when she wanted to fuck and when she wanted to cuddle, not her body or this chemical reaction driving her insane.

"Not yet." She closed her eyes, fighting her tears, fighting her body.

It was her body, dammit. It had a mind of its own lately and it was killing her.

Callan watched her a moment longer, then with a sizzling curse stalked from the room again. Merinus sighed, her breathing rough now that he was no longer in the room. She couldn't control the soft whimper that escaped her lips. She was only thankful the television masked the sound.

She was breathing hard, fighting to draw air into her lungs as her inner flesh clenched, demanded relief. Her clit actually throbbed and her nipples were torturously hard, aching for the warmth of his mouth. Her hand moved, her fingers running over the hard points lightly, her body trembling at the incredible pleasure the action brought her.

Her head ground into the pillowed headrest. She felt her juices pool between her thighs. Suppressing her groan, she sat up on the couch, bracing her elbows on her knees as she raked her fingers through her hair. Her fingers dug into her scalp. She shivered again. Even that tiny pain was exciting.

She could control this. She took a deep breath, reining in the madness that threatened to whip through her. She could make it. Self-control, that was all it took. If a person could get through drug withdrawal, surely she could get through Callan withdrawal. It was just a matter of controlling the urge. That was all.

She nodded firmly. The action shifted her shirt again, raking her sensitive nipples and she bit her lip to hold back her moan.

Something cold to drink. One of Callan's beers. Hell, he had a whole fridge full. She stood to her feet, a shudder working over her body as her panties pressed against her clit. Oh God, she was going to come from thong friction alone. She was pitiful.

Stepping carefully, she moved into the kitchen and jerked one of the beers out of the refrigerator. She twisted the cap, hearing the faint hiss. She turned the bottle up to her mouth, taking a long, cold drink. Then she held the frosted bottle between her breasts, taking a deep breath as she leaned against the appliance for support. This was bad. Really bad.

"Where's Callan?" Sherra stepped into the kitchen, her eyes narrowed as she watched Merinus drink from the beer.

"In bed." She would have shrugged if she could have handled the sensation of cloth rasping over her breasts.

"How long since he fucked you?" Sherra asked bluntly.

Merinus rolled her eyes. "Long enough to suit me."

Yeah. Right. Not in this lifetime.

Sherra's lips firmed.

"It's not a good idea to deny this when it's so strong, Merinus. You know how bad it gets." Sherra moved to the sink, pouring herself a glass of water and drinking it quickly.

"How would you know?" she asked bitterly. "I don't see you crawling all over some man trying to get off."

Sherra looked away, her expression cool, but a glimpse of tormented eyes filled Merinus with remorse.

"I'm sorry, I didn't mean that, Sherra. But it's my body, my decision," Merinus reminded her, then tipped the bottle up and finished the beer. It wasn't enough. She needed something to chill her out now. She opened the refrigerator and grabbed another.

She popped the lid quickly and took a long drink.

"Dangerous, Merinus." Sherra walked toward her, frowning at the drink. "We don't know how alcohol will mix with this chemical reaction between you and Callan."

"Guess we're about to find out then." Merinus laid the bottle along her temple. It was cool and comforting against her flushed skin. "Can you turn the a/c down a little further, Sherra?" She asked. "It's hot in here."

She closed her eyes, the appliance now supporting her as she breathed heavily. It was stifling, and only growing warmer.

"It's not the a/c, Merinus," Sherra told her, her voice quiet. "It's the reaction. The withdrawal. You need to go to Callan."

"I can control this," Merinus said, more to convince herself than Sherra. "It will just take time."

She took another drink of the beer, finally feeling the effects of it beginning to penetrate the haze of lust. Mating frenzy, what a hell of a name to call it, she thought. She had never seen her damned cats act this way. They screamed and squalled and got it on and then were done with each other. This was ridiculous.

"Merinus, the alcohol could have severe affects—" Sherra began to caution her.

"So could sex with Callan," she argued. "For God's sake, Sherra, his little soldiers are counteracting the contraceptive you keep poking in my arm. His sperm is changing and becoming normal, and only God knows when I'll start ovulating, if I'm not doing so on a daily basis. I do not want to end up pregnant by a man who doesn't love me or need me other than to scratch some fucking chemical itch that's developed between us. Why can't you guys understand that?"

Merinus could feel the anger raging inside her now. It did this before. She remembered that. That day in the lab, when Sherra and the doctor wouldn't stop touching her, poking at her. She eased over to the table and sat down. The pain had come next. Great blinding waves of erotic pain that left her weak and gasping. Then Callan had kissed her. The taste of him, male and spicy, so hot, had made her crazy to beg him to fuck her. But it had eased the terrible craving. Maybe all she needed was a kiss?

She could handle a kiss. His lips rough and hot, his tongue plunging into her mouth, caressing hers, mimicking the movements his cock would make later, driving her insane for more. Or his tongue plunging between her legs. That's where she wanted it. Lapping at her, fucking into her needy pussy as he growled against the folds of skin. She finished the beer quickly.

"I'm going to go lay down." She stood up, sagged momentarily, but gathered her strength and toddled to the couch. Damn, a few beers had never affected her this way before.

"I'll sit here with you for a while," Sherra sighed, following close behind her. "You should let me help you into bed at least, Merinus."

"Nope. I am not getting within three rooms of Callan. Damn him. A whole house isn't enough space right now."

"It would be if you would stop fighting it," Sherra suggested.

Merinus collapsed on the couch. She tucked herself against the back, folding her body tight, feeling the waves of aroused pain beginning to build.

"Go away," Merinus muttered. "I don't need this right now."

The first wave rocked her body. Merinus closed her eyes, fighting to relax against the heat, the hard slam of rushing demand that washed over her. She breathed deeply, feeling her vagina spasm in a harsh wave, and her juices ease from her body. Her panties would be soaked in no time, she thought with a depressed sigh.

This was unlike anything she had ever known could exist. They should bottle whatever it was Callan had that did this. It could make a fortune. An aphrodisiac unlike any other.

Sherra didn't leave. Merinus was aware of her sitting quietly beside her on the couch, watching her closely. Like a damned germ under a microscope, Merinus thought snidely. That was how she was beginning to feel. Minutes later she was aware of Sherra rushing from the room. It didn't take her long to return. Of course, she had her little basket of goodies with her.

"Open your mouth."

Merinus groaned, but did as she was asked. A swab stroked over her dry mouth. What good it was going to do them, Merinus had no idea. Then she clenched her teeth, trying not to fight the next wave of lustful demand. It was harder than the last, pulling at her womb, tightening her cunt. Damn, she would strangle Callan's cock if he got inside her now.

"Vaginal sample." Sherra moved towards her.

"Try it and I'll kill you," Merinus gasped. "Leave my damned pussy alone. It has enough problems right now."

But she didn't fight when the swab eased quickly past the leg of her shorts and swiped through the juices at her vaginal entrance.

"I'm a fucking sex experiment," Merinus groaned.

"I really need a blood sample now," Sherra worried. "It's really important."

"You guys should have been vampires," Merinus bitched, but she held her arm out as Sherra pushed the coffee table close to the couch for her to rest it upon.

"I won't touch you unless I have to," Sherra promised

"Damned good thing. But wait just a minute," Merinus gasped.

A shiver began in her womb, slowly working over her body, building, almost like a climax until Merinus was gasping for breath, her fists clenching as her body was rocked by a demand that took her breath. She heard Sherra curse violently as she moved back from her.

Merinus wasn't certain how long it lasted, how long she fought to breathe. Her eyes were wide, her vision fuzzy as the waves of pulsing lust swept over her again and again. It was going to kill her. She knew it now, she would die, a slow, miserable horny death right here and now.

CHAPTER EIGHTEEN

"Fucking stubborn woman," Callan's curse seemed to echo in her head.

She was jerked from the couch into his arms, her breasts crushed to his chest, her thighs clenching around his hips. His lips covered hers, his tongue sweeping into her mouth as his flesh seared her. Her arms went around his shoulders, her hands spearing into his hair, fisting there, pulling him closer, unconcerned with any pain she would cause him. She wanted it to hurt. She wanted him to know what he was doing to her, wanted him to feel the violence rising inside her, the need, so sharp and agonizing it was like death.

He carried her through the house, his lips hard on hers, grinding her lips against her teeth, his tongue a dominating force as it tangled with hers, licked at it, stroked her lips. His erection was hot, uncovered, pressing against the fragile barrier of shorts and panties as he stalked through the house. It was driving her crazy. She wanted his cock inside her, now.

She arched against him, her hands still pulling at his hair as he dragged his lips from hers, stroked them down her neck as he bore her into the dark bedroom. His teeth nipped at her. His tongue rasped over her skin, the faint roughness making her press herself tighter against him, grind harder against his cock.

"Stubborn bitch," he cursed her breathless, his voice an animalistic rumble as his hand caught in her hair now, pulling her head back, making tingles of pain shoot through her head. Damn, that felt good. Too good.

Then he released her. He tossed her on the bed, watching through narrowed eyes as she came to her knees. She faced him, breathing hard, heavy.

"I won't be gentle," he warned her, his voice rough.

"Neither will I." She whipped the shirt over her head.

Watching him, she licked her lips as her hands smoothed over her stomach, moved up, then cupped her breasts in her palms, groaning at the sensation, at the startled wildness in his expression. Her hands didn't ease the desperate need for calloused warmth, but the expression on his face eased the terrible emptiness that had been building in her soul. He wanted her, craved her as desperately as she craved him. He could be tempted, teased as well as she could. He could be pushed to the limits of his lust, and she intended to push him.

Her hands moved to her shorts, pushing beneath the waistband, stripping them and her panties off quickly. She tossed them to the floor, her eyes never leaving his face. She wasn't willing to lay down submissively, a sacrifice to the reactions tearing her body apart. She wanted him, all of him. The man and the beast. She wanted to take him instead of leaving the control of their passion to him alone.

"How wild are you?" she asked him, amazed at the low, husky sound of her voice.

The fingers of one hand ran in a slow, teasing stroke from between her breasts, over her stomach, then between her thighs. His eyes flared, his face flushed as her fingers dipped into the heat and dampness glistening over the inner lips. His lips parted, his breathing rough and harsh.

"Too wild for what you are attempting, baby," he warned her.

"I won't submit." She smiled teasingly as she brought her fingers to her lips, tasting herself as a hard growl slipped from his chest. "If you want it, you have to take it."

She extended her fingers to his lips then. They parted, the heat of his mouth sucking the taste of her body from them. He moaned, his fists clenching as he watched her. She arched her neck, allowing her hair to cascade down her back, her swollen breasts to tempt him as she brought her hands to them, her fingers raking over her nipples.

"Why are you doing this?" he asked her, his tone dark, wildly sexy.

"Do you want it bad enough to take it?" She went on all fours, staring up at him, her mouth now level with the straining length of his erection. "I do."

"Merinus, don't make me hurt you," he whispered, though instead of pleading, his tone was warning.

"Don't make me hurt you, Callan." Her tongue stroked the bulbous head of his cock.

A warning hiss erupted from his throat. Merinus smiled in satisfaction, her lips parting, one hand gripping the base of his wide cock, her mouth easing over the head, her lips raking the hot flesh as she swiped over it with hot little licks. She had read enough about oral sex, heard enough, that she knew the basics. She thought she could improvise the rest. Her lips closed on him and she began a deep suckling motion that milked at his cock, her tongue swiping over it lazily. Evidently she was doing something right.

Callan's hands tightened in her hair, his hips thrusting against her mouth jerkily. Her tongue probed beneath the head, feeling a curious pulse, a hard, harsh throb at the bottom of the head, beneath the smooth, sensitive skin. His cock jerked, pulsed harder.

"God, Merinus," he cried out her name, half growl, half beseeching groan. "Don't do this. I can't control the need."

Her hand gripped the base of his cock, the other cupped his tight scrotum, her grip massaging, caressing as she began to move her mouth up and down the bursting flesh, caressing with lips and tongue, glorying in his strangled growls as he fought to keep from impaling her mouth with his flesh.

* * * * *

Callan's fingers were tight in her hair, pulling at it, rubbing the silken strands over his abdomen as he fucked her mouth. It was exquisite, the moist heat caressing him, her tongue stroking over him, caressing the hidden barb that would emerge when his orgasm neared. He could feel it throbbing now, fighting to override his control, eroding his need to worship, demanding that he dominate. That he fuck her mouth hard, as he would her cunt, hold her to him, shoot his semen into her mouth in the most intimate of orgasm. He had never done that. Never allowed a woman to suck him to climax. He wanted Merinus to. Needed it. Had to know that she was his in every way. He was tortured in that need, to take her, possess her in every way that a man could possess a woman.

That need had only been growing over the past days. He fought it. Each time he saw her bend over, or watched her tongue lick her lips. He fought the visions of taking her, of fucking her mouth, her ass. That tight little forbidden hole beckoned him, just as her lips did.

She was sucking at him now, drawing his balls tight against his body, his barb throbbed. He shook his head, sweat pouring from his body. Heat wrapped around him, stroked by his lust, fueled by her touch.

"Merinus, enough, baby." He couldn't drag her from his erection, from her sucking pleasure. He didn't have the control needed, and she was ignoring him quite well.

She slurped on the hard, thick cock, drawing it to her throat, then back to her lips, and back again to her throat. Her tongue raked, caressed, drawing his climax nearer with each stroke.

He couldn't control it. He couldn't fight the need, the hot rushing demand. He felt the flesh swell, the barb emerge, harden, tighten. She groaned over his flesh as her tongue raked it, her lips sucked it. His teeth clenched, his hands gripped her head. He couldn't fight it, couldn't fight her. God save him, he was the beast those bastards had created. His balls tightened, his cock jerked, then he cried out, holding her head still as he buried himself as deep, as hard as the hand wrapped around the base of his swollen flesh would allow before he erupted.

He wouldn't let her pull back, but she didn't try to. Her lips were clamped on his thrusting cock, her tongue like a lash of fire over the bursting head. He felt his semen explode from the tip, splash into her mouth. Long, thick streams that ripped his insides apart with pleasure as a hiss of completion, then a hard, male growl echoed through the room.

He was fighting for breath, his chest heaving, his body tight as he drew back from her, shaking as her lips drew snugly over his flesh when he pulled from her. She stared up at him, her lips damp, her eyes dark and glittering with sensuality.

She was the most beautiful creature on the face of the earth. Inordinately graceful, even in her lust. Her hair was tangled around her flushed face, her lips parted as her tongue ran over them slowly, as though savoring his taste.

He was still hard. His climax had eased the most pressing demand, but he needed more. He needed the taste of her, sweet and hot filling his mouth. Before she could fight him, he had her on her back, coming over her, his eyes locked with hers as he lowered his head, taking her lips in a kiss so hot it singed his toenails.

His hands cupped her breasts, his fingers gripping the hard points of her nipples and pinching them gently. She arched tight against him, her hands in his hair again, wrapping the strands around her fingers as she held him to her.

No, tonight she was no willing sacrifice to their frenzy. She was in no way submissive. She met each kiss with a greed of her own, stroking her body against his, moaning, crying out at each touch.

"You will burn me alive," he whispered at her neck, his mouth rasping over the mark he had left on her earlier that day. She shivered at the caress.

"We'll burn each other then." Her voice was husky, filled with wonder as her teeth scraped his shoulder in retaliation after his scraped her neck.

He liked the feel of her teeth on his flesh, raking, feasting on him. Her tongue was like a stroke of silk across his skin. Hot, moist silk that made him mad for more.

He moved lower on her body, his mouth moving to her breasts. He loved the sound of her breathless scream as he sucked the hard little tips of her nipples. The way her hands gripped his hair, holding him close. The way she rode the thigh he tucked in close to her wet cunt. He was starving for her. He couldn't wait much longer to move lower, to lick down the narrow, closed slit, to plunge his tongue deep into the tight depths of her vagina as he drew all her silky cream into his mouth. There was nothing so intoxicating as the taste of his woman's pleasure.

"I'm going to eat you alive," he growled against the swollen curve of her breast as he began his downward trek. "Shall I show you the torture you showed me, baby?"

She moaned, the sound low and pleading as his lips skimmed her flat abdomen. His hands moved to her thighs, moving over the warmth of her skin, parting them wide as he lowered himself between them.

He could smell her heat. It was unlike anything he had ever known. Sweet, just a hint of cinnamon, wild and elusive. He was a man dying for a taste of ambrosia, and she held the only source between those slender thighs. His head lowered, his tongue moving slowly through the slick essence that coated the soft inner lips.

* * * * *

The touch of his tongue was like a bolt of electricity searing her womb. Merinus gasped at the sensation, her body tightening, drowning in the pleasure that washed over her. There had been nothing like it in all her life. She bucked against his mouth, feeling his tongue circle her aching clit, his lips suckle at it. His hand parted the folds, his finger running through the juices that wept from her body, caressing a path from her hidden entrance then lower, shockingly lower, to the tight pucker of her anus. She jerked. He growled warningly into her flesh, sending vibrations of ecstasy echoing over her body. She arched. His tongue stabbed into her vagina, his finger slid a forbidden inch into the lower entrance.

"Oh God, Callan."

She gripped his shoulders, her nails digging into the muscles as her vagina tightened, desperate to hold his tongue in place as she marveled at the feel of his finger lodged just past the entrance of her ass.

It didn't hurt. She would have thought it would. He moved it, pulling free of her body's grip, his fingers moistening themselves in the juice that ran from her cunt, then returning to slide into the tight hole once again. All the while, his tongue thrust hard and fast inside her, driving her closer to completion, as his finger drove her closer to insanity.

She tossed, bucking against him, her hands in his hair again, pulling him close as she felt the bite of sensual pain in her ass, the thrust and drag of his rough tongue in her vagina. Torturous need clawed at her insides, burning her alive as he fucked his tongue hard and fast inside her gripping channel.

She was going to come so hard she knew she would die with the sensations of it. She gasped, burning, reaching, she screamed out at the agonizing pleasure and exploded into his mouth as his finger forged deep inside her ass an instant before her muscles clamped tight in orgasm. Fiery fingers of electricity sizzled her insides, as her hands anchored in his hair and he eased his finger free of her anus, before rising quickly over her.

His cock slammed inside her vagina. Stretching her, filling her as they both cried out at the clawing, greedy lust that had taken control of their bodies. There was no time to ease into their race for completion. Their bodies were frenzied, locked together in a dance of agonized pleasure. His hips drove his erection deep, thrusting hard and fast. She felt the small thumb of flesh that began to grow tautly erect on it just under the head of his cock. It raked the gripping muscles that milked his shaft until with one last heavy thrust it fully emerged, locking him in deep, jerking, pulsing against the sensual trigger deep within her body as his sperm erupted from the head of his cock.

Merinus saw stars. Her climax was like a ravaging beast as it ripped through her body this time. She couldn't breathe, she could only convulse against him as his teeth bit into the skin between her neck and shoulder, just enough pain, just enough edge to drive her into madness.

It was long moments later before she felt Callan collapse to the bed beside her, drawing her tight against his heaving chest as he dragged the blankets over their cooling bodies. He held her close to his heat, his hand pressing her face into his chest, his body wrapping protectively around her.

"I'm sorry," he whispered, his voice agonized. "Oh God, Merinus, I'm so sorry. I'm so sorry."

She pulled back from his chest, staring into the tortured depths of his golden eyes. She was sated, relaxed. Her body no longer throbbed, lust no longer clawed at her insides.

"For what?" Her hand lifted weakly to caress the hard line of his jaw.

"I hurt you." He laid his hand over hers, pressing it close. "I don't want to hurt you."

"Hmm," she murmured. "Hurt me again some more next time then. You must have found a cure."

"What?" His voice was shocked.

"I can sleep now." She closed her eyes to do just that. "It doesn't hurt anymore, Callan."

She snuggled against his chest, feeling his arms come around her with a hesitancy that brought tears to her eyes. She kissed his chest weakly, then let the darkness and the incredible warmth of his body lull her into peace. For the first time since seeing his picture on her father's desk weeks ago, Merinus was at peace.

CHAPTER NINETEEN

It was barely dawn when Callan brought Merinus quickly awake. With his hand over her mouth, his voice a quiet hiss in her ear, he warned her to silence. Staring up at him in surprise, Merinus nodded her head, barely recognizing the savage standing before her.

His expression was hard, frightening in the dim light of the room. What was even more terrifying was the fact that he was dressed in dark fatigues, his hair tied back, his amber eyes glowing with an eerie light within the darkness of the room.

"Here." He jerked her shirt over her head as he pushed her shorts into her hands. "Dress quickly."

He was already dressed. As she dragged her shorts nervously over her hips, he handed her socks and her hiking boots.

"Hurry," he urged her as she pulled the socks and boots on and laced them with trembling fingers.

As she rushed to dress, Callan was stuffing small boxes in a backpack, his movements hurried but controlled. Muscles bunched beneath the clothing, tight and hard, his body tense in preparation for danger. This was not a relaxing wake up call.

"What's wrong?" Confusion filled her voice, though she fought to keep it at a low whisper.

"We have company. Soldiers." He grabbed her hand when she tied off her boot and drew her quickly to the door.

It was then Merinus saw the dull glint of the gun he carried in his hand. Small and lethal, the silver black color gleamed subtly in the darkness, reminding her of the death that always surrounded him. She took a deep, steadying breath, following him as he drew her from the bed. Keeping his other hand wrapped carefully around her wrist, he pulled her from the bedroom, heading cautiously down the dark hallway.

Merinus couldn't hear anything. She strained to detect any sound out of the ordinary, but all she heard was total silence, and the dull thud of her own heartbeat. They moved carefully along the hallway, staying flat against the wall as he drew her towards the kitchen. Drawing her down to a crouch, Callan moved her into the kitchen and over to the door that led into the garage. There, he turned the doorknob silently, standing alert as he inhaled slowly.

He jerked the door opened and rushed her across the concrete floor to the hidden door. It opened before they could reach it. Sherra waved them in quickly, dressed in fatigues as well, a gun in her hand.

"Get her dressed." Callan pushed Merinus towards Sherra as he headed to where the doctor was packing equipment in desperate haste.

"Leave anything you don't have to have. Samples and notes only, Doc." Callan grabbed several cases of just that and rushed them to a waiting Jeep parked at the end of the cavernous room. "We don't have time for the rest."

"How close are they?" Sherra pushed pants and a T-shirt at Merinus as she glanced back.

"They'll be through the security system in a matter of minutes. It will take them no time to find the hidden door," Callan barked. "Get your shit together and let's get out of here. Taber and Tanner are keeping track of them and they're working on the doors now."

Merinus hurriedly took her boots off, jerked her shorts over her legs, then her T-shirt over her head. As she struggled to put the boots back on then, she glanced up. Only then did she see the small earphone and mic that he had over his head. He talked quietly into it for a second as he loaded another box into the Jeep.

"What about Dayan?" Sherra questioned him as Merinus jerked on the pants and pulled her boots back on.

"Out of contact." Callan's voice was hard, cold.

"He ran again?" Sherra questioned in amazement, anger pulsing in her voice. Evidently it wasn't unusual for Dayan to be out of the line of fire when trouble arose.

"Packed." Callan ignored her question. "Sherra, you and Dawn get the doc the hell out of here. Get to the safe house and wait for me there. You know what to do if you don't hear from me."

Merinus felt fear crawling through her body. What would they do? What about Kane? Sherra was supposed to meet with them that morning, she knew.

"You promised Sherra would meet Kane." She stared across the room at Callan's cold expression.

"And we weren't attacked until I talked to that cutthroat brother of yours," he snarled. "Until I know if he's the one who betrayed us, then he can cool his heels where he's at. This isn't a team, Merinus, like before. This is a full assault, over a dozen soldiers. They aren't taking chances this time."

Merinus shook her head at the accusation in his tone.

"Kane didn't do it. He didn't know where we were."

"Kane is a soldier, Merinus," he growled. "He could have had a trace on that fucking cell and pinpointed us within minutes. Had I not been so concerned with your worry and fears, I would have thought of that. I've risked us all with my own ignorance."

Merinus bit her lip as he strode quickly to her, pulling a large backpack over his shoulders and carrying the smaller on his shoulder.

"We have to go." He grabbed her wrist, pulling her along behind him as Sherra and the doctor rushed to the Jeep. "Hopefully, the soldiers will see the signs of the Jeep and follow it as far as they can. Sherra and the doctor will have no problems when they emerge outside, because the area is heavily used by hunters and the road into here is unknown. There's a smaller, hidden corridor on up here that takes us out into the mountains."

"How will that help us?" She fought to keep up with him as he rushed through the narrowing tunnel that led through the mountain they were currently in.

"Because I know the fucking area and they don't," he told her fiercely, his gaze burning into hers as he turned back to her. "We're not safe anywhere else, Merinus. Only here."

"Call Kane," she gasped when he pulled her into a shadowed crevice.

He pushed a large rock out of the way, drew her into the dark corridor, then rolled it closed once again. Seconds later, a small beam of light lit the way.

Merinus could feel nerves and panic washing over her. Callan thought Kane had betrayed him, she knew he did, and she couldn't think of a way to convince him otherwise. She knew her brother would have never, ever put her in a position that could get her seriously hurt. Bruised a little, but never hurt.

"Maybe it wasn't soldiers." She struggled for breath as he loped along the narrow passageway, pulling her behind him, forcing her to keep up. "Maybe it was Kane and my brothers."

"Then they came in the wrong way," he said harshly. "Whoever was out there was packing weapons, Merinus, and plenty of them. It was the first thing I smelled. They were outside our bedroom window right before I woke you. If it were your brothers, they should have fucking knocked. And Taber would have recognized your family."

"Kane wouldn't try to hurt you," she argued.

"Dammit, Merinus, the bastard has enough sense to know that an animal is fucking his baby sister. He was furious on the phone. If it were me, I would have already killed him."

She flushed at the knowledge. Of course Kane would know, but still, she couldn't see him rushing in and doing anything so impulsive without assessing the situation first. It just wasn't like him. But she didn't have the breath to argue further with him. He was moving them quickly through the passageway, his steps silent as she fought to keep her own movements just as quiet. Her boots were soft-soled, but still there was a shuffle, a scrape of leather over stone that seemed to echo around her.

It seemed they strode though endless miles of weathered stone before he slowed the fast walk they were in. He began to move slower, easing her through the corridor, his head tilted as he listened carefully.

"We're getting ready to move out of the tunnel. I want you to stay quiet, Merinus and stay right behind me," he warned her as he stopped and laid his mouth at her ear to speak. "No matter what I tell you to do, you do it, and do it quickly. Do you understand?"

His voice was quiet again, that throb of savagery in it making her heart beat out of control. She nodded her head quickly as he glanced back at her. His eyes glittered in the darkness, a dull gold, furious, cold.

He extinguished the penlight and eased around a corner, moving silently toward the dim light ahead. He stilled, his fingers going to her lips as his head tilted, listening intently. He pushed her against the wall, indicating she should stay there, stay silent.

He was going on without her. Merinus shook her head violently, her fingers gripping his arms. Then she heard a sound, a shuffle of feet, a light scrape against stone. Her eyes widened, terror flooding through her. Callan's eyes narrowed as he pushed her tighter into the stone, a warning in his expression as he pulled the gun from his belt and began to move away from her.

Merinus took a deep, silent breath. She fought to keep her breathing normal, her heart rate slower. She couldn't hear anything past the desperate drum of blood rushing through her body. She was terrified. Her own fear was like a separate entity choking her, strangling the breath in her throat as Callan moved silently away from her. She watched his face, seeing the cold threat in his expression. This wasn't the lover she had known in the past days, or the teasing, elusive prey she had stalked the weeks before. Callan was now the creature those damned scientists had created. Cold, hard, his body primed and ready to fight.

Stay! He mouthed silently.

She nodded, unwilling to worry him. Kane had warned her many times of the danger of a soldier allowing his concentration to fracture under fire. He had to be able to fight without the baggage of internal or emotional conflict. She pressed herself tighter against the stone, watching him desperately, praying he knew she would stay put as he warned her to.

He smiled softly, approvingly, then disappeared from sight as a tear fell from her eye.

* * * * *

Callan could smell them despite the camouflaging scent they stupidly thought would mask their presence from him. There was no way to hide the stink of sweat and the desire to kill. They were good, he gave them that. Had it not been for the smell, he would have never known they were there before he heard the shuffle of feet. And that would have been masked by his own rush through the corridor. The men sent after him were well trained and determined. A hazard.

Taber and Tanner were still on the other side of the caves ensuring Sherra and Doc Martin's escape. There would be no help there. Only God knew where Dayan was. As usual, he had disappeared when trouble came calling. There were three of the soldiers waiting for him in the small cave where the corridor emptied out. The good thing was that they seemed to think they would hear him in time to react. They weren't hidden, rather in plain sight.

Callan slid a hunting knife from the sheath at his thigh, palmed it carefully, then stepped into view. The weapon went flying into the shoulder of the man whose weapon came up first. He dropped to the ground as Callan turned his gun on the other two, another knife whipping from sheath to hand and flying to the arm of another.

"I don't want to kill you bastards, but I will," he announced softly, his gun trained on the injured, more than surprised soldiers. He looked to the last one left standing, watching coldly as the man held his hands carefully at shoulder height.

"We're not here to kill you, Lyons. We just want the girl." The surprising statement had Callan growling low, dangerous.

"Why would you want the girl?" he asked him softly.

The soldier shrugged. "Council orders. They didn't give a shit about you on this one."

Could the Council know? How could they have known unless Kane had relayed the call to them?

"Throw me the restraints." Callan indicated the plastic ties the soldier carried in his belt.

He moved carefully. Callan saw the bunch of his muscles, the intent in his eyes. He pulled the last knife, aiming it as the soldier stilled.

"The next bastard who tries gets it in the heart," he warned them. "Now do as I said, real damn careful."

The restraints landed at his feet. He threw two back to the standing soldier.

"Take care of your buddies." He watched impassively as the ties were placed over the soldiers' wrists then jerked tight, but not tight enough to restrict blood flow. "Sit down. Hands behind your back." Callan waved the gun at him, indicating the floor.

They sighed and did as he ordered.

"Why do they want the girl?" He repeated the question as he restrained the soldier, then placed the straps on the feet of all three men. "And answer me this time or you'll shed blood, too."

He could hear the gnash of teeth. They had been taken out efficiently, easily. It wouldn't look good on their records.

"All I have are the orders." The soldier shrugged, his weather beaten face resigned. "We don't know why they want her. Just that she's your woman, and they now consider her Council property."

Rage burned in Callan's stomach. Council property. Disposable merchandise. If they knew Merinus was his woman then her life was in more danger than his was at the moment. He moved around the men, pulling lethal knives from hidden sheaths and boot straps. Little daggers came from under shirt collars and shoved in sheaths beneath shirtsleeves. There were a million places to hide a weapon and he could only hope he found those the soldiers carried.

"When did the order go through?" Callan asked him, his voice hard.

"Late last night. We were rushed in on a Council jet and brought here."

"Where were you rushed from?"

The soldiers grunted. "Now, Callan, you know better than that shit."

They wouldn't tell, they never did.

"You made a mistake."

"Naw, you did when you killed the last team," the soldier told him quietly. "They reported your rescue of the girl, when they showed up dead, you proved she was more than just a nosy journalist. You should have known better, man."

Callan took a deep breath. He didn't know this soldier, but he was like all those he had known. They knew what he was, who created him. They knew the main goal was capture, but the Council would accept his death if there was no other way. And now, they knew about Merinus.

"Tell the Council and your buddies, playtime is over," Callan told him quietly as he moved back to the corridor entrance. "I won't be playing anymore. I'll be killing."

He paused, listening carefully. He could smell Merinus' fear, and the beginning lust in her body. Damn, he wasn't moving fast enough. He had to get her to safety, fast.

"Merinus," he called out to her softly.

She rushed to him, her hands reaching out to the broad palm he extended to her. He wrapped his arm around her, watching the soldier carefully. The man's eyes went immediately to the mark on Merinus' neck.

"Shit, you mated her." The soldier shook his head as he watched Callan wrap his arm around her body, censure lining his voice. "You may as well kill her now, man. She'll never survive the tests those bastards force on her when they catch her."

Callan felt Merinus jerk in fear.

"Shh, say nothing," he warned her, his breath at her ear. "Let's get out of here."

He moved her through the cavern, careful to skirt around the soldiers. They were well trained and still more than dangerous, even restrained. If they got their hands on

Merinus, they could easily use her to force his compliance in any area and he knew it.

Dawn was barely peeking over the ridge as he moved her through the forest. The soft chirps of morning, the sounds of animals awakening, feeding, moving about freely assured him that the danger had yet to stalk them too close. He had to get her out of the area and to the Jeep he kept carefully hidden. Even the others had no idea of some of the safeguards he had in place. That Jeep, carefully hidden and packed for emergencies, would get them far enough away for him to ensure Merinus' safety and to pay her brother back for his betrayal of her.

He had to get her to one of the safe houses though. Already her body was heating, needing his, just as he was beginning to need her. Even in the danger of the moment, he could feel his need for her pulsing in his blood.

"How did they know about the mating?" she questioned him as they moved through the thick growth of forest, following what appeared to be little more than an animal trail.

"My ignorance." He sighed regretfully. His mistakes were going to end up costing him the life of the woman who was beginning to mean everything to him.

"You didn't do anything," she argued breathlessly, but she still kept up with his fast pace. He had to get her as far from the damned cavern as possible before those soldiers got free and managed to call their buddies.

"The mark on your neck, the fact that I touched you. Pulled you into my arms," he said roughly. "I rarely touch, and only during the actual fuck do I embrace a woman. They know this. The soldiers know everything about my DNA, my training, my habits. I gave us away."

He was filled with self-disgust and impotent anger. He had made his first mistake in killing the soldiers. He had never gone searching for them, and only killed when given no other choice. He should have known the bastards had reported Merinus and her probing questions to the Council. He should have thought, dammit, rather than letting fury guide his actions. The animalistic urge to protect and shelter, to retaliate against any danger to his woman had rode him hard, even then. It was getting worse. It had been all he could do to keep from killing those men in the cave. Only his knowledge of Merinus' reaction to it had swayed him from doing it. Her emotional connection to him wouldn't have survived the bloodshed.

CHAPTER TWENTY

Sherra stood silently in the shadows of the motel, watching carefully, her eyes narrowed as the nine men parted company and went to their respective rooms. They were furious, but one was coldly dangerous. She had watched them at the airport after dropping Doc off at the safe house, then followed them to Sandy Hook and watched as they checked in.

Kane didn't remind her of Merinus in any way. He was darker haired, the color nearly black, with intense, cold blue eyes. His strong jaw and high cheekbones gave a hint to Native American ancestry, his hard, graceful body hinted at extensive military training. She knew the look, the way a killer moved. She had grown up among them, been raped by them more than once. But this one, she knew personally.

This man had brought her pleasure. Despite her pleas, despite her wishes to the contrary, he had taken her beneath the unfeeling eye of a camera, riding her from one climax to the next, his lust fueled by hers, and hers by his touch.

Had it only been seven years ago? Sweet heaven, that night tormented her, even now, as though it had happened only yesterday. The dark soldier who had sworn to help her, to rescue her. He had come to her, holding freedom in one hand, her heart in the other, and spent the night teaching her the pleasures of her woman's body. When he left, he never returned. But the doctors had. With the video, snickering, jeering at the things Kane Tyler had done to her, that she had done to him, all in the name of science. Rape had not impregnated her. They had wondered if pleasure would.

Her hands clenched into fists of rage as he lingered outside his room, lazily finishing a cigarette he had lit moments earlier. She wanted to kill him now. She had sworn she would kill him if she ever found him again. Sworn she would see to it that he paid for every moment of pain she suffered all those years ago. She had sworn he would pay for lying to her, and for doing it so easily without her knowledge. He had betrayed her, just as he had betrayed his sister.

His expression hardened when the last door finally closed and he was left alone with her.

"Where's Merinus?" His voice was savage, pulsating with a fury that sent a fission of unease down her body. "And why the fuck weren't we met at the airport as promised."

"I have a better question," she said from the safety of the shadows. "Why would a brother betray a sister he swears to love on the eve of promised help?"

He turned around slowly, casually, until he was facing her. She saw hard purpose in his face, and surprise.

"What the hell are you talking about?"

"A full team of soldiers swept over Callan's house. A dozen men. All I know for sure is that they didn't get him or Merinus. But I know they want her. They know about her."

"Know what, for God's sake?" He raked his fingers through his hair, his voice quiet but rough with fury. "Why the hell would they attack now?"

"They know your sister has mated with Callan," she told him carefully. "Just as you knew."

Or had he? She watched his face pale alarmingly, his blue eyes widening.

"That bastard touched her?" he snarled.

"No," she drawled mockingly. "He mated with her. Surely you remember the concept? And now the Council no longer cares if they take him alive or dead. They want the woman and any child she carries. But you already knew that, didn't you, Mr. Tyler? Why else would they attack mere hours after talking to you?"

He shook his head slowly.

"I never betrayed my sister. I wouldn't." His voice sent a chill over her spine.

Sherra frowned.

"I came to kill you, Kane Tyler," she said carefully.

He didn't seem surprised now. His mouth edged with mockery.

"Perhaps you could delay that little attempt long enough for me to save my sister's ass," he suggested. "What the hell is this mating shit?"

"Later," she growled. "Now is not the time for explanations. Now is the time for you to tell me how the Council learned of the mating, if Merinus didn't tell you of it."

And Sherra was nearly certain he hadn't known. He was a liar, but in this one instance, he was telling the truth. Her gifts had grown through the years, with maturity and desperation. She could now smell a lie as others could diseased trash.

"Who are you?" His voice sizzled. "And you're going to have to be a little more forthcoming than you are, woman. I can't help Merinus or Callan with so little information."

Taking a deep breath, Sherra stepped from the shadows. She watched his eyes widen, saw the suspicion turn to knowledge.

"You weren't killed," he whispered, blinking, trying to assure himself she was there.

Bitterness filled her with a wave of pain so intense, she threatened to drown beneath it.

"No, lover, I wasn't killed. But that doesn't mean you have much longer to live."

And Sherra faced her past as she never had before. Nightmares and broken hopes fragmented around her, drawing her soul into a bleak, dark void she feared she could never escape. She felt the surging lust, the need, just as Callan and Merinus knew it, thundering through her blood, through her very being. Before her stood the man who had betrayed her years before. In a bleak, cold lab, his body laboring over her, throwing her into pleasure despite every barrier she put up against it. Her mate. The father of the child she had lost. The one man she had sworn to kill.

* * * * *

It was dark before Callan made it to the hidden Jeep. The precautions he insisted on taking and the rough terrain they were going through had turned a half-day's hike into a full day's. He pushed Merinus into it, cranked the engine with a prayer, then a sigh of relief when it turned over easily. Pulling out of the small, deserted shed at the edge of a logging camp he started down the road at an easy pace.

Merinus was lying in the back seat, tired, drained from the run and the drugged lust raging through her body. Callan had quickly replaced his camouflaged T-shirt with a plain white cotton shirt. His hair was pushed beneath a baseball cap, and his gun lay in easy reach. The drive to the next town wasn't far and if he stayed on the main road, well away from the paths he was known to take, then he might get out of this relatively unscathed.

His safe house was tucked away several hours from his home. On the edge of a large town, unassuming, with only a few neighbors and it was fully stocked. He could hide there long enough to figure out what the hell had happened.

He pulled into the garage hours later, sighing wearily as the garage door closed automatically behind them. Merinus had slipped into a restless sleep earlier. She whimpered occasionally, shifted around, but the weariness dragging at her body had been too much.

"Are we there?" She rose slowly from the seat, her voice drowsy, aroused. God, he wanted her.

She was ready for him, her body wet for him. He took a steadying breath. He had to get her in the house first.

"Come on." He jumped from the Jeep then helped her out, lifting her carefully into his arms and stalking to the door.

"I can walk," she protested, but she pressed herself closer, her mouth finding the warm skin of his neck as he fit the key into the lock.

"And I can carry you," he told her, feeling something in his chest tighten as he held her close.

The house was dark, silent. He flipped on low lights as he walked into the kitchen, inhaling carefully to be certain no surprises awaited. All he detected was the closed scent of the house and hot, wet woman.

"Hungry?" He stepped into the living room, placing her on the couch as he stepped back.

She raked her fingers through her hair as she stared up at him.

"Yeah. And a shower. I need a shower bad," she sighed. "Where are we?"

"Other side of Ashland," he told her quietly. "Come on, I'll show you where the shower's at so you can bathe. I'll use the other one and get dinner together when I'm finished. It won't take long."

He led her to the master bedroom. The heavy wood furniture and spotless appearance gave it an impersonal feel. He never cared much for the place, but the very fact that it was the opposite of what he would have personally chosen made it that much safer.

"Go on." He nodded to the large master bath and its garden tub. "I'll lay a shirt out for you to wear. I'll use the other bathroom."

She turned to him, her eyes heavy lidded, weariness dragging at her, and she was still the most beautiful woman he had ever laid eyes on. He lifted his hand to smooth his fingers over her cheek, staring down at her, longing for her. Only the fact that she was worn to the bone, tired and hungry, kept him from putting her on that big, unused bed and pounding into her.

She pressed her cheek to his fingers, a smile lifting the corners of that pouting mouth."

"Take your time." Callan bent to her, his lips whispering over hers in a gentle kiss. "I'll go ahead and start supper after my shower. I'll come up for you when it's done."

"I love you, Callan."

His heart broke. He felt it shatter, the pieces slamming into his soul as she stared up at him, her eyes slumberous, her body filled with need, her life in more danger than she could know, and still she whispered those words to him.

He closed his eyes, wanting to block the site of it from his mind, from the beast that howled out in misery.

"No," he whispered, shaking his head. They were already bound, forever tied together in their need for each other, in the danger that stalked them. This burden he could not face.

She felt his fingers on her lips. They trembled. He opened his eyes and saw the tear that fell from one eye. It eased over her cheek, bleak and lonely as it made a track through the dust and grime on her face from their run through the mountain.

"Yes." Her voice shook as she fought more tears.

He wanted to scream out at the injustice of it. At the laugh fate was having on him. In one hand lay all his dreams. In the other lay his death.

He pulled her to him, crushing her against his chest as he fought his own tears, the cries of the beast suffering within him.

"I just wanted you to know, Callan, even before the mating, I loved you. When you were just a picture, a story, a man I couldn't stop dreaming about." Her words pierced his heart. "I don't want us to die without you knowing that I love you. That I loved you even before you touched me."

Callan shuddered. His arms tightened around her, his face burying in her neck. His lips pressed to the small wound there where his teeth kept going during the height of their passion.

"When I first saw you, you were standing in that greasy parking lot of the station, wearing those damned jeans and that shirt that flashed your stomach," he said hoarsely. "My cock damned near came out of my jeans, and my heart bled. Because I was looking at the woman I would have taken for my own, if my life were my own."

His life wasn't his own, but she was. Nature had taken the choice from him. And it would kill him if he failed to protect her. Callan knew the chances of protecting her were growing slimmer by the day. The Council knew about her now. They knew about the mating.

He pulled back, unable to bear their touch any longer, unable to bear the uncertain future staring him in the face. Damn their souls to hell, Merinus was better off dead then risking her life this way. She didn't have a chance. Eventually, they would get her. Just as they always captured him. Eventually. He turned from her, heading for the bedroom door.

"Bathe," he whispered, his voice tight, the ache in his soul nearly strangling him. "I'll have something to eat soon."

He heard her sigh behind him. A lost, aching sigh that speared through him, hurting him more than he was already hurting. She was so innocent. Too damned innocent for the horrors awaiting them. How could he assure her safety? What could he do to keep the degradation and pain he knew she would suffer from her future?

Go in as she asked? That question haunted him. He could bear the humiliation, the tabloid stories and the judgments against him. He could risk the chance he would be branded sub-human for her safety. If it brought her safety. If her brother had been the one to betray her, then it wouldn't. But, if his other suspicions held true, then it wasn't her brother at all.

Weariness pulled at him, hopelessness beat a discordant note in his brain. It had been there in the cave with those soldiers. An elusive scent nearly hidden by the stink of men of evil. He hadn't noticed it at first, and only later, after Merinus fell asleep in the Jeep had it come to him. There had been the smell of another, a man who wasn't with the soldiers, a man Callan knew well. His chest tightened with that knowledge, despite his need to deny it.

That sheltered cave was not used for a reason. It was barely known, even to the residents of that area of the mountains. And none knew of the linking caverns, for Callan had closed them off years before. He stripped quickly, adjusting the water and stepping beneath the spray. He wanted to wash away the memories of horror and pain, but it wasn't possible. He wanted to wash away the evil of his conception, the stench of the crime against humanity that they had used him to commit, but once again, he could not. All he could do was wash away the grime of yet another desperate flight to safety, and pray to God he was wrong about his betrayer. Enough blood stained his hands and his soul, he didn't want to compound his past sins with the sin of killing one of the few people he loved.

"Callan." He jerked in surprise as a silhouette appeared outside the glass door.

Shapely, small and fragile, Merinus stood outside the steamy chamber, her voice hesitant, beckoning. He opened the door, sliding it across the tracks until he could see her. She was radiantly naked, hope and need glistening in her eyes.

"Merinus," he sighed, shaking his head.

"I need someone to wash my back." She held up her washcloth, her expression hopeful, her body aroused.

Would he ever be able to deny the scent of her need? Callan knew he couldn't. He never would. It was as intoxicating to him as his taste was to her. He stood beneath the water, feeling it caress his skin with its heat, and knowing it was nothing compared to the heat to be found within her body.

"I'll fuck you," he groaned.

She smiled sadly, stepping into the cubicle with him, closing the door behind her.

"And I'll love you," she whispered.

Her hands went to his chest, smoothing over his skin, her fingertips testing the muscle beneath. Taking the washrag from her, he dropped it carelessly on the small shower shelf beside him. He watched as her eyes closed, the water cascading over her hair, her pale face. She luxuriated in the heat of the water, moving her head to allow it to soak every strand.

"Let me wash you then, beauty," he told her, his voice soft. Too soft for his own peace of mind. How he wanted her. His body ached with his need, both physical and emotional.

Into his cupped palm he deposited a generous amount of shampoo and began to work it into her hair. His fingertips caressed her scalp, drawing the wet silk through them, stroking the tender skin of her head. She moaned in pleasure, her body brushing against his as she leaned into his chest, her tongue washing over his flat male nipple with slow sensuality.

His body tightened, growing hotter by the second. He moved her beneath the spray once again, watching as suds rinsed from her hair, rolled slowly over her shoulders, her full breasts. Caressing her as he wanted to caress her. Kissing her skin with satin softness, hiding the hardness of her rosy nipples for the briefest second. When the last of the suds had washed away, he retrieved the soap from the shelf. He left the washrag. He wanted nothing but the smooth slide of suds between his hands and her flesh.

He worked the soap between his hands as he stared down at her. Her eyes were passion glazed, her body trembling with weariness and passion.

"You're eating before you go to sleep," he told her softly, an involuntary smile edging his mouth.

The smile disappeared when he touched her. She gasped, arching against the hands that cupped her breasts, the fingers that gripped her nipples. Slowly, inch-by-inch he covered her body with creamy lather until he was kneeling at her feet, pressing her legs apart, his fingers running over the slick flesh of her smooth pussy.

"I love the way you touch me," she gasped as his fingers began to stroke her, wash her. Suds rolled down her thighs, mixed with the heady scent of her feminine need.

Callan laid his head against her abdomen, one arm wrapping around her upper thighs as he held her steady, the other parting her legs further. He had to taste her. He could wait no longer. His tongue swiped through the satiny folds, then curled around her swollen clit.

She shuddered in his grasp. Her hands dug into his hair, holding onto him as he teased the little bud with soft strokes, careful to keep the rougher portion of his tongue well away from it. With only the tip he stroked around her clit, feeling her shudder, her stomach contract. He sucked it into his mouth then, applying just enough pressure to have her grinding her hips against him, her needy moans filling the shower stall as he teased her.

"Callan, please." She bucked against his mouth as he pressed her against the wall, then lifted her thigh to his shoulder.

She screamed out as his tongue speared into her. Deep, hard, spreading the muscles of her vagina as he sought the addicting taste of her desire. The fingers of one hand continued the teasing strokes against her clit as he ignored her demand for instant gratification. He didn't want to rush this, he wanted to savor the taste and the touch of her.

He licked at her gently then, moaning as her juices coated his tongue and his lips. So ready for him. She wept for him, pleaded with him, her muscles clenching on his invading tongue as she reached for the release she would only ever attain with him.

"Mine," he groaned against the folds of flesh, licking in swifter, firmer strokes.

"Mine," she cried out, her hands clenching in his hair, her voice wild with her need to climax. "Always mine."

And he was. Hers. She was his. He came to his feet, lifting her to him, pushing between her thighs, his cock plunging inside her in one quick stroke that took him to the hilt. Callan gritted his teeth at the fiery pleasure that washed over his body. She was tight, gripping him in a silken fist so damned hot it took his breath.

A wail of pleasure sounded from her lips. She tightened, rocked against him. He pulled back and thrust hard again. She climaxed instantly, her release raining over his erection, destroying his self-control. He held her close in his arms, his hips powering into her then as he fought to get deeper, closer. God help him, she was all that mattered to him now. Being inside her, heart, soul, body. This was all he dreamed of and more than he had ever believed possible.

Stroking desperately inside her, he heard her building moans of renewed need, felt the emergence of the barb and knew ecstasy was only seconds away. He held her tighter, thrust harder, faster. Merinus tightened in his arms once again and as his cock lodged deep, his seed spurted into her, he heard her scream and felt her climax rush over her for the second time. And in her arms, for those few endless seconds, he found peace.

CHAPTER TWENTY-ONE

They stayed buried in the house for two days while Callan paced the floors and checked the hidden email account he had. Everyone had checked in. They were secure but two of the messages had his instincts raring in self-defense. The first from Dayan, swearing Kane and the Tyler men were seen meeting with the soldiers, coordinating a search for Callan that covered every inch of the mountains. The other from Sherra, informing him that she and a relative were desperately searching for them to relay information. He cursed violently when that email came through. He told her to stay put, to put off the meeting with Kane Tyler. Why had she taken this into her own hands? And who was lying? Sherra or Dayan? For the first time since their births Callan began to question the loyalty of the Pride.

"Is everything okay?" Merinus stood between the kitchen and the living room, watching him in concern.

Her hair was tangled around her face, drowsiness still flushed her skin. He had left her sleeping in the bed hours before after another bout of sex that damned near left him drained.

She was dressed in one of his T-shirts. The hem of the blue cotton covered her thighs and hung on her slender shoulders. The intimacy of her wearing his clothing left a gut punch of desire that he couldn't deny. Possession, raw and hot flared in him. His woman.

"Everything's fine," he assured her quietly, unwilling to worry her further.

He saw the concern in her eyes though, and knew he hadn't fooled her. Their lives were hanging by a thread now, the dangers inherent in the situation terrified him. Merinus had no scope of the evil that inhabited the Council and he prayed she never learned.

"We need to contact Kane, Callan," she broached the one subject he wasn't willing to discuss yet. "He's going to be worried out of his mind. That's not a good thing, either."

He could see her absolute belief in her brother reflected in her expression. She thought of her family before she thought of herself. She trusted them when she could trust no one else, especially that damned soldier brother of hers.

"I have to be certain he didn't betray us first, Merinus." He shook his head, staring back at Sherra's email.

He could assume the betrayal came from Kane, or from one of his own. Which was more likely to want to see him and Merinus captured or dead?

"Kane wouldn't betray me, Callan," she told him quietly.

There was no anger in her tone, no doubt. She trusted her brother implicitly.

"How can you be so certain, Merinus?" He sighed roughly. "The attack came hours after your call to him."

"I know because I know Kane." She shook her head, moving further into the room.

She went to the couch near him, sat down and regarded him solemnly.

"Kane went ape shit when Dad showed him the box your mother had sent to him on her death," she revealed.

"I don't know why, but I know he was hurt. Hurt and angry, but not at you. He spent months gathering evidence, working to reveal the Council members. He has a list from your shoulder to your elbow and a stack of proof against them that would terrify you."

Callan narrowed his eyes on her.

"Why didn't you tell me this before?" he asked her.

"I tried to tell you, but you never wanted to hear it." She rolled her eyes at his abrupt question. "I told you we had everything taken care of. Did you think I would lie to you?"

"The hell if I knew what to think then, or now," he grunted, shutting down the email program and pacing the floor. "I know we've been betrayed by someone close to us, and accusing your brother is a hell of a lot easier than the alternative." Better than believing that one of his own would do it.

He couldn't get the thought out of his head that one of his own had betrayed him, or the memory of that scent in the caves, lingering on the flesh of the soldier.

"Who is the alternative?" Merinus asked him carefully. "Callan, Kane didn't know we had mated, or whatever this is. He wasn't even certain we were having sex. He suspected it, but he didn't know it was anything deeper."

"He would have known." Callan frowned. He knew Kane had at least suspected that his sister was too emotionally involved with her lover to leave. The Council would have suspected the rest based on that.

Merinus sighed. "Maybe he would have, but he wouldn't have betrayed me or you. He's put too much into this, taken too many risks himself."

"Why?" Callan snapped. "Why would he do this, just for a story? He didn't need anything more than the proof Maria had to run it."

Merinus bit her lip thoughtfully.

"I don't know why," she finally admitted. "All I know is that he did. And I know he's been very upset since this came about, almost obsessed with it. He wouldn't betray you, not just because of the risk to myself, but because of whatever is driving him as well."

Callan growled low in his throat.

"That is such a sexy sound." He turned in surprise at the aroused amusement in her voice.

She was watching him, her body relaxed for a change, her head tilted thoughtfully.

"What is?" he asked her carefully.

"That growl in your voice," she said, watching him with heavy lidded desire. "It makes me shiver, makes my body want to rub over all yours."

Her heat wasn't upon her yet. He smelled the air carefully. The scent of warm, willing woman was there, but not the desperate lust he was used to smelling when she wanted him. Callan watched her carefully, seeing nothing in her expression that would indicate that the chemically induced needs were riding her. There was no smell of it on the air, no desperation or tense muscles showing that would hint at her need.

There was something elusive, though. Like the faintest fragrance of spring. He admitted to being more than a little confused now.

"Why are you looking at me like that?" She pushed her fingers through her hair, attempting to restore it to order. She still looked sexy and tousled though, warm and beckoning.

"You want me." He was more than a little amazed by that fact.

"Well, duh," she gave him a look that suggested she was beginning to suspect his intelligence. "Just figure that one out, Sherlock?"

Callan frowned.

"Woman, you are a snide creature." He allowed the rumble in his chest to echo in his voice.

Her face flushed, but her expression showed her knowledge that he was tempting her.

"I'm a bitch." She was clearly laughing at him. "Ask Kane, he'll tell you."

The mention of her brother sobered him. He tucked his hands in the pockets of his jeans and paced to the window that he kept covered with heavy curtains. He didn't look out. There was no need to. There was enough wildlife in the area that if he were being stalked here, he would know it. The birds would stop singing, and the frogs would ease their early evening serenade.

"Do you have a way of contacting him, other than the cell phone?" he asked her.

She sighed, sobering. She was filled with laughter and hope, despite their circumstances. Her innocence amazed and terrified him.

"No, not really." He glanced back as she shrugged. "Kane secured the phones we were using before I left so the calls couldn't be hacked or traced. Both units have an indicator on them, in case the impossible happens and someone locks onto the channel. He took every precaution with them."

Merinus' unit was tucked in his pack. He had felt the vibration of it earlier in the morning when he had dug out the ammunition for his pistol.

"Either your brother or mine has betrayed us," he told her, watching her face go blank with shock. "We're in trouble here, Merinus. The Council knows I've mated with you; they will stop at nothing to take you now. They did everything to breed us while we were in captivity, thinking our children would be easier to control than we were. If they take you, then they have me willingly, and they know that."

He watched the fear that washed over her face. She swallowed tightly, her hands gripping the material of the shirt at her waist, her fingers turning white with the tension that invaded her body.

"What do we do?" she asked him.

He breathed out roughly. "I have two choices, neither are secure. We could leave the country and disappear, but that's not a guarantee they won't find us. We'll never be truly safe and neither will our children. Or I could trust your family and do as you came to ask me to do, but still, no guarantee. Both choices are rife with danger, Merinus. There will be no peace for us, whichever way we go."

Hope filled her expression. She had such belief in her brothers and her father that she thought they could solve any problem. He wondered what it would have been like to be raised in such a secure, protective environment. To have such faith in someone other than yourself.

"Kane knows what he's doing, so do the others, Callan," she promised him desperately. "I have seven brothers, each one of them has been working on this for over six months now. Gray is with the FBI, Caleb is a private investigator, Kane has all kinds of contacts in the C.I.A. and across seas. They have boxes of proof, but need you to back it up. You can do this, Callan. We can do it together."

Her expression was beseeching, her eyes wide and so filled with confidence. This time in him. She watched him as though he could solve this problem by his will alone. He wanted to curse her innocence, but found himself desperate to believe in it as well. Surely, it couldn't be so simple. After years of running, decades of doubt and hopelessness, could it really be so easy? Of course it couldn't, but what choice did he have left?

"We will wait one more day," he finally sighed, glancing back at the computer, the emails he had received bothering him more than he wanted to admit. Tanner and Taber had done a copy of theirs to each of the others of the Pride. Sherra had not. The email had come singly and carefully coded. She trusted no one now, except Kane Tyler and himself.

"I believe Dayan has betrayed me," he finally told her softly. "His scent was in the cave and on the soldiers within it. He knew of the mating and has been furious over it. His instability may have driven him over the edge."

He hid his rage, his pain. If Dayan had betrayed the Pride, then it would fall to Callan to kill him. Dayan would become the hunted, something Callan swore the others would never be again.

"Callan." Merinus came to her feet, her expression bleak, filled with pain for him.

He shook his head, moving away from her. He didn't want her tenderness right now, not while he was filled with this rage.

"I took them out and covered their escapes with the deaths of scientists, soldiers and doctors," he whispered. "The screams of the dying still echo in my ears, the deaths of the babes incubating in their tubes still tear at my conscience." He dragged his hands through his hair, fighting the years-old horror and regret.

"You did what you had to do, Callan." She gave him total acceptance, when he didn't even have that for himself.

"I swore they would never be hunted again," he whispered, fighting the ragged wound opening up in his soul. "I would not like to hunt my brother, Merinus. To know that the beast overcame him does not give hope for the rest of us."

"Are you serious?" Incredulous anger colored her tone. He turned to her in surprise.

Her hands were propped on her hips, her brows drawn into a frown as she stared at him as though he had lost his mind.

"In what way?" he asked her carefully. Damn, she could be mercurial.

"The beast overcoming him?" She snorted in a less than ladylike fashion. He could likely blame Kane for that habit. "More likely his human nature coming out. Dammit, Callan, animals do not betray each other. Check out the Discovery Channel a little more often. You need to research, hon. Only humans sell each other out, only humans kill for no reason. It would say that perhaps

Dayan got a little more human coding than the rest of you did."

She crossed her arms over her breasts, staring him down as though he were a child in need of a lecture. Where was this woman's fear? Her respect? Even the scientists had shown him greater fear.

He lifted a brow at her. She didn't understand what the scientists had created, how they had attempted to train them. He could forgive her the ignorance, he decided.

"Oh, look at that brow arching," she said mockingly. "Lion-O thinks he knows better."

Callan clenched his teeth.

Merinus threw her hands up in defeat.

"Fine, believe what you want to," she snapped. "Just like a man, you will anyway. But I'm telling you right now, and you'll find out I'm right, Callan Lyons, Dayan is a typical psychopath. It's there in those beady little eyes of his. I never did trust him."

"There is such a thing as a typical psychopath? Did you see this on the Discovery Channel as well, darling?"

Her eyes widened at the little dig, her head tilting, considering.

"I'm sure it aired and I'm certain I'm right. I have a brother that's into pop psychology, he would know all about it and I'm sure he would agree with me."

Figured. Was there anything those brothers of hers didn't do? And did they ever disagree with the little imp standing across from him? It occurred to him that she might be just a bit spoiled by those brothers of hers.

"So what are you going to do?" There went those hands on those slender hips again.

Her breasts pushed out against the T-shirt, the hard nipples like a beacon to his eyes. How was a man supposed to think when confronted with such a sight?

"I told you, I will decide by tomorrow," he growled, fighting a lust that had nothing to do with any scent of need coming from her body. For a change, the lava hot scent was barely present. What he detected now though, was much more destructive. A woman irritated, angry, and just plain, pure aroused. His cock throbbed.

"Well, you know what I think. Now I'm going to go take a bath and you can sit here and brood all you want to. Then I'll fix dinner. I make a great pasta salad."

She swept from the room before he could snarl. Pasta salad? He didn't think so.

CHAPTER TWENTY-TWO

Merinus made her pasta salad to accompany Callan's steaks and baked potatoes. They ate silently, then cleaned the kitchen together. Pouring her a glass of wine, Callan led her back to the living room.

His silence wasn't nerve wracking. Merinus could tell he was thinking, weighing the options they had. Not that she saw many options. Kane was going to have to be called, whether he liked it or not. Her family was their only hope.

She sat on the couch while he paced the room and ignored the heat building between her thighs. She more than admitted that the normal desire she felt for him was bad enough, but this building tension, this wildness that seemed to get worse with each fucking was making her crazy.

"Take off the shirt." His voice was strained, rough with his demanding sexuality.

Merinus glanced up in surprise as he stalked toward her. His movements slow and graceful, the jeans hugging the bulge between his thighs that seemed to grow larger as he came closer.

His expression was intent, almost feral. His eyes were bright, glowing in the deep tan of his face. Merinus felt her heart beat quickly, her breathing becoming deep and rough as she licked her lips in anticipation. This would be a mating. The times before had been sheer lust, an easing of the burning fire that raged between them. But this time would be different—she could feel it.

She crossed her arms over her chest, drawing the shirt over her head with a languid movement as she lifted her legs to the couch, leaving them slightly bent, closed. She wouldn't submit to him easily. For a moment, it worried her, the feeling that rushed over her body. She felt almost animalistic, the need for him going beyond simple desire, her determination to hold her own with him rising as hot as her lust.

He stopped at her feet, his eyes narrowing as his hand went to the snaps of his jeans. Merinus' hands went to her breasts; she cupped them slowly, her fingers teasing her nipples as she arched her breasts towards him. A move meant to tease, to entice. He growled low and deep, his lip lifting in a mild snarl. Merinus smiled at him, her eyelids lowering as she licked her lips with her damp tongue, watching as the thick, proud length of his cock emerged from the opening of his jeans.

"Open your thighs," he ordered her, the grumble of his voice a sensual rasp over her nerve endings.

Merinus rose to her feet instead. She wouldn't give him anything willingly this time. If he wanted her, if he wanted to take her, make her his, then he would have to fight for it. Where the wildness came from, she didn't know. What made it rise like a demand in her body, she wasn't certain. But it was there and refused to be denied.

"You aren't undressed yet," she said a bit coyly. "Would you take me still dressed, with your cock the only bare skin touching me?"

His eyes followed her movements carefully.

"I'm on the edge, Merinus," he warned her, his voice dark. "This demon has risen too quickly, too hard inside me. Lie down and don't fight me. I don't want to hurt you."

She tossed him a look over her shoulder as she skirted a wide path around him.

"Perhaps you're the one who will end up hurt," she suggested, her voice low, pulsing with the arousal of this new and intriguing desire rising inside her. "Why should I submit? You lie down, and allow me to have my way with you."

Her hand smoothed over her buttock as she passed by him, well out of arm's reach. The sensation of her own hand against her buttocks sent a tingle of pure heat rushing over her body. As she watched him over her shoulder, she drew her nails across her skin, knowing she left the soft blush of the abrasion.

His face flushed, his eyes glittered. He moved without rushing, stripping his jeans from his body, the powerful muscles of his legs and thighs tense and hard as he tossed the material to the couch.

"I won't be easy, Merinus," he promised her, moving around behind her, stalking her, his intent clear in his expression.

"Neither will I," she promised him.

She knew before he pounced. She watched the muscles of his chest bunch. An instant before he moved she was streaking for the stairs. She felt her heart pounding harsh and loud in her chest, her blood raging through her body, desire wrapping around them, urging them into a desperate game of domination.

He caught her halfway up the stairs. The heat of his body blanketed hers as he snagged her around the waist, bringing her to a stop, bending her to her knees. Merinus bucked against him. She felt his erection slide between the cheeks of her ass, heating the narrow crevice with his incredible heat. He was thick and hard, and it would be so tempting to tilt her hips and allow him to thrust into the wet, needy channel he sought.

She allowed him to believe that was her intention. She relaxed, moving against him, and when his arms lifted to clasp her hips, she scrambled up the steps. Of course, he only let her go, she wasn't fool enough to believe she had actually escaped.

Merinus glanced back from the landing, watching as he came up the steps behind her. He was moving fast, his expression savage. She sprinted for the bedroom, intent on slamming the door behind her, locking him from her, leaving him only the scent of her incredible lust to beckon him. She made it as far as pushing the door halfway closed, then he was there, pushing past it, slamming it closed behind them.

"Would you like to try hiding under the bed?" he suggested silkily as she backed up from him.

"Would you like to try my knee in your nuts again?" She smiled, watching him almost wince. His face definitely tightened.

"You want me," he accused her with no heat. "I can see your juices gleaming on your cunt."

She licked her lips, running her tongue over them slow and easy as his eyes flared at the action.

"So take it." She shrugged. "If you can."

He smiled.

"You think it will be easy again, Merinus?" he asked her, his voice low and dangerous. "You think it will merely be another hard, fast fuck before my barb anchors me inside you?"

Her vagina clenched in anticipation. But he only shook his head at her.

"Not this time," he warned her. "This time, I will make you submit."

"And just how do you intend to do this?" she questioned him archly.

His hand went to the thrusting flesh of his cock. He stroked it slowly, his movements unhurried.

"When I am done, Merinus, there is not an entrance in that sweet body of yours that I will not have taken." He edged closer as she backed away from him, watching him warily now.

"I will have you on your knees, your lips wrapped around my cock until I cum inside your hot mouth. I'll fuck your lips like I've dreamed of doing since the other night when you stole my control. And when I've given you my first load there, I'll lay you on your stomach, stretch your ass and fuck it until I'm anchored there, filling you with more of my seed. And we both know I'll still be hard when I'm finished." He ignored her widening eyes. She couldn't even imagine him fitting there. "Then, I'll raise your hips and I'll fuck that hot little pussy until you're hoarse from screaming, your body pulsing with so many orgasms you'll beg me to stop."

"Quite an itinerary," she told him sweetly. "You were doing fine until you brought up the anal thing, Callan. We both know it won't fit, so don't make promises you can't keep."

He smiled a second before he rushed her. Merinus had time to squeak out a cry of alarm before he had her on her knees before him. His hands anchored her shoulders, holding her fast despite her struggles. His cock was poised at her lips as one hand left her shoulder to grip her jaw, holding her still.

"You will," he groaned.

The head of his erection pressed against her damp lips, his fingers opened her mouth until he slid home with a low cry. She would suck him, Merinus knew, but his climax would not be easily attained. Not with her. Not yet.

She refused to tighten her lips on him. Her tongue caressed him with slow, easy strokes, her body tightening as his flesh jerked within her mouth. A low, sexy growl filled the silence as he held her head still, his hips pushing against her, then pulling back as he sought relief in the humid depths of her mouth.

The thick shaft stretched her lips, seared her with its heat. She drew on it with a slow, lazy sucking motion of her lips, staring up at him, watching his face contort in pleasure. His hands were in her hair, kneading her scalp; his short nails scraping the skin erotically. Merinus moaned in rising excitement, then felt the shiver that worked over Callan's body at the vibrations against his erection. The mounting tension and excitement was burning her alive.

Merinus felt poised on the edge of an arousal unlike any she had known before. The feel of his thick shaft stroking in shallow thrusts in her mouth, her position, the dominance in him combined to edge the passion higher. His scrotum tightened against the base of his cock and a rough groan of sheer delight whispered over her ears. She licked him like candy, from base to tip. Her lips caressed and stroked, spreading the moisture of her mouth over the heavy veined cock as she sucked it with light pressure.

She refused to tighten her lips. She wanted to tempt and tease. She wanted him wild and hot, wilder than he had ever been before. Her fingers encased the taut sac beneath his throbbing erection, her nails scraping the crease of his thighs, her tongue painting intricate patterns over the flesh of his cock as she ignored his near desperate moans.

"Suck it, Merinus," he growled at her, his hands clenching in her hair. "Damn you, suck it."

She watched him from beneath her lowered lips, tempting him to make her, daring him to punish her. The sexual game was heating up in a new and dangerous way. She felt a measure of nerves at her own actions, but the overriding demand inside her refused to let her give in easily. She circled the head of his cock with her tongue, then stroked the soft, incredibly sensitive area where the barb pulsed just under the skin, threatening to emerge, pleading for the desperate stroke of her mouth to bring it to life.

"This is a dangerous game, baby," he whispered as she smiled up at him.

Merinus felt her uterus contract, felt the slow slide of her juices leak from her cunt. She was wet and burning. Her own orgasm would be only a few strokes away if he were to impale her with the thick, rose-headed weapon she held in her mouth. And what a sensual torture tool it was.

Placing her tongue flat along the rising stiffness, she encased it snugly in her mouth and drew on it again. Slowly. She refused to give into his heated moans.

"Merinus, baby, you're killing me," he panted as her fingers joined the play, caressing and teasing his scrotum with light strokes and gentle rasps of her nails.

His hands kept her in place, refusing now to allow her to draw back, to continue the torture of her tongue swiping over his erection. His thighs were rock hard now, planted wide apart, his hips arching into her suddenly slack mouth.

"Damn you," he growled hoarsely. "You will pay for this, Merinus. Suck my fucking cock."

He pressed the length of his flesh into her mouth, nearly touching her tonsils before she clamped down on it, her teeth rasping the silk encased steel, her mouth enclosing it tight and hot as he began to fuck her with shallow strokes.

"Yeah. Yeah. Like that," he whispered, his voice hard, sounding tortured with pleasure.

He was watching her, his gaze intent as he stroked in and out of her mouth. His eyes were heavy lidded, his face sensually flushed, his lips parted and full as he breathed hard and deep, a growl whispering past his chest every so often. Merinus wrapped her hands around the base of the thrusting weapon, moaning in rising need as she felt the beginning erection of the barb. She would have loosened the pressure then, but Callan's hands were suddenly cupping her cheeks, her jaw.

"No more teasing," he snarled down at her erotically as he pushed his cock dangerously close to her throat.

The threat only incited her desperate lust. She began to suckle him deeper, her tongue caressing it with quick strokes as he began to stroke harder into her mouth. He was wild now, savage in his sexual intensity. The hard angles of his face were pulled into desperate lines as his teeth gritted with the rising need for orgasm. Merinus felt his cock pulse, the barb emerging, stretching the bit of looser skin over it as it began to come fully erect.

The need was on her now. She wanted the taste of him. She wanted to hear his desperate cries as he pulsed and spurted his seed into the waiting depths of her mouth. She wanted to taste him, love him. She wanted to show him, prove to him that she accepted him, all of him, every desire, every act he would have with her.

"Merinus." He was pumping harder, faster, only her hands braced at the base of his thrusting erection kept him from driving it down her throat.

A low, agonized growl tore from his throat as his breathing became harsh and deep. Perspiration dotted his forehead, his hands were back in her hair, clenching in the silken strands. Merinus felt the full erection of the barb, at least half an inch in length, stiff, pulsing. She curled her tongue around him, her body tightening at his animalistic cry as she caressed it, raked it with her tongue. He pushed against her desperately now, his body trembling, lust overtaking him. He was so wild, so desperate for release that when she felt the first hard blast of his semen spurt into her mouth, she heard the loud, feline cry of pulsing satisfaction that was torn from his chest. He climaxed long and hard, filling her mouth with the hard jets of his release.

Merinus still refused to ease the soft strokes of her tongue. His body shuddered each time she licked the head, the throbbing barb, small pulses of his cum tearing from his body with each stroke, for long moments. Finally, the small appendage withdrew once again, but the hard state of his cock remained. He pulled back from her, his eyes wild, his expression savage as he reached down and pulled her quickly to her feet.

"Mine." His voice was rough, demanding in his possession.

She smiled slow, tempting.

"So prove it," she whispered.

CHAPTER TWENTY-THREE

The beast in Callan roared at the challenge that whispered past her lips. He snarled down at her, now past the point where he could be shocked at his own actions. The beast inside him was in control and no matter how hard he tried to fight it now, he could no longer rein it in. And Merinus was tempting it. Deliberately, systematically destroying the control he fought to keep.

He pulled her up, his hands no longer gentle, though he fought to keep from hurting her. He didn't want to hurt her. He didn't want to bruise her delicate skin, but he knew his grip was too harsh as he dragged her against his chest.

Her nipples poked at his flesh. They were hard, hot, tempting. He lowered his head, his lips going for the seductress' smile on hers. He growled when she refused to open to him. His teeth nipped at her. He felt her nails bite into his shoulders, but still she refused him entrance.

"Merinus, do not do this," he pleaded with her, his last reserves of restraint slowly slipping from his grasp as she continued to tease him.

Her lips curved into a small smile, her dark eyes glittering from beneath her lowered lashes as she licked her lips. His hands tightened on her arms. The beast clawed for freedom, raking his loins with a demand he could no longer deny. He jerked her closer, his teeth rougher as he nipped at her lips again, drawing a surprised cry of pleasure from her. That sound gained him entrance.

He slanted his head, grinding his lips on hers as he speared into her mouth. He could feel the glands along his tongue, swollen, the intoxicating hormone of his race ready to release into her system. He stroked her tongue and she refused to play. As with his cock, she refused to draw on him, taking the release into her. She struggled against him, her nails raking his shoulders, though her hips thrust desperately against his shaft as it pressed against her lower stomach.

He drew her tongue into his mouth, his mouth drawing on hers in example, then sent his spearing into her mouth again. A tempting sound of laughter vibrated against his lips as she refused yet again. One hand went to her hair, fisting in the strands, jerking her head back. He knew the light pain warned her of his intent, yet still she refused to draw on his tongue. His savage growl shocked him, as did his actions, but he no longer had even a measure of control to ease his way.

He backed her quickly into the wall, jerking her against him, moving his cock until it raked the tender folds of her soaked pussy. She was so slick and creamy, so hot and tempting he couldn't stop the aroused snarl of pleasure that pulsed through his body. His hands gripped her buttocks, his fingers smearing through the lubricating cream before he eased a finger inside her tight anus.

"Do as I want," he ordered her savagely as she cried out, arching at the small penetration.

"Make me," she dared him again, a siren, a seductress out to destroy.

"Don't do this, Merinus." His finger slid deeper inside her ass, his cock jerking at the tight, heated depths of that channel. "I know more about forcing what I want than you could ever dream. I don't want to hurt you."

She nipped his lips, her lips curving, her gaze beckoning.

"I want all of you. Man and beast," she whispered when he jerked back in surprise from her rough caress. "I won't submit to you any longer."

The beast howled in joy, the man trembled in pleasure.

How long had it been since his passions had been given free rein? He knew it hadn't been since the labs, where the women brought to him were well versed in all manner of painful sexual acts. The beast had raged then, when his sexuality had first been emerging. But not since his escape had he allowed it free again.

"I'll hurt you." His finger drew back, drawing more moisture, then plunging its full length up her ass once again.

Her body arched, her mouth opening on a low scream as she shuddered with the pleasure/pain he brought her.

"You will do as I want, Merinus," he commanded her, his voice a graveled rumble now as man and beast merged. "Do as I wish. Suck my tongue into your mouth."

His tongue throbbed with the need to release its essence into her body. The aphrodisiac would fill both their bodies then, spurring their lusts, releasing the beast from the last fragile bond that held it.

"No," she cried out, her head tossing, her body jerking against him as she fought to accustom herself to the impalement.

"Then I will stop." He eased his finger free of her.

"No. No. Don't stop." She fought to follow the slow retreat, to keep his finger buried within her.

"Do as I ask, Merinus," he ordered against her lips, then his tongue stroked over them, the rough rasp more pronounced now with the hormonal need surging through his body. "Do it, Merinus."

Her head tossed as he rubbed his cock against her clit. He could feel the little pearl trembling against him, swollen, desperate for release.

Her lips ground against his, her mouth accepting his tongue, drawing on it slowly, sensually. The taste of spice filled his senses as she drew the drugging hormone from his tongue. She cried out, her nails piercing his back, her legs tightening around his hips as he plunged his tongue in and out of the silken lips encasing it.

When the glands no longer pulsed, he jerked back from her. She was breathing hard, her breasts rising and falling in hard breaths, her nipples raking his chest, her hips squirming against his as she fought to force his cock inside her hot pussy. She stared up at him, her cheeks flushing as the potency of the hormone began to invade her system. His. She was his woman. His mate. This proved it.

"Mine," he growled again, his hands clenching on the cheeks of her ass as he ground her against the torturously hot shaft that screamed out for relief. "Say it. Tell me you are mine."

She smiled. That smile had his heart nearly bursting from his chest. The mix of tenderness and challenge was nearly more than he could bear.

"You are mine," she whispered.

His eyes narrowed.

"You will say the words before this night ends, Merinus," he swore. "You will scream them to me and beg for me to hear you."

"No, you will scream them for me." Sultry, her voice low and husky, her body hot and wild as she raked her nails down his chest, watching him through half closed eyes.

She was smiling that smile again. The one that had the beast raging, growling low and deep. She licked her lips, spreading the taste of her over them. She wanted to tempt and tease. She wanted to push the beast and shred the control the man had fought for years to attain. So be it. The beast was free. It snarled down at her, not in violence, not in rage. In demand.

He moved then, rubbing her silky, slick folds of skin over his erection as he moved her to the bed. He watched her eyes dilate, her face flush as his hot cock stroked her clit. He heard her breath catch and gloried in it. When he reached the bed he dropped her to it, staring down at her for a long moment. He knew the ways to achieve what he wanted. He could throw her into pleasure so intense, so burning and deep that she would beg him for his possession, beg him to allow her to belong to him. He would show her this night who was master of their bed.

He moved to the nightstand and opened it slowly. He didn't have all the sensual devices in this house as he did at his home, but he always kept on hand a large tube of lubricating jelly. He pulled it out and came back to her.

She glanced at the tube, then at Callan. He returned her stare, moving carefully onto the mattress beside her. Then he flipped her over. He threw one leg over her thighs to hold her in place, his upper body kept her shoulders against the mattress.

"I could tie you down," he whispered, nipping at her neck as she struggled against him. "Restraints can drive the pleasure higher, Merinus. Would you prefer this? Or would you prefer to give me what I wish?"

She was breathing hard and heavy, and just under the scent of her arousal, he could smell her trepidation. She was breathing hard and rough, her body tense as he held her carefully in place for the touch to come. She jerked when his hand smoothed over her buttocks. The rounded pale globes enticed him to caress, to fill his hands with their warmth, and he did just that. Then his fingers traveled through the narrow crease. He smiled in tight anticipation as her breath caught.

"I'm going to take your ass now, Merinus," he breathed against her ear. "I'm going to prepare you carefully and show you how much pleasure the pain of that possession can be. Whenever you are ready to submit, darling, just say the words."

Her protest was a strangled groan as his fingers found the tight little entrance. She was feeling the effects of his kiss now. He could feel her muscles relaxing, despite her attempts to keep it from happening. Flipping open the cap of the lubrication he moved his hand back, spreading the gel in a thick line over his fingers.

"Callan?" Her voice was filled with nerves when his slickened fingers found the tight entrance once again.

Callan lay with his head between her shoulder blades, parting the cheeks of her ass with one hand as his fingers began their sensual invasion. The first finger slid in easily. He heard her moan vibrating at her back as he slid in and out in easy strokes for long moments. Then a second finger joined in the play. She stretched easily for him, her body bucking against him, her skin dampening with perspiration as he held her still. When the third finger joined the first two long moments later, she jerked at the tight fit, the pull of the tender muscles, the burning pleasure he knew that was beginning to invade the tight channel.

"Relax for it, Merinus," he soothed her. "Feel how readily your body accepts it. How easily my fingers slide into you."

He pulled back, then returned with a swift, deep penetration. She nearly screamed with the sensation, pushing back on his fingers, her body trembling with need.

"I can't stand it," she cried out, bucking against him.

"Tell me what I want to hear then," he told her gently, though he knew nothing could save her from the possession to come. It had been more than a decade since he had taken a woman in such a way. He remembered the tight heat, the heady sensation of the forbidden suddenly attainable. Watching his cock sink in, female flesh stretching to take him, accepting this ultimate intimacy.

Merinus was no whore purchased merely for his pleasure, though. She was not practiced, nor well versed in the pleasures and the pain of lust. She was new to this touch and her womanly hesitations only spurred his need higher.

"No." She tossed her head in denial.

"You will not orgasm until I have what I want, Merinus," he promised her, filling her slowly once again. "I know a thousand ways to make you scream for ease. Give in to me now."

He had to have her submission.

"No." Her hips followed his fingers back as he retreated.

The beast snarled out in impatience, the man moved quickly, his fingers retreating, his body moving to straddle her thighs, his cock lodging in the crease of her ass. She gasped at the move, her body tensing in expectation.

"Are you ready, Merinus?" he crooned, his voice gentle despite the sandpapery roughness of the tone. "Are you ready to take me there?"

He stroked his hard flesh along the crease, watching the tight globes part until he found the little pink hole he sought. She jerked against him as he moved between her thighs then, separating them quickly, his hands jerking her hips to the proper position.

She tried to move away from him then. With a lithe, graceful movement, she was nearly out of his arms, rolling to her back and attempting to roll from the bed. Callan laughed in victory as he caught her, dragging her back to the center of the bed, staring into her dilated eyes as he moved between her thighs once again.

"We can do it this way as well," he assured her.

He gripped her ankles, then pulled them to one shoulder, angling her hips to the side. As one hand held them there the other re-positioned his cock. Merinus was breathing hard and heavy, watching him with wide eyes filled with a combination of fear and anticipation. Waiting no longer, he tested the readiness, the slick preparation of the tiny hole then placed the head of his cock at the entrance.

"Submit to me," he ordered her, his body tightening at the thought of the bliss to come.

"Callan," she cried out as his hips lodged the broad head into the tender opening.

"Submit."

"You submit," her cry was a plea for mercy.

He pushed against her, feeling her muscles part, stretch as her trembling moan turned into a low, long cry of building pleasure/pain. Callan clenched his teeth, fighting his overwhelming desire to drive into her flesh. He stroked in slowly instead, watching her eyes widen, feeling her ass clench on his flesh, then he stroked through the tight, resistant ring of muscle that was his last hurdle.

* * * * *

Merinus couldn't scream. She could only stare up at Callan as she fought for breath, feeling the thick length of his cock as it impaled her ass. The pain blended with the pleasure, making her hips buck against him, driving him deeper, keeping her poised on the edge of orgasm as he stretched her, stroking nerve endings she never knew she had.

Her fists were clenched in the blankets, her head tossed as she fought to deny him further.

"Give in," he whispered.

She couldn't give in. Not until he did. Not until he was taking her as she knew he wanted to. Not until all control was gone.

"You give in," she pleaded as he began to stroke slowly inside her.

She couldn't stand it. The sensations were terrifying. The mix of pleasure and pain would kill her. Callan held her legs to his shoulders, parting them, his eyes going to where he invaded her. His face was contorted with absolute animal pleasure. His eyes glowed with it.

His hips moved slow and easy, stroking his cock in and out of her, his scrotum slapping at the cheeks of her ass with every downward stroke. Merinus clenched on him, hearing him growl. She pushed back to him, almost insane now with the need for a deeper, harder stroke.

"More," she finally cried out. "Please, Callan, harder."

"Submit to me." She was more than shocked when his large, broad hand struck the cheek of her ass from the side.

Her eyes widened at the burning pleasure.

"No," she denied him again.

He thrust against her harder, deeper, his hand striking her smooth flesh once again. Merinus cried out, driven nearly to the brink of orgasm with each powerful stroke in her ass, each small slap to her buttocks. She jerked against him, fighting for more, harder. She needed desperately to climax. Her fingers went to her clit, intending to stroke it to release, but Callan laughed. He laughed at her as he gripped her hand, pushing it away.

A groan of frustration tore from her lips. Her head tossed as the pleasurable pain was being stroked in her lower channel, she was crying out on every stroke, almost begging.

"Submit to me," he ordered her again.

His fingers glanced her clit and she bucked. They circled the little pearl, pumping it with easy strokes, but never enough to bring her release. The caress only threw her deeper into the morass of insane arousal. She could feel her cunt clenching, weeping. Her muscles straining for release, her body pleading for it. She shook her head, unable to speak now as she fought for climax.

"You will." His fingers moved as his erection continued to impale her anus.

He spread the lips of her cunt, his eyes narrowed as he kept her legs raised to his shoulders. Then two diabolical fingers plunged inside her.

So close. Her body tightened, orgasm a breath away, and still he wouldn't let her have it. He merely stretched her vagina, filling it, his fingers twisting inside her as she bit her lip and fought her body's demands that she give into him. Give into him now, her body screamed out the demand.

"Mine," he told her again, his eyes narrowed, wild. His face savage as he watched her, teeth clenched on a snarl as he allowed one more thrust of his fingers.

"Yours," she screamed out to him, desperate now, her body assaulted by so many sensations she knew they would drive her insane. "You're...oh God, Callan, let me—"

His fingers pumped into her hard and fast in a rhythm that matched the cock buried in her ass. She felt the smaller erection emerge, his barb stretching her ass further with a burning pain that tipped her over the edge as she heard him growling in his own release. A second later, she felt the hard blast of his semen spurting inside her, she exploded in such mind consuming pleasure she wondered if she would survive. Over and over again, her cries weak and strained as she clenched on his flesh, on his fingers, her body shuddering violently with the wild release that quaked over her.

And Callan was by no means immune. The beast was loose. He threw back his head and roared his victory over her as the last pulse of his seed shot into her behind. He was lodged deep inside her, his cock jerking, the barb pulsing as it held him locked to her. His hair was damp, his facial expression tight as his body arched into her once again, trembling in the aftershocks of his release. Long moments later, she felt him slide from her, still hard, still throbbing, only the barb had lost its erection. His cock was still engorged, thick and heavy with his lust.

She was too weak to open her eyes to see where he was going, but moments later she heard water running in the bathroom. When he returned, he turned her to her stomach gently. She couldn't protest, whatever he wanted he could have. She was boneless, mindless with satiation. But it was the warm roughness of a cloth between her thighs that she felt. First over the saturated lips of her cunt, then through the narrow cleft of her ass.

He cleaned her gently, his hands slow, the strokes thorough.

"Are you okay?" he asked her finally, his voice soft, hesitant.

"Mm." She didn't want to use breathing energy on actually speaking.

He was quiet behind her then. His hand was warm on her buttocks; his silence though, was filled with tension.

"I'm sorry." She could barely hear the apology.

Merinus took a deep, strengthening breath. Damn, men and their phobias. She turned on her back staring up at him drowsily.

"Why?" she mumbled.

Callan frowned.

"I lost control—"

"So?" She yawned. Damn, she was tired now. "I wanted you too. Now lay down here and cuddle me, dammit. A woman is supposed to be cuddled after mind blowing sex, not attempting to make sense of some man's psyche."

Uh oh. She watched that expression of male offense cross his face. Now, how the hell had she managed to wound his poor little ego?

"My psyche is not the problem," he informed her with an overload of pride.

Merinus rolled her eyes.

'Then what is?" She pulled weakly at the other side of the comforter as a chill began to replace the warmth of her body.

"I lost control," he said again.

"And I said: So?"

"I hurt you."

Merinus looked up at him. He was perfectly in control again, if still a little horny. He sat beside her, his amber eyes glittering with regret.

"You didn't hurt me," she argued. "I liked everything you did."

"Dammit, Merinus, I smacked you," he whispered painfully, dragging his hand roughly through his hair. "I do not hit women."

Merinus smiled. She remembered well the pleasure of that particular little spanking.

"Yeah, I know," she sighed in contentment. "Cuddle me for a while and you can do it again."

The shock on his face would have been comical if she had the energy to laugh.

"You wanted that?" He seemed confused by it.

Merinus sighed. "Callan, I want all of you. I want you wild and growling, purring and contented, and even roaring in release. I don't just want a small part of you. I love you. The whole package."

He shook his head as though to deny her claim.

"But you are mine, too," she told him firmly. "Remember that. Or I really will neuter you. Or I'll have Kane do it. And I bet he won't use anesthesia."

He winced. Good. Then he brought his hand to her face, his expression filling with tenderness. Damn, he better not make her cry. She really didn't have the energy.

"You humble me," he told her roughly.

"And if you make me cry, I'll smack you." She kissed his palm though, and sighed peacefully before whining. "Now please get me warm and comfy so I can sleep. I'm killed here."

Callan moved hesitantly, pulling the blankets from beneath her and getting in beside her. Merinus moved against him instantly, his extra body heat a balm to her cooling body.

His arms went around her, holding her close to his chest, his chin resting atop her head. He was thinking, she could tell. She didn't consider that a good thing, considering it was the incredible sex of moments before that he was thinking so hard about.

"I did it deliberately, you know," she finally said in exasperation as he reached over to switch the lamp out.

"I know you did." He wrapped his arms around her once again.

"So why are you so damned put out over it?" She frowned.

"I could have hurt you, Merinus," he sighed. "I know how. I was beyond all control with you. That's dangerous."

"Evidently not." She shrugged. "Callan, I'm not your enemy, nor am I threatening your life. Get over it. You did an amazing job of making me submit and I'll be eternally grateful. Maybe later we can even play again."

"You will drive me insane." His voice was resigned.

Merinus was quiet for long moments. Funny, her father and brothers used the same tone of voice and the same words often. What the hell did she do?

"I'm going to sleep." She would figure it out later. "Men are just too confusing for me to figure out right now."

She thought she heard him chuckle, but it could have just been the vibrations of the soft purr she could hear beneath her cheek. Definitely more soothing than snoring.

CHAPTER TWENTY-FOUR

Callan held Merinus for a long while after she fell into a deep sleep. Her body curved close to his, soft and tempting. His hands smoothed over the curve of her back, his eyes closing in pain. He should have walked away from her the moment she came into town. He should have packed and disappeared as he meant to do. Instead, he had given into the temptation of brown eyes filled with laughter, and a temptingly curved body that hardened his cock in seconds. And then, he had thrown her life into chaos.

He grimaced, knowing the past week had been more than hard on her. The demands her body was making on her had to be confusing, frightening, but she never gave into it. She had still laughed, she had still fought with him, tempted him. She had given him her body willingly, even during moments when the 'frenzy' was not upon her. Her passion burned him alive then. What had happened less than an hour before terrified him.

He couldn't find a reason why he had suddenly demanded her submission. The scent of her lust had struck him like a bat to heat, triggering some primal instinct inside him. It had become imperative that she submit and accept that she was his, and she had refused. He had to hear her admit she belonged to him, and she had refused. For a while. And her refusal had broken his control.

He grimaced, remembering the exhilaration, the pleasure of releasing the beast inside him. It pounded through his blood, his cock, his heart and soul. The climax had been so intense he thought his head would explode as well as his cock. And she had loved every minute of it. There was no mistaking the mask of ecstasy that had covered her face. Her pleas for more. Her desperate, strangled screams of release. Damn her. She had bound him to her. Taken his will to walk away from her. He was tied to her now, with no hope of escape, and no hope of safety. He couldn't run far enough, or hide long enough now to keep the Council from taking her eventually. There was only one choice, one chance to save what he had found with her.

He moved away from Merinus carefully, tucking the blankets around her, touching her hair regretfully. It would never be as easy as she wanted it to be. He could never give her peace, or true safety.

Pulling on a pair of shorts, Callan left the bedroom and returned downstairs. The computer was still running, his mail program logging his messages in. He saw he had the reply from Sherra that he had been expecting. She was still with Kane and his family. An army themselves, she assured him. She trusted them. But she didn't trust Dayan. Callan rubbed his hands over his face. The truth was finally sinking in and he hated it. Sherra was waiting with Kane for a call from him. As Merinus had said, the cells were secured and Kane would know if they were being hacked.

He had slipped the phone out of his pack earlier. It lay on his desk now. He glanced at it, sighing wearily. Picking up, he keyed a secured number in, watching the indicator at the back. It stayed green, positive for a secure line.

"Merinus?" The line was answered quickly by a very irate brother.

"She's sleeping." Callan wanted this first conversation just between the two of them. "Where is Sherra?"

"Right here," Kane answered. "Tell us where to meet you, Callan. The shit is getting deep now, we have to get you to D.C. fast."

"Let me talk to Sherra first. Then I'll talk with you." Callan would know by her voice if the man was to be trusted.

There was a pause, the sound of a low feminine voice.

"Callan," she spoke quietly. "Kane isn't lying to you. We have major problems here."

Callan breathed roughly, both in relief and in aggravation. At least she was safe.

"Where's Dayan?" Callan asked her coldly.

There was silence.

"Sherra?" he asked her carefully.

"He's disappeared, Callan. Taber and Tanner are tracking him, but he's staying just out of reach."

"What happened?" Something had, Callan knew, or the others wouldn't be after him.

"He attacked Dawn."

Callan was silent, feeling rage work through him, over him. After the horrors Sherra and Dawn had both faced, he had dared to hurt her.

"How bad is she?" he asked her carefully, fighting his fury.

"Bad enough. But she'll live through it," Sherra sighed. "We have her in the safe house with Doc now. He'll take care of her. Taber and Tanner will take care of Dayan. We have to get you and Merinus to New York. Kane's setup is as secure as it gets, Callan. He has all the evidence in place, all we have to do is get you to the Senate meetings this week on genetic engineering in D.C."

Callan grimaced. He would have to stand before the world and claim he wasn't quite human, not quite animal. Sickness burned in his stomach. The only thing worse would be what would happen to Merinus if they got hold of her.

"Are you at the location I gave you?" he asked her, referring to his coded directions in the email he sent.

"I'm here, as are Merinus' brothers and her father. Tell us what to do, Callan."

"Put Kane on."

"How do you want to do this, Lyons?" Kane's voice was set and determined.

"There's an airfield about four miles from you. A small one. Very private and deserted. Have a private plane there at noon tomorrow. Merinus and I will meet with you where you are now, and go to the airport together. When we get there, your pilot will vacate the craft and I'll fly us to an undisclosed location outside D.C. If I can still trust you that far, then we'll go ahead with your plans."

"Trusting bastard, aren't you?" Kane snarled.

"Kane, if the Council gets your sister, they will destroy her, painfully. There will be nothing left of her, alive or dead when they are finished. I refuse to take a chance on that. And don't think the Council isn't watching you, too. They know about Merinus and they know who she is, and if Dayan has betrayed us, the plans your family has made as well. There's no safety for us, or for you and your family until this is finished."

"I know what the Council is, Callan, and I have my own safeguards in place," Kane assured him. "My sister is everything to myself and the rest of her family. You can count on that."

"As long as I can. Remember, noon tomorrow." Callan disconnected, then flipped the phone to the desk.

He breathed in roughly. Terrified to trust even someone Sherra was backing. He trusted no one but himself and Merinus now. Especially now when the danger was so much closer.

He rose to his feet and paced the room slowly. The motel Kane and Sherra were staying in was one of the best and he knew she would have taken precautions in checking in and disguising herself. They would be aware that the Council had been watching them, their soldiers trying to track them. That was no guarantee they had taken enough measures, though. There was no foolproof answer. His muscles bunched with the tension that knowledge sent through him. The roads between here and D.C weren't any safer. There would be hidden Council operatives all along the line, if there weren't already.

Son of a bitch. He snarled with anger. He could have escaped on his own, but not with Merinus —

"Callan?" She stood in the doorway, dressed in his shirt again, concern etched across her face.

He breathed out roughly, turning to her, opening his arms for her.

She came to him as naturally as breathing. Her arms going around his waist as he held her close to his bare chest.

"How do I protect you, Merinus?" he whispered roughly against her hair. "I'm terrified of losing you. Terrified I can't get you to D.C. safely."

"How would you do it if I weren't with you?" she asked him, raising her head to meet his gaze. "I can keep up, Callan. I'm not weak and I'll try like hell not to slow you down. Do what you would do if you had only yourself to deal with while getting there."

"There is safety in numbers," he sighed. "Your family knows this, that's why they are gathered together for you now. I just hope the Council isn't willing to risk everything to stop them. A public massacre would only give credence to the proof your brother has and would serve them no purpose."

"Then we need to keep this public," she said with a frown. "Why try to sneak to D.C.? I'm certain Kane can arrange a public statement, and then Uncle Brian can arrange an escort to D.C. Why be covert about it?"

"Because—" Callan could go no further.

He stared down at her, tilting his head, her idea turning over in his head. Why hide? That only gave the Council the opportunity to try to take them. He had hid for so long, fought covertly for so long, that he knew nothing else. Knew no other way to fight.

He grabbed the phone from the desk and hit Kane's number. The light indicator flashed green.

"Callan?" Kane's voice was questioning.

"Do you have contacts with the television stations around here?" Callan asked him quickly.

"Several are affiliated," Kane answered him cautiously.

"Do you have any of the proof you gathered easily accessible?"

"Most of it." Once again, the voice was cautious.

248

Quickly, Callan outlined the plan forming in his head. The bastards couldn't touch them if the whole nation was watching their trip to D.C. It would be perfect.

"That would work," Kane told him, his voice edging into excitement. "It will take a while to set up. I'll call you back with the details. If you can bring yourself to answer the phone."

"I'll answer it," Callan growled. "Get it set up. Have the reporters standing by for the location to meet us."

"Callan, what about the others?" Kane's voice was guttural now. "Sherra, Dawn, and the two men."

"There are three other men," Callan reminded him.

"Not for much longer, if I know as much about you as I think I do," Kane said wearily. "Will you reveal them as well?"

Callan took a deep breath. "This will be their decision. Have Sherra contact the others. They can stand with me, or I will do all I can to continue to hide them. Whatever they decide."

There was a tense silence across the line.

"Is Merinus doing okay?" Kane finally asked.

Callan glanced at Merinus, seeing her worried expression.

"She's fine. But I want to get off this line before you're hacked. We've talked too long this evening already. Contact me when you have this set up and we'll give you our location."

Callan disconnected the phone.

"You're really going to do this?" Merinus whispered hopefully. "You'll really come forward and make them pay?"

Callan grunted. He had no illusions about this. The Council would never truly pay.

"I am going to go forward. I will submit to their questions and ultimately their exams, for a while," he promised her. "But the danger will never be over, Merinus, you must understand this. We'll have to always be careful, always be within the Pride. Our strength is within our numbers."

"And if the others don't come forward?" Merinus asked.

"They will." He knew them all well. They would stand beside him, no matter what.

He pulled Merinus into his arms once again, holding onto her, praying for a miracle he didn't really expect. Peace would be too much to ask for. So he prayed only for her safety with everything in his heart and soul. He prayed just for that.

* * * * *

Kane disconnected the phone then checked the indicator light carefully. It was still green. He breathed a long, tired sigh, then looked up at the others in the room. Sherra he found immediately. She was sitting in a far corner, lounging in one of the comfortable chairs that the suite afforded. His brothers were watching him expectantly, his father's face, lined with worry and pain, was confident though.

"We set up a news conference. Caleb," he addressed the second oldest brother. "Get on your line and pull in reporters from D.C. and New York. We want top names down here. I don't want a shoddy affair." He turned to Sherra then threw the phone he carried at her. She caught it gracefully, her lithe body never tensing or jerking in surprise. As though she had been expecting it all along. "Call your brothers and Doctor Martin. Get the others here where we're all together. Callan wants the search for Dayan dropped. He also wants each of you to decide if you're willing to reveal yourselves, or if you prefer to stay hidden."

"Do we notify our Council contact?" Gray, the youngest brother, and the one that resembled Merinus the most, asked.

"No, let it come from their moles in the newspapers and stations." Kane shrugged. "We'll have enough fish to fry here. My unit is ready to move to provide security and protection to Callan and his family. Now let's get things moving."

The twelve-man group of ex-special forces followed Kane to each job he took, personal or business related. They were at present bunked in each room surrounding the two Kane and his family had taken.

"How much trouble do you expect?" John Tyler, Patriarch of the Tyler clan questioned him sternly.

Kane breathed out roughly.

"I expect at least one attempt on them during the news conference," he admitted. "I want Merinus in armor and all angles accessible to them covered. I'll have my men take care of that. It could go easy, but I never expect easy."

"The Council will want them dead if possible. If not, they'll try damage control instead." Sherra came to her feet as they turned to face her. "They won't expect the proof Kane has on them, so we may all be safer than we think."

That was what Kane was praying for. When the shit hit the fan it would smear more than one government figure in several countries, as well as a handful of billionaires. Damage control wouldn't be easy to provide by then.

"Okay, let's get everything ready," John said tensely. "I want this taken care of and I want my daughter home. Get moving."

And of course they did. No one ignored John Tyler, or disobeyed him. They got moving. Everyone but Sherra. She had made her call, did her part, and Kane watched her as she moved restlessly around the room. She had been like this all day. Almost nervous, unwilling to stay in one place for long. Not that he expected her tension was the same as his own. Every muscle in his body was tight with arousal, and had been since she had stepped from the shadows the other night.

He couldn't forget the touch of her. The taste of her silken skin, those damned throaty growls she made while he pounded into her body. She liked her sex rough, her teeth to nip, hands to grip. She was no shrinking violet or weak-kneed virgin, even when she had been a virgin. She had been a temptress, a seductress, her body conforming to him, urging him on in heated demand. He wanted to fuck her again so badly he could barely stand it. Feel that hot pussy stretching around him, her cream soaking his cock and balls. Damn her. He hadn't been this horny since his time at the labs.

And that was why she hated him now. She never understood why he was there. And she wouldn't listen when he tried to tell her why he hadn't come back for her as he swore he would. Hard to rescue someone when you were half buried in a pit, fertilizing it with your blood. Bastards had known what he was up to somehow and nearly killed him for his efforts. The only thing that saved him was the fact that, at the time, they had no idea who he was. And by the time he healed, he had been forgotten. Only the scientists and lab soldiers had seen his face, and Kane was careful to stay out of any limelight, any public appearances. He had been working on this for ten years and he would, by God, see every bastard behind it destroyed. Just as they had destroyed.

He looked at Sherra again, pain striking his chest, guilt eating him alive. What had they done to her? Callan had rescued her not long after the attempt made on Kane's life. He had taken her out, saved her, but something else had marked her. It was there in her expression, the careful shift away from him when he got too close, the secrets that swirled in the shadows of those dark green eyes. She no longer trusted him and he couldn't really blame her. She had waited for him, believed in him, and he had failed. It didn't matter why.

"Sherra, what did your people say?" He moved closer to her, trying to control his anger as she backed away.

"They'll be here in a matter of hours. Taber and Tanner were already on their way to Dawn. Dayan slipped away from them."

He saw her fists clench. She had been enraged when they learned Taber had barely made it to the other girl in time to save her from the man's brutal rape.

"Will they stand with him?" Kane questioned her, knowing that the group would make more of an impact than one man.

"We have always stood behind Callan. Just as he has always protected us." She shot him a feral look.

Another cut at him. Before she was finished he would be lying in figurative shreds at her feet.

Lora Leigh

"That's all I needed to know." He nodded, rather than trying to spar with her in front of the others. He turned to Caleb. "Caleb, we have a possible group, not just one. Let's keep the information sketchy but impossible to resist."

Caleb nodded as he made another call.

The Tyler men moved about the room performing their various assignments. Sherra watched it all with a half snarl on her lips.

"Chill out, baby, we'll take care of everything," he told her softly.

Her eyes darkened, her expression tightened with fury.

"I am not your baby," she sneered. "So stop with the cutesy shit, Kane. I know you and I know what you are, so stop trying to suck up to me."

Kane felt his control begin to erode. Eight surprised expressions turned to them, watching the byplay carefully. His eyes narrowed on her, his fists clenching at the urge to jerk her into the next room and give her something to fight about.

"Baby, when I start sucking it won't be an attempt," he said warningly, turning away from her. "Fuck it, I'll deal with you later when I have time."

"No, you will not deal with me period." She brushed past him, heading for the door.

"Where the hell do you think you're going?" He grabbed her arm as she headed for the exit, swinging her around to face him.

Fury outlined her body as she looked down at the hand gripping her arm, then looked up at him as though the touch sickened her.

254

"Take your hands off me." Her voice vibrated with anger, but he was damned if he didn't see need flaring in her eyes as well.

He jerked her across the room, pushing her roughly back into the chair. When she went to push her way back to her feet, he slammed his hands on the arms of the seat, forcing her back.

"You are not going anywhere," he raged furiously, watching her face flush now. "You can sit your ass here or you can run and hide in the bedroom, but you will not leave this suite. Do you fucking understand me?"

"Kane." His father's sharp voice protested behind him. For the first time in his life, Kane ignored his father.

"Do you hear me, Sherra?" he asked again, never breaking their stare.

Her lips thinned, their little pout almost tempting him to possess them with a strength of a desire nearly tearing him apart.

"Fine," she literally growled at him, her eyes shooting sparks of fury as she drew back as far as possible from him. "But your sister is right, you're an asshole."

Kane's eyes widened in surprise, then he frowned in irritation.

"Does she fucking telling everyone I'm an asshole?" He heard his voice rise in incredulity, then turned to look at his family for an answer.

They were staring at him with a mixture of surprise and disbelief.

"Maybe she likes warning the world of the potential," Sherra sneered. "It's not like it's easy to miss."

He swung around to her again.

"Kane." The order in his father's voice was impossible to deny. "Leave that girl alone, she said she wouldn't go anywhere. Get the hell out of here and make sure you're ready so we can all get some rest before morning. Which is only a few more hours away."

John faced him, a scowl on his face as he watched his oldest son with no small amount of confusion.

"Sherra, you leave this room and I swear I'll hunt you down," he told her fiercely, staring into her eyes as they widened in shock. "And I promise you, you won't like it much when I find you."

She snarled silently, revealing the longer than normal canines at the side of her mouth.

"Be a good kitty, baby." He smiled mockingly. He turned and left the room before she had a chance to retaliate, but her furious curse followed him into the hall.

He breathed out harshly then, running his hands over his short black hair and stomping to the next room. Dammit. He had no desire to fight with Sherra. He didn't want her mad. He wanted her hot and horny and begging him. And eventually, he would have it.

CHAPTER TWENTY-FIVE

Callan lay beside Merinus smelling her need, her heat. The scent had changed, and he felt his chest tighten with that knowledge. He lay still, not touching her, staring at the darkened ceiling in misery. The "mating frenzy" was completing its cycle. Merinus was ovulating.

She tossed against the mattress, still sleeping, despite the arousal beginning to rage within her body. She would awaken soon, and when she did, she would need his passion, his seed. The desperate lusts would ease then, according to Dr. Martin and become more normal, but she would carry his child. That was in the email Callan hadn't shown her. The conclusions of the tests the scientist had been running had come through late last night. The uncertainty over the pregnancy hormone easing the frenzy was now certain. Despite the earlier indications it wouldn't, the test samples had finally shown proof that the frenzy was nature's way of ensuring breeding within the Pride.

His fist clenched at that knowledge. Equal parts hope and rage surged through his body. Like any man, he dreamed of having a child with the woman who had stolen his heart. A child filled with laughter, with happiness. But could a child of his ever have a life that carefree? A child whose DNA was infected by its father, a child they would call a freak of science?

Merinus rolled against him, her silken hand found his abdomen. He grimaced at the rising heat in his own body, the pleasure he found in her touch. He could feel his tongue throbbing again, the glands along his tongue enlarging. A fucking aphrodisiac, to ensure the "frenzy". Nature was having the last laugh on them all. Somehow, she had found something worthy in the Breeds science had created and was determined to keep them around.

He ignored the burning moisture in his eyes, his hand smoothing over her slender arm, loving the feel of her. The warmth of her. He had found acceptance from her, but he knew she would be terrified when he revealed the truth to her. A truth he was praying was a mistake. But his sense of smell didn't lie. How he knew what the scent was, he was uncertain, but he knew. It was the smell of rebirth, as light and elusive as spring.

Merinus moaned low and deep, her hand moving lower, dangerously close to the erection throbbing between his thighs. He was harder than he could ever remember being. Throbbing, desperate to sink inside her, to bury his cock as deeply inside her as possible before spilling his seed.

"Merinus," he whispered her name, turning to her, his hand going to her cheek as he awoke her.

Her eyes blinked open, a sensual smile shaping her lips as she moved closer to him.

"Wait," he whispered, holding her still. "We must talk."

"Later." She rubbed her breasts against his chest, her hard nipples burning his flesh.

"No, darling," he denied her. "We talk first. You have to listen to me."

He saw her frown in the predawn shadows of the room.

"So talk. But hurry." Her leg caressed his as she moved against him, her breathing becoming deep, laborious.

"Merinus, if I take you, you'll conceive tonight." He stared down at her intently, watching her eyes widen.

"What?" she asked him nervously. "You can't be sure of that."

She shook her head, but he smelled her growing hotter. The spicy scent was an aphrodisiac all its own. As though the thought of carrying his child wasn't as abhorrent as it should be.

"I'm certain, Merinus." He allowed his hand to smooth over her cheek, his thumb to trace her lips. "The need you're feeling will only grow worse, more painful without my sperm coming inside you. But you must know what will happen when it does. I cannot stop it, Merinus. I cannot protect you from this."

He wanted to howl with his rage, his pain for what he was putting her through.

"You aren't to blame, Callan." Her smile trembled, her eyes glistened with tears. "It's not your fault."

Her lack of anger towards him cracked his soul. How could she be so accepting, so loving to a man who had all but destroyed her life?

"I love you, Merinus. I want you to know this now," he whispered. "You are my soul and you are my life. I could not survive without you now."

"I know that." A tear fell from her eye. "I know Callan, because it's the same for me."

He laid his forehead against hers, breathing roughly, staring down at her as he fought to come to grips with what this night would bring. A child. He had never thought to know that joy, that fear.

"I will protect you and our babe as best I can," he told her roughly. "With my life, Merinus."

Her hand was shaking as it moved to cup his cheek. He could feel her fear now, her uncertainty. Suddenly the complications were growing with each second. It was no longer just their lives at risk, but the life of an innocent.

"It's really bad this time." She breathed in hard as her body shuddered with the heat. "I'm scared, Callan."

He moved her to her back, looming over her, wishing there was some way to take her fears from her.

"We will make it okay, love," he swore to her, though he had no idea how. "Somehow, someway, we will keep our child safe."

He lowered his head, his lips whispering over hers as he fought the need to plunge his tongue deep into her mouth. To possess her in every way, to make her take the hormone that would drive her need higher, make her body burn, make her release tear through her body and drive her quicker to fertility. Dr. Martin had been certain that this was the reason for the hormone. All tests when combined together fused to produce a single result. A child.

Wanting this night to be remembered, not just for the fear of conception, but for the beauty of their pleasure, Callan began to tease her lips. He didn't want to tempt with the crazed needs of long love play. He didn't want her mindless. He wanted to pleasure her, love her. His kissed her gently with only his lips, sipping at hers; staring into her wide eyes as his hands caressed her swollen breasts, her hard nipples. Then his tongue brushed her lips, slipped inside and allowed the effects of science and nature to begin.

She accepted the invasion, her eyes closing with a groan as the taste of spice filled both their mouths. It would begin now. And he feared where it would end. But he didn't stop kissing her. He couldn't. He wanted the contact to last, to linger forever in his mind. That when he gave her his child, he loved her, worshipped her.

Within minutes their breathing increased, perspiration coated their bodies, lust rippled through them. Callan groaned as his hand lowered, testing the rich cream that prepared her for him. She was slick and hot, ready for him. He moved between her spread thighs, lowering himself against her, positioning his erection for the first hard thrust. He knew what she liked, and he would be certain that every stroke was made to gain her ultimate pleasure.

"I love you, Merinus," he groaned against her lips as he thrust deep and hard inside her.

* * * * *

Merinus felt the shock of his entrance, the sudden stretching of her vagina, the pleasure/pain that drove all other thoughts from her head. Heat seared her body, spasmed her womb. Her muscles clenched on his cock as he whispered his words of love against her lips.

She climaxed on the second stroke, but still the heat built. She bucked against him, her hips thrusting her cunt harder against the invading erection that pumped hard and fast inside her. Callan was moaning, his head lowering to her breasts, his rough tongue licking at her nipples as his mouth suckled each in turn. His cock kept a smooth, hard rhythm as he thrust in and out of her. Each stroke stretched her, filled her. Her head tossed, her body shuddered.

Then he was moving faster, harder. His mouth went to her neck, to the little wound that never seemed to heal, his teeth locking on it, his tongue stroking as she began to feel the final phase of his possession. The hardening of the barb that would lock him inside her seconds before his ejaculation. The firm, stiff flesh that would allow no withdrawal and would ensure the conception that nature intended.

She cried out as the firm thumb began to stiffen, raking her flesh erotically as he began to pound inside her mercilessly. She could feel the heat building in her stomach, knotting her muscles. Her vagina clamped down on his cock, milking it, demanding his release as she felt a harder, stronger orgasm building inside her own body. Her nails bit into his back as the deep strokes had her crying out for ease. He was growling low, her cries echoed through the room The barb lengthened then, and on the last hard stroke locked into her sensitive flesh and sent her into an explosion so hard, so deep she screamed out his name as she felt his seed erupt inside her.

His arms trembled beneath her shoulders as he gasped for breath. Merinus lay there, trying to catch her breath and frowned. Heated moisture dripped against her shoulder. Not much, a few fragile drops. She felt tears build in her eyes, her arms tightened about him, and she wished she knew what to say, knew some way to ease the pain inside this strong man.

"You humble me," he whispered, his face hidden in her neck, his voice husky. "You amaze me, Merinus."

"And how do I do this?" she asked him gently, her hands threading through the tawny strands of his hair.

He shook his head. "Your love. Your acceptance."

His voice strengthened, the hoarseness of his emotion leaving it slowly. He shook his head, took a hard breath and lifted himself from her. She felt him ease his cock from her body and sighed in regret. She would keep him there forever if she could.

He moved away from her, sitting on the side of the bed, gazing into the dim light of the room as morning slowly made its way toward them. She watched him, seeing the strength in his body, the way he straightened his shoulders, ready to face the new battle coming their way as surely as daylight was edging through the sky.

"It won't be easy." He stared toward the window and the thick curtains covering it. "I can't make any promises, other than I'll always love you. I won't leave you. I'll do what I can to protect you."

"No one could ask more of you, Callan," she told him, her voice soft. "I don't expect more of you."

"You should." He breathed roughly, dragging his fingers through his hair. "You should have run from me screaming when you first realized you desired me, Merinus."

She laughed softly, remembering the day she had watched him masturbate on his back deck.

"I don't think that was possible," she said with a smile. "I was too busy admiring your gorgeous body."

He flashed her a quick, embarrassed look, then frowned at her sternly.

"I'm being serious," he chided her.

"So am I, Callan." She smiled. "I'm not weak, nor am I so timid I can't face whatever life throws at me. We're together for a reason. We'll face whatever life brings us as best we can."

She sat up, curling her legs beneath her as she leaned against his shoulder, staring up at him as he stared back at her. She let her lips caress his muscular shoulder, her hand smoothing over his back.

Callan took a deep breath. "I never expected you." He shook his head with an edge of amusement. "You are a dangerous woman, Merinus Tyler."

"Naw, just a determined woman." She grinned against his shoulder. "I know a good thing when I see it jacking off."

He flushed. Shooting her a look of mingled confusion and exasperation, he shook his head as he turned and pulled her into his arms. He held her tight against his body, relishing her warmth, the way she relaxed against him, looked up at him so trustingly.

"We should shower and begin to prepare for what's ahead of us," he told her softly, thinking of the news conference to come, the days ahead that would be filled with endless tests, questions and danger. He prayed Merinus' brother knew what the hell he was doing, because if anything happened to her, then Callan knew his rage would be satisfied with nothing less than blood.

"You never did return the favor as you promised," he reminded her, his brow arching suggestively. "When we come together again, you will have to make this up to me."

Merinus flushed then. She felt the heat along her cheeks, but a flame of desire between her thighs. That tingle of lust reminded her, though of the possible conception this night may have wrought. She couldn't say she was comfortable with the idea of it happening so soon.

She would have preferred to wait, to know they were reasonably safe before bringing a child into the lives they would share for the first few years.

"I'll see what I can do you for ya, sugar," she drawled, imitating the slow southern drawl she had finally grown accustomed to hearing.

"Well, you just do that, fine thing," he mocked her, and Merinus had to admit he sounded a hell of a lot more authentic than she did.

They were silent then. Holding each other, watching the light slowly filter into the room as the day eased ahead.

"I don't want to let go of tonight," she finally whispered regretfully. "I wish we could just stay like this, forever."

Callan sighed slowly, his hands smoothing over her shoulders, her back. He kissed her forehead, a soft caress of regret and longing.

"Come on, we'll shower and get breakfast. Then I need to contact the others. It will be over soon, Merinus. Then perhaps we can make a life for ourselves."

Merinus swallowed tightly, battling her fears and her regrets. She hadn't had enough time with him. The time she needed to store her memories in case the worst should happen. She wasn't a fool; she knew the danger that lay ahead of them. She had known the dangers that faced Callan from the beginning.

He rose from the bed, pulling her up beside him as he kissed the top of her head once again.

"Go ahead and shower, I'll use the other one or I won't be able to keep my hands off you." He pushed her towards the bathroom. "Go. I'll start breakfast when you come down."

"What if I beat you?" she asked him archly.

He gave her a look that clearly doubted that was possible. Merinus narrowed her eyes at him. She would show him. She shrugged rather than saying anything and went on into the bathroom, followed by his indulgent male chuckle.

CHAPTER TWENTY-SIX

She beat him. Merinus snickered as she scampered past the spare bathroom, hearing Callan still involved in his shower. He must have been delayed getting in, which meant he had been up to something before he started. She frowned. He was going to have to learn to be a little more forthcoming than she had a feeling he was.

Dressed in a pair of sweat pants and one of his big shirts she headed for the kitchen. She could at least get breakfast on. She was starved, and morning was starting to shine brightly outside the heavy curtains that covered all the windows.

A second of panic filled her at the thought of the coming day. It wouldn't be easy, letting Callan stand before the world to announce who and what he was. She knew how he treasured the solitude of his life, the peace he found when he wasn't being hunted. He would never know that again.

She flipped the light on as she entered the kitchen to dispel the deep shadows of the room, then came to an abrupt halt. Her heart jumped in fear at the man standing before her. But what terrified her most was the gun aimed at her stomach, and burning rage that seemed to flicker with dark flames in his brown eyes.

"I knew he would bring you here," Dayan smirked, his handsome face twisted with horrific fury as he approached her. "He thinks no one knows about this place, but I did. I know he comes here to hide, and I knew he would bring you here."

Merinus watched him approach, backing away from him until they entered the connecting living room, praying she could get him into a position where Callan could jump him when he came downstairs.

"Do you want to die, cunt?" he sneered.

She shook her head desperately, watching the gun nervously.

"Are you breeding yet? Gut wounds hurt real bad whore, and they would kill the abomination you're likely carrying by now."

Merinus covered her stomach with her hands, an instinctive reaction she wasn't able to halt as his eyes followed the action knowingly.

"Please—" she whispered. "Don't do this, Dayan. Callan will kill you for it."

Dayan sneered. "My dear, Callan is going to die as well. I won't let him destroy everything I've worked for since we escaped those labs."

Merinus swallowed tightly. She could feel fear drumming through her veins in time to the harsh beat of her heart. Her chest tightened as she fought to breathe past her panic, to find a way to think clearly and help Callan. God, this would kill him. Dayan was his family.

"Callan risked his life to save you, to keep you and the others hidden," she gasped. "How could you betray him like this?"

Merinus couldn't understand the depth of evil that it took for Dayan to do this.

"Because he betrayed us." Dayan's voice rose in fury, and he wasn't even aware of it. Merinus prayed Callan heard it. "He's going public, and the others will follow him like the mindless children they still are. Like he's

King. Like he is the last word. He doesn't know what he's doing. I told that stupid bitch Maria and she wouldn't listen. So she had to die for it. She almost convinced him last year. I won't let him do it. I won't let him destroy everything like this."

"What do you suggest he do then, Dayan? The Council won't stop." She edged around the room, moving carefully beside the dubious protection of a chair. If only she could protect her stomach, protect the child that may or not be forming even now.

"He should have gone back for us," Dayan raged. "I could have led the Pride. It was my right. I suffered the most for them. I should have led and he should have let them capture him."

The furious words made Merinus sick. She remembered the reports she had read of the labs. The barbaric tests, the training to condition Callan to kill, to be no more than a disposable weapon. The women that were brought to him to breed, then killed when he refused. The horrendous pain he suffered in their punishments when he refused their orders. Only a twisted, evil mind could even consider that he should have gone back. Only a monster could have killed the woman who helped raise him for trying to secure their safety, such as Dayan had done to Maria.

"You weren't strong enough to lead, evidently," Merinus snapped. "Only an animal would have suggested he do such a thing. How did they create you, Dayan? How did they manage to finally succeed in the creature they were after? Perhaps Callan should have sent you back."

Pain and fury vibrated through her body. Callan had nearly given his life countless times for this bastard, only to have him turn on him, betray and deceive him.

"Oh, they succeeded beyond their wildest imaginations." Dayan laughed. "Only, they have no idea how well they did succeed. I'm their dream child, Merinus, and once the Pride is under my control, Sherra and Dawn breeding my cubs, then I'll let them know. They will agree to my every demand in exchange for the services I can provide for them."

Merinus stared at him in disbelief.

"Dayan, what makes you think you can do this? The breeding isn't voluntary; you know that from Callan and me. It's hormonal. If Dawn or Sherra were your mates, you would know it by now."

"No." He shook his head, a maniacal smile crossing his face. "See, I know something you don't. The women don't go into heat like you did, Merinus. They don't mate like Callan mated you. When they ovulate any bastard can breed them, your brother and Sherra proved that."

Merinus blinked. "What the hell does my brother have to do with this? Which brother? Dammit, I have seven of them and every one of them will skin your ass alive and tack your hide on their wall for a trophy if you don't stop this shit. That is if Callan leaves anything left of you."

He smirked at her, the gun never wavering.

"Brother Kane was a soldier at the labs, Merinus. He was chosen to rape her when she went into heat the first time, and he did an admirable job. Even planted a cub inside her. I, of course, had to rid her of it. I can't tolerate another man's offspring within my Pride."

Merinus wavered in shock. She felt her knees go weak.

"You're lying," she gasped. "Kane wouldn't do that. He would never hurt an innocent woman."

Dayan shook his head in pity.

"But he did Merinus. Didn't you ever wonder how Kane knew about a supposedly Top Secret experiment before your father received Maria's box of evidence? How he knew when everyone associated with that lab was dead? He survived my attack somehow. Survived my rage. But he'll pay for it soon enough, for good."

"I don't believe you." She believed Kane might have been there, but not for the reasons Dayan said, and sure as hell wouldn't believe he had raped anyone. She knew her brother too well for that.

He frowned at her darkly. "I have no reason to lie."

"You have every reason to lie," she told him angrily. "You're a traitor to your own people, Dayan, there's no honor in you. You couldn't be trusted to give the weather accurately."

"You have a smart mouth, bitch," he snarled. "If I weren't already determined to kill you, I'd kill you for that alone."

"And you're a fucking prick with some real faulty illusions of grandeur." She glimpsed Callan's shadow moving slowly along the steps from the corner of her eye. "The others will take you apart themselves. You won't be able to hide the scent of Callan's blood on your hands. Their senses will pick it up, Dayan. They'll know."

She saw the glimmer of uncertainty enter his eyes.

"They won't know," he growled, but his protest wasn't as strong as it should have been.

"They can smell blood. They know the scent of their own; their DNA ensures it. Do you think you can wash away the scent of their deaths from your body? Do you really think they won't know?"

"Only Sherra and Dawn will be left." He shrugged. "I'll kill Taber and Tanner myself."

Merinus laughed at him, shaking her head as Callan moved closer. She had to keep his attention on her.

"You won't get within a mile of any of them," she told him mockingly. "They're smarter than you are—"

"Callan wasn't," he denied. "I caught his woman."

"Have you?" she asked, jerking back, falling to the floor as Callan's roar sounded through the room.

She scrambled around the chair as she heard the scream that erupted from Dayan's throat. The gun went flying when Callan tackled him. Merinus grimaced as it flew in the opposite direction of the chair. Breathing roughly, watching the struggling men carefully, she began to crawl around the room.

Feral growls filled the room, crashing furniture, flying fists. Dayan was like a savage animal, but Callan more so. With feet kicking out, fists hammering into flesh, the two men fought around the room, vying for supremacy. As Merinus reached the gun, she heard a scream of resounding pain that sent a chill down her back.

Callan had managed to tackle Dayan, maneuvering the other man in front of him, his arms locked around his neck. As Merinus' eyes widened in horror, Callan gave a final, savage wrench. The sound of the other man's neck breaking had bile rising from her stomach. Dayan's eyes were wide with surprise and defeat, horror washed over his dying expression as Callan allowed him to drop slowly to the floor.

Merinus raised shocked eyes to her lover. He stared at her, his expression cold, brutal. He never blinked, he offered no apology, but she saw the misery and grief in the glitter of unshed tears in his eyes.

He was covered in blood. His bare chest marked with the scratches of Dayan's longer, sharper nails. He wore only a pair of blood-splattered sweat shorts. His feet were bare; his legs marred with ugly cuts and bruises, splayed apart, the muscles still tight, taut with the danger that pulsed in his body.

Merinus was breathing harshly, her heart pounding in her chest, her hands clutching the forgotten gun.

"Fuck, you need another shower now," she whispered as she swallowed tightly, then grimaced at the inane comment. "Oh God, Callan—"

Her hand went over her mouth as she fought the sickness rising in her throat. Dayan stared at her, his eyes vacant, wide in that last second of horror as he stared at her. She dropped the gun, her body shaking so hard she could feel her bones trying to rattle.

"Merinus." Suddenly he was kneeling beside her, not touching her, his voice broken with his grief, his regret. "Did he hurt you?"

She shook her head desperately, fighting her tears.

"Oh God, how do I help you?" She turned to him, heedless of the blood that marred his body. His blood and Dayan's.

His arms came around her hesitantly as she threw herself in his arms.

"Help me?" he whispered, his voice rough as he touched her hair, her back, as though frightened to embrace her. "You're safe now, Merinus. It's okay."

She shook her head against his chest, the tears finally falling from her eyes, humiliating her with her weakness in the face of danger. She was such a wimp, she thought. He had saved both their lives, scarred his soul with the necessity of taking his brother's life, and she needed his comfort. She should be comforting him instead.

"I'm so sorry," she gasped through her tears. "I'm so sorry. I'm so weak, Callan. I'm so weak."

She clutched at his shoulders, too weak to stand, fear still echoing through her system, the horror of the violence quaking through her system. As Callan tightened his arms around her, the sharp sound of the front door splintering tore them apart.

Merinus screamed as the door flew inward. Callan shoved her towards the chair, his sharp order lost amid his growl of rage as he dove for the gun Merinus had dropped.

"Merinus. Callan." The harsh voice of her brother had her swinging around in time to watch Callan come up in a lithe, graceful move to his knees, the pistol gripped in both hands, his face a mask of rage.

"Callan." She fell toward him; terrified he wouldn't stop in time.

He was ahead of her. The gun went up, his finger falling quickly back from the trigger.

Dazed, breathing hard from shock and reaction she watched the way he crouched as the room began to fill with the presence of others. Her brothers and father, even her uncle, Senator Samuel Tyler was there, along with the vaguely familiar near dozen men who followed Kane. Taber and Tanner, Sherra and Dawn and Dr. Martin brought up the rear. Everyone but the Senator and the

Tempting the Beast

good scientists were armed to the gills, weapons showing, bodies taut and ready.

"God. Talk about fucking testosterone overload," Merinus groaned as she collapsed on her ass, staring around as her brothers and Kane's military group swept through the room, upstairs, making certain of security, she assumed. Shit, she didn't know what the hell those black clad strangers with hard cold eyes were doing, let alone her brothers.

"Don't touch her." Suddenly Callan turned furious, feral eyes on whoever had dared to move behind her.

Merinus glanced up in time to see Kane raise his hands and step away quietly. Callan moved across the space of only a few feet and jerked Merinus in his arms. His body was blazing with heat, his muscles tight with tension.

"Give him a few minutes to cool off." Dr. Martin moved among the men commandingly. "Get away from them. Get Dayan's body to another room away from him now. Let him settle down or he'll never find his control."

Merinus looked back at Callan. His face was flushed, his eyes closed as he held her close.

"Callan?" she whispered.

"I could have lost you," he answered, his voice ragged, harsh. "If it had been Council soldiers, if it had been anyone else, I would have lost you."

His hold tightened as he fought for breath. "God help me, Merinus, I can't lose you."

Merinus breathed out deeply. She struggled to turn in his arms, finally succeeding as he loosened his grip only marginally. Her arms went around his shoulders, her head

275

cushioned on his heaving chest. Around them, people moved, spoke, asked questions and demanded answers.

"How were we found?" Callan suddenly jerked his head up, his eyes blazing in suspicion as he looked at those around them.

"Kane had a tracker on Merinus' cell," Sherra answered him coolly. "I didn't know, Callan, until this morning when he tried to call and his readout indicated the phone had been destroyed."

Vaguely, Merinus remembered seeing the broken remnants of the phone on Callan's desk. Dayan must have destroyed it, thinking he would keep them from calling for help. Callan had no phones in the house. No way to track any communications he made.

Callan took a deep, steadying breath. Merinus felt his control slowly reassert itself. His body relaxed marginally.

"Callan, you need to get cleaned up." Kane stood several feet from them, staring down at them broodingly. "We're going to call the police in on this one, do some damage control. Uncle Sam," he nodded to the Senator, "came out here on the midnight flight to personally escort you back to the Senate hearings on genetic altering and DNA engineering. We have a lot of work ahead of us."

Callan rose slowly to his feet. His arm wrapped around Merinus, refusing to let her go.

"Merinus can stay here with us," Kane told him forcefully.

"I don't think so." Merinus didn't trust the cold smile Callan sent her brother. "Merinus stays with me, Kane. Period. You can talk to her after we both clean up."

Merinus rose to her feet alongside Callan, watching the two men stare each other down, both intent on having his way. They were like two pit bulls getting ready to fight over the same bone, but for different reasons. Kane wanted to hoard her, keep her a child, his innocent sister forever. Callan wanted the woman he had made and he was damned determined to keep her.

Kane opened his mouth to speak. Merinus knew whatever came out of it would only make the situation worse.

"Don't start, asshole," she snarled, seeing the mockery that flashed across his eyes, an indication that something stupid was getting ready to come out of his mouth.

He flashed her a dark look. Merinus took a deep breath.

"I need another shower, anyway, and so does Callan. Do whatever you guys have to do to get things ready to go. I can't deal with it right now."

Her mind was too dazed, shock and fear and fury still running through her veins. Adrenaline overload was turning into a bitch.

"At least try to hurry." Kane raked his fingers though his short hair, impatience tightening his body. "We have to get a story together and get things started here, Merinus. I need you for that."

He speared her with a commanding look.

"You'll just have to wait," she told him, accepting the arm Callan wrapped around her as her legs trembled beneath her. "I can't right now, Kane. I just can't."

She was aware of the concerned, worried looks on the faces of her family. She should have been more eager to reassure them then she was to find a moment alone with Callan, to soothe the beast that still fought for release.

"Come on." Callan turned without addressing the other man again and drew her from the room.

When they reached the stairs, he didn't make her climb them herself. He picked her up in his arms and carried her to the big bathroom off their bedroom. He didn't speak, his expression didn't soften. But he was hard. His cock was like a poker, steely and hot against her hip. His eyes blazed with lust. He locked the bedroom door behind them, then with a simple jerk at her pants, bared her from the waist down.

"I can't wait." He backed her up to the wall, lifting her, pushing her pants free with one foot.

He spread her legs then plunged his cock deep. Merinus gasped, unaware how ready she had been for him. Her vagina clasped his erection with a hot, slick grip as tight as a fist as he buried himself inside her.

Her head fell back against the wall, her hands gripping his scratched bloody shoulders as he bent, buried his head in her neck and began to pound into her. He was groaning with hoarse pleasure with each thrust. His erection was hard, scalding hot, driving her into a passion as natural and as deep as love itself.

Heat and fire seared her body, pleasure rushed over her in a tidal wave of sensation, sweeping away any doubt, any residual fears left in her. His hands gripped her hips, her thighs clasped his and his cock buried itself over and over inside her. Stretching her, he filled her, burned her with his need. This was no hormonal demand, no kiss to encourage the heat, no preliminaries, just hard, honest passion.

His teeth bit at her neck in the place he had marked as his own. His rough tongue stroked her. Callan grunted harshly as Merinus' moans rose in intensity. She could feel her climax building, gathering inside her, the explosion only moments away.

Fighting for breath Callan increased the pace of his thrusts. Wet flesh slapped together, her cunt made suckling sounds as his cock slid easily inside her over and over again. Then she trembled, shook, she fought her scream, and managed to keep it down to a loud cry when she felt the barb emerge, lengthen, harden until it locked him deep inside her. That hot caress sent her careening over the edge. Her orgasm struck hard and deep, tightening her body as she felt him spurting his release inside her, distantly wincing as his satisfied roar echoed around them. Boy, Kane would definitely have problems with this.

* * * * *

Below, Callan's sexual roar was clearly heard. Sherra grimaced as eight men flushed with anger, glancing at the stairs, their bodies stiffening with outrage.

"She's not a child," she informed them all. "You may as well get used to it now."

John Tyler turned to her with a fierce frown.

"Young lady, that is my child," he snapped angrily.

"No sir, right now she's Callan's mate," she argued tightly. "Her life was nearly lost and his DNA demands he reassert his claim. Get used to it, get over it before he gets down here, because if all of you crowd him, with your male pride all upset, you will merely force his instincts to the forefront. He's just claimed her, let him get used to that before he has to deal with your possessiveness."

Sherra ignored Kane's sneer. She had been doing that for two days now.

"We have other problems here," Samuel Tyler spoke up, distracting brotherly and fatherly outrage. "Let's get our priorities straight and go from there. Four hours till the press shows, we have plenty of work to do."

EPILOGUE

"Wayne Dubrow, reporting from Washington at the Senate hearings on DNA engineering and research. Callan Lyons, the alleged Breed, created by a group of scientists working in genetic reengineering appeared before the Senate committee this afternoon on genetic research. Accompanying him is his fiancé, Merinus Tyler, daughter of John Tyler of the National Forum. Also accompanying him are a dozen doctors, scientists and DNA specialists brought in weeks before to verify his claim.

Mr. Lyons, and four other members of his family, also experiments in these horrific tests, gave their stirring testimony before members of the Senate and the press."

The reporter stood stately, somberly before the Senate Building, his voice rough, emotionally charged as he detailed the testimonies given, especially those of the two young women. The world was held spellbound by the beauty of the quiet blonde, the shy, fearful frailty of the golden brunette. But it was the men, their faces perfection in male curves and angles that struck them with the truth of the story being told.

Callan Lyons, the head of the family, proud and striking, his amber eyes direct and straightforward as he informed the Senators and various lawmakers of the horrors he had endured. The deaths, the cruelties, the identities of mercenaries, soldiers, billionaire, political and public figures involved. Those political figures were noticeably absent from the hearings.

Scientists spoke, among them, Dr. Martin, the DNA specialist who had treated each member since birth and followed after their daring escape and the death of his own family. The Tyler's weren't unarmed themselves. Years of research and evidence had been gathered. No stone left unturned. The story was horrific, moving, garnering international sympathy and support for the proud members who had fought their lives for peace.

* * * * *

Deep in the African jungle, a satellite link pulling in the story, a couple sat silently watching. The male, an older version of Callan by several years, was quiet, tense. The woman, a small dark haired doctor, wept silently. Their story was being told. This male, Callan Lyons, had been victorious where they had not.

They clasped hands, and the male, Leo Vanderale, knew that they would be making their own journey soon, and with them would go the son they had borne thirty years before. Perhaps their son would finally be free of the past then, and the danger they had hidden from him for so long.

* * * * *

Deep in the mountains of Mexico a different scenario was taking place. Mexican and U.S. agents were swarming a hidden lab. Fire erupted as scientists attempted to destroy evidence and lives as they were overtaken. Babies cried, their mewling sounds both human and animal, adult members of the experiments snatched their children in the commotion and ran for cover. Fighting their way through smoke and ash to avoid the agents attempting to round them up, the soldiers attempting to kill them.

Hard gray eyes surveyed the scene as half a dozen men and women, and four children escaped the mass destruction. He followed them quickly; his Pack could hide for as long as needed. He would be damned if he would let them be rounded up like animals.

* * * * *

General Morris Goveny stood over the still form of his security officer. Agents covered him, guns trained on him, the hard eyes of Mexican and American officials condemning him.

He was the pride of the Genetics Council, his lab supposedly the most secret, the wolf hybrids they had bred the most exceptional specimens yet. And it was all falling down around his ears.

His security officer had been shot by the bastards storming the labs, his head doctor had deserted the labs at the first round of gunfire. The General considered himself much smarter. He raised his hands above his shoulders, staring back at the condemning expressions of those who had come for him.

"They're animals. Tools and nothing more," he muttered as the television droned behind him, the reporter listing the traits of what he called Human Genetic Hybrids. "They aren't human. Not really."

Not humans, animals, created to serve, to obey dictates of their masters. His eyes narrowed on the bank of monitors by the television as he glimpsed the Jeeps racing from the compound. Of course, they had escaped. His creations, his pets. For the moment he was defeated, but he swore the day would come when they would pay.

"General Goveny, you are under arrest." A tall American official stepped forward decisively.

Goveny's lips twisted as he sneered at the censure he glimpsed in the other man's gaze.

"You will learn, they are not society's pets," he said. "They are animals. Savage, inhuman. They must be trained, confined…"

"You, Sir, will be the one confined." Cuffs snapped over his wrists. "Due to your criminal disregard and insane orders, the labs are destroyed, as well as everyone in them. Your breeds are dead, but I promise you, you'll pay for the crime of their birth."

He hid his smile. He hid his plans. They weren't dead. But he promised himself that they would soon wish they were.

About the author:

Lora Leigh is a 36-year-old wife and mother living in Kentucky. She dreams in bright, vivid images of the characters intent on taking over her writing life, and fights a constant battle to put them on the hard drive of her computer before they can disappear as fast as they appeared.

Lora's family and her writing life co-exist, if not in harmony, in relative peace with each other. An understanding husband is the key to late nights with difficult scenes and stubborn characters. His insights into human nature and the workings of the male psyche provide her hours of laughter, and innumerable romantic ideas that she works tirelessly to put into effect.

Lora Leigh welcomes mail from readers. You can write to her c/o Ellora's Cave Publishing at P.O. Box 787, Hudson, Ohio 44236-0787.

Also by LORA LEIGH:

- Aiden's Charity
- Heather's Gift
- Jacob's Faith
- Marly's Choice
- Menage a Magick
- Sarah's Seduction
- Seduction
- Shadowed Legacy
- Shattered Legacy
- Submission
- Surrender
- Wolfe's Hope
- Law and Disorder 1: Moving Violations – with Veronica Chadwick

Why an electronic book?

We live in the Information Age—an exciting time in the history of human civilization in which technology rules supreme and continues to progress in leaps and bounds every minute of every hour of every day. For a multitude of reasons, more and more avid literary fans are opting to purchase e-books instead of paperbacks. The question to those not yet initiated to the world of electronic reading is simply: *why?*

1. *Price.* An electronic title at Ellora's Cave Publishing runs anywhere from 40-75% less than the cover price of the <u>exact same title</u> in paperback format. Why? Cold mathematics. It is less expensive to publish an e-book than it is to publish a paperback, so the savings are passed along to the consumer.

2. *Space.* Running out of room to house your paperback books? That is one worry you will never have with electronic novels. For a low one-time cost, you can purchase a handheld computer designed specifically for e-reading purposes. Many e-readers are larger than the average handheld, giving you plenty of screen room. Better yet, hundreds of titles can be stored within your new library—a single microchip. (Please note that Ellora's Cave does not endorse any specific brands. You can check our website at www.ellorascave.com for customer recommendations we make available to new consumers.)

3. *Mobility.* Because your new library now consists of only a microchip, your entire cache of books can be taken with you wherever you go.

4. *Personal preferences are accounted for.* Are the words you are currently reading too small? Too large? Too...ANNOYING? Paperback books cannot be modified according to personal preferences, but e-books can.

5. *Innovation.* The way you read a book is not the only advancement the Information Age has gifted the literary community with. There is also the factor of what you can read. Ellora's Cave Publishing will be introducing a new line of interactive titles that are available in e-book format only.

6. *Instant gratification.* Is it the middle of the night and all the bookstores are closed? Are you tired of waiting days—sometimes weeks—for online and offline bookstores to ship the novels you bought? Ellora's Cave Publishing sells instantaneous downloads 24 hours a day, 7 days a week, 365 days a year. Our e-book delivery system is 100% automated, meaning your order is filled as soon as you pay for it.

Those are a few of the top reasons why electronic novels are displacing paperbacks for many an avid reader. As always, Ellora's Cave Publishing welcomes your questions and comments. We invite you to email us at service@ellorascave.com or write to us directly at: P.O. Box 787, Hudson, Ohio 44236-0787.

Printed in the United States
75054LV00001B/74